DEATH *DREAM VALLEY*

All the big signs in Dream Valley were dead now and the luminescent surface of the pedway had faded to dark gray. But a pleasure palace had been set afire just a few blocks away, and the wild, crackling flames cast a lurid yellow glare.

Further along the pedway I heard smashing sounds, screams, and something heavy being dragged. Looters, I guessed. In a world of surplus wealth, theft was pointless; but that wouldn't stop anyone.

For jaded senners who had lived all their lives under the eyes of the Protektorate, crime would be the most exotic, forbidden snap . . .

PROTEKTOR

CHARLES PLATT

AVON BOOKS • NEW YORK

PROTEKTOR is an original publication of Avon Books. This work has never before appeared in book form. This work is a novel. Any similarity to actual persons or events is purely coincidental.

AVON BOOKS
A division of
The Hearst Corporation
1350 Avenue of the Americas
New York, New York 10019

Copyright © 1996 by Charles Platt
Cover art by Tom Canty
Published by arrangement with the author
Library of Congress Catalog Card Number: 95-94738
ISBN: 0-380-78431-9

First AvoNova Printing: February 1996

AVONOVA TRADEMARK REG. U.S. PAT. OFF. AND IN OTHER COUNTRIES, MARCA REGISTRADA, HECHO EN U.S.A.

Printed in the U.S.A.

RA   10 9 8 7 6 5 4 3 2 1

ACHNOWLEDGMENTS

I pay tribute here to John W. Campbell's *Analog*, which imprinted me with the methods of science fiction; to Fred Beyer and Hal Pollenz, who opened the world of computers and computer programming to me; to Vernor Vinge, who defined the problem in science fiction of taking into account (or evading plausibly) the imminent singularity of artificial intelligence; to Hans Moravec, for *Mind Children*; to Eric Drexler, for *Engines of Creation*; to my editor, John Douglas; and most of all to Alfred Bester and Dashiell Hammett, the two American storytellers whose work I most admire—from afar.

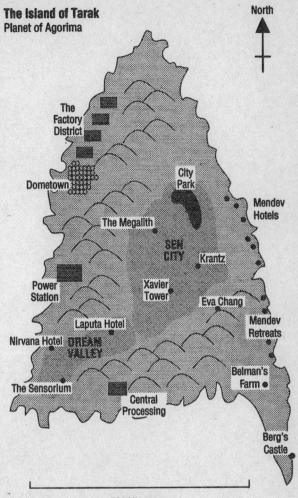

The Island of Tarak
Planet of Agorima

North

The Factory District

Dometown

City Park

Mendev Hotels

The Megalith

SEN CITY

Krantz

Power Station

Xavier Tower

Eva Chang

Laputa Hotel

Mendev Retreats

Nirvana Hotel

DREAM VALLEY

Belman's Farm

The Sensorium

Central Processing

Berg's Castle

500 kilometers

000000

Our transit vehicle sank through the night. Beneath us, pedpaths were a tangle of neon veins embracing the organs of the city. Towers shimmered in the heat; highways were smeared with light; fliers around us winked like fireflies.

The western sky rippled with distant auroras—vapor signs beckoning to the pleasure zones of Dream Valley. I imagined hundreds of thousands of seekers partying there, barely aware of the vast network of services that sustained and safeguarded them. Throughout their lives the systems had fulfilled every need, always functioning faithfully, never giving any real cause for alarm.

"We have overload at Traffic Control," a calm, measured voice said beside me—the voice of Lee, my auton. "Two fliers have been allowed to converge. I'm unable to intervene."

I looked through the transparent canopy of our vehicle and saw nothing. Then a flash like a giant strobe bleached the sky. As the lightburst diminished I blinked through its phantom residues and saw flaming embers falling. A low rumble rolled across the landscape, and a moment later our little vehicle rocked in the shock wave.

Somewhere in the support systems on this planet, a parasite was loose. Already, it had begun to damage its host.

"Take us to the crash point," I said.

0000001

We fell out of the sky and the city turned like a wheel, the web of lights rushing up from below. "Is Life-Support responding?" I asked.

"A rescue vehicle has been dispatched," Lee told me.

The biggest chunk of wreckage hit a building directly beneath us, sprayed fire across its roof, then rolled over the edge and crashed to the ground.

I looked up and saw bright pinpricks circling— thrill seekers eager to view the disaster. Meanwhile, a red-and-white beacon was racing from the south.

"What's the status now at the Mains?" I asked.

Lee paused, using his wideband radio link to interrogate the giant systems that controlled this world. "Traffic Control shows no further lag time," he told me. "The overload has disappeared."

Such a wild fluctation made no sense; yet I wasn't entirely surprised.

"Does Central Processing have any trace on us?"

"No. We are not logged in."

"So take us to that little landing field upwind from the flames."

Our transit vehicle sideslipped and kicked briefly in thermals as we passed over the burning wreck. There was a faint jarring, rasping contact as we finally set down. I checked my dart gun, feeling acutely conscious of its inadequacy. Then I retracted the canopy and stepped out.

0000010

My first breath of air on the surface of Agorima brought me the soft, rich odors of dark soil, flowering succulents, hot, dusty streets—and the acrid tang of burning plastics.

Blue flames were licking the crashed flier, and there were sharp cracking sounds as its shell fractured in the heat. I stared at it, wondering if anyone was still alive in there and feeling sick at my inability to get them out. Then the rescue vehicle from Life-Support swooped down and opened like a metal flower, disgorging spotlights, peekers, and a swarm of meks.

I moved toward the sudden white glare of emergency lighting and watched the machines as they scuttled around the wreckage. One of them doused the flames with white gas while two more levered apart glowing segments of the passenger compartment and a fourth extended flexible arms to probe inside.

A human figure climbed down from the rescue vehicle. "Hey," I called.

He turned toward me, his fireproof suit glittering like a chromed cocoon. "Keep back," he shouted. It was an amplified, metallic voice. "This is a hazardous area." He took a step toward me. "There's a flight barrier up. How'd you get down here?"

"I didn't notice any barrier," I said, making myself sound casual. "Seems like all kinds of things are screwing up, the last couple of days."

"Just keep out of the way," he said. Either he saw no pattern, or he saw no reason to talk about it.

He turned his helmet and paused, motionless, interacting over his radio link with his crew of meks. Evidently I wasn't going to get anything out of him unless I identified myself—which I had no intention of doing.

I noticed another flier coming in. I switched my eyes to infrared and activated my private link with Lee. "Who's the newcomer?" I sent to him silently.

There was a barely perceptible pause as he browsed Traffic Control. "A reporter. Eva Kurimoto. She has emergency clearance."

That was good. That was exactly what I'd hoped for. I stepped back into the shadows.

0000011

Kurimoto's flier touched down and she jumped out, a slim silhouette against the white lights. She saw the man monitoring the rescue team, went over to him, and started gesturing, pointing at the wreck. I heard nothing and assumed she was communicating with him over an emergency channel, but I had little interest in that. Judging from the man's body language, she wouldn't get any more than I had; so I moved quietly across the area till I was standing between her and her flier, and I waited.

She was persistent. It took her a couple of minutes to give up and turn away. She started back toward me, a slim, booted silhouette in a belted robe that rippled as she moved.

I showed myself. "Eva," I said.

She stopped short. Her face was shadowed but I saw a red pinpoint wink near jawline—some sort of scanning device. "Who are you?" she asked, sounding cautious.

"Is she on-line with her employers?" I sent to Lee.

"No, she's a freelance operator. She's logging

five-sense data in her personal storage, and she's copying it through the Mains to a file server at her residence."

"Block that transmission," I said, and waited a beat while Lee accessed the input buffers at Computer Central, located Eva Kurimoto's signal, and intercepted it.

I moved a little to one side and saw her features limned with white. She looked young, smart, and suspicious. "My name's Tom McCray," I said quietly. "I work for the Hub Digislature. I'm a Protektor."

"Really." Her tone was heavy with disbelief.

I moved one step closer. She was dressed decadent. Her thickened black hair swirled around her face, semisentient like her robe, sustaining itself by filtering trace nutrients from the air. Her fingernails were luminous yellow. Her knee-high boots glittered dark red, made from shrink-fitting stuff that conformed so snugly to her skin, it looked as if it was sprayed on.

Her image job looked more suitable for a Dream Valley greeter than a reporter on assignment—but on the pleasure world of Agorima, I reminded myself, normal standards did not apply. "Access her stats," I said to Lee, voicing it this time, loud enough for her to hear.

"Her residence is in Greenview, the opposite side of the valley," Lee answered, following my lead and speaking audibly. "Her bio age is fixed at twenty-seven, chrono age forty-two. Her family immigrated here when she was fifteen and were quickly consigned to the local dometown as a result of gambling debts. Since she emerged from that environment she has worked in casino management, real estate, sim scripting, and last year underwent training as an independent gatherer for the SenTel network with five-sense sim implants. She has placed eleven feature items, more than one hundred human interest fillers. She was natural-born, but prefers—"

"Stop," she said sharply. "Who's that with you?" Her voice sounded hostile, now. She stepped closer to Lee.

"My auton," I told her. "He enables my privileged access. All data in the Mains are open to him."

She paused a pace away and reached up to touch Lee's face. Plainly dressed, with androgynous beige plastic features, he looked like a fashion-window manikin.

She turned back to me, and I saw that her skepticism was gone, replaced by a look of intent interest. Protektors were rare enough; it had to be newsworthy that I was here.

"Why did you come to this crash site?" I asked her.

She hesitated, reluctant to answer the question. Then she gave a little shrug. "There've been—bug reports, the past two days."

"Do you think there's a pattern?"

"How should I know?" She waved the question aside. "What do you think? Is that why you're here?"

Behind us, there was a whine and rattle of machinery as the remains of the crashed flier were winched into the rescue vehicle's cargo bay. The glaring lights suddenly died, and night closed around us. Bulky dark forms of meks scurried back to their compartments and stowed themselves.

I decided Eva Kurimoto was satisfactory for what I had in mind. "I need to talk to you," I said. "Privately, at your residence."

"Why?" She made it sound combative.

"There's a serious situation here on Agorima," I told her. "Far more serious than anyone realizes."

"So—you want background from me, or what?"

I nodded. "You can help me with some information, yes."

She thought about that. "And do I get to ask you any questions?"

"To the extent that time permits."

She thought about it some more, then nodded decisively. "All right," she said. "My place."

0000100

I closed my eyes as we drifted across the sparkling valley. Lee estimated our flight time at ten minutes, which allowed me to view some clips from Central Processing's input buffers—the holding areas in the Mains where surveillance data were received from billions of peekers and servers scattered across the city.

My hearing faded and my vision blanked. Then—

SIM FREAK

I was floating, staring down from a point near the ceiling of a room painted midnight blue. The perspectives were distorted; the walls seemed to curve in. The floor was strewn with squares of white and black: hardcopy and lek components. I saw wires, data screens, and a man squatting in the center of it all.

He was long-haired, naked, and unshaven. There were black beads in his ears, a black collar around his neck, and he was adjusting a pair of cheap optic-nerve inducers. It was a low-rent VR rig. He looked like a hard-core user who couldn't afford implants because he spent all his credit on sims and all his time in simspace.

I watched as he caressed a black tablet in his lap. There was a moment of silence. Then he screamed. He struggled up onto his knees, groping like a blind man. A moment later he fell backward and went into convulsions. Blood welled up around the black beads in his ears and started trickling down the sides of his jaw. The lights went out as his shelter's support system sensed his distress and shut down the power—too late.

WASTE DISPOSAL

I was in the center of a two-lane highway, a few millimeters above its polished, resin-coated surface. In the night sky, distant clouds flickered with rainbow backwash from the signs of Dream Valley. Landscaped hills loomed like the lumpy body of a great black beast. The highway glowed with its own cold phosphorescence.

A car hissed past, a sleek glittering thing that quickly receded into the distance.

A sanitation mek came onto the highway from an on-ramp and moved along with its warning lights flashing. But its function was inverted; its motors whirred and it started spewing filth, a fountain of trash and dirt. The residues blurred my vision, finally eclipsed my eye as the machine rumbled over me.

EMBARRASSMENTS OF RICHES

I was floating through a palace in Dream Valley. Men and women in harlequin togas were riding ramps that curved up among drifting clouds of colored steam. Everyone was laughing, giddy on stimulants. My viewpoint drifted among them, unnoticed and ignored, then passed through a light curtain. I looked down and saw a man and a woman in a privacy cubicle caressing a soft pink quivering thing that might have been a pig before it had been genetically modified. Its head was the size of a pimple, and its body was augmented with a dozen different organs and orifices. It quivered with pleasure as the humans coupled with it.

I passed through another light curtain into a hall where circles of pastel radiance drifted lazily across a floor of purple velvet. The space was crowded with naked silver statues whose bulging transparent bellies were crammed full of archaic gold currency. Revelers fed the statues more gold, manipulated their limbs, and here and there— with melodic cries—the statues allowed a few coins to trickle out of their mouths and genitals.

Then the lights dimmed almost imperceptibly and in response to some unspoken, universal command the statues began yielding their entire reserves of wealth. At first the revelers shouted with delight, gathering handfuls of money. But as the payout continued, and continued, laughter turned to screams. Men and women floundered helplessly under the shining metal torrent, engulfed by it. Quite soon, blood began flowing among the gold.

0000101

There was a moment's disorientation, like a transmission break in a simcast. I blinked and found myself back in my transit vehicle, drifting toward a sparse scattering of homes on a hillside thickly layered with vegetation.

I touched my palms to my chest, my thighs, my cheeks, restoring my body awareness. The status lights on the control panel were a familiar mosaic of blue and green, the drive was humming gently, and the seat was vibrating almost imperceptibly under me. There were no system malfunctions here. I had no personal cause for concern.

"Give me a malfunction summary," I said to Lee.

"Eleven deaths have occurred in the past two days. There have been almost one hundred injuries, and the rate of increase is exponential. Early editions of tomorrow's zines are now referring to a freak run of accidents. Citizens' groups are logging complaints with the planetary digislature, but no one is openly speculating, yet, that the systems could be corrupt."

I saw Eva Kurimoto's flier setting down ahead of us on the little landing field outside her home. The citizens of Agorima made smooth, effortless landings like that every day, simply by telling their fliers where they wanted to go. Traffic Control at Central Processing did the rest, monitoring and controlling the exact position of every vehicle and providing remote power via focused microwave beams. Without a doubt, my transit vehicle was the only one under independent power and guidance.

If Central's errors continued to multiply, midair collisions such as the one we'd seen would become increasingly frequent, until the city became littered with dead bodies and burning debris.

0000110

Set on a hillside dense with tropical forest, the house was a skewed stack of six rectangular slabs, each edged with windows overlooking the wide, shallow valley. I sensed the newness of it, the walls fresh from some factory on the other side of

An Electronic Bureaucracy

At the beginning of the twenty-sixth century there were more than 100,000 human-inhabited planets in our galaxy and thousands more under development. Linking them was the Protektorate: a system of government that had survived without major changes since the early 2100s. It was composed entirely of systems that lacked sentience or free will but had a limited degree of artificial intelligence.

According to historical records of life on Earth, the first primitive computers were used mostly for bureaucratic functions such as census-taking and accountancy. The development of semi-intelligent machines took far longer than anyone had predicted, as software design continued to lag behind the power of hardware; but by 2050, expert systems were moving into managerial positions in the same areas of government where computers had originally served as mere counting and adding machines a century previously.

It made good sense for the new, semismart computers to take over the jobs of bureaucrats. They were meticulous, obedient, unimaginative—and they always followed the rules.

the world, the land untouched by sentient life until less than a century ago.

I walked with Lee and Eva Kurimoto up a steep, curving path bordered with thornbushes and wild roses. There were no insects here; no crickets among the tailored vegetation. Our footsteps seemed loud in the total stillness.

A door slid open in front of us. We stepped into an elevator, rode it to the top floor, and emerged in a space the size of a ballroom. I looked up and saw that the ceiling was a mosaic of slanting facets—triangular transparent panels refracting the night sky.

"Where does her money come from?" I sent to Lee.

"She is not wealthy by local standards. Homes such as this are relatively common here among people working for the entertainment media."

As the room lighting slowly brightened around us I looked at her and tried to evaluate what I saw. She seemed friendly and relaxed, and she looked at me directly, with no hint of shyness or affectation. She had delicate features, and I wondered if the name Kurimoto implied a genuine family lineage or if she'd merely chosen to refeature her face Asian.

Her eyes were intent. She was watching my face as closely as I was examining hers. "Are you doing image capture?" I asked her.

"Of course. Any problem with that?" She frowned, and the furrow between her eyebrows was an unexpected intrusion in the perfect, unlined symmetry of her features.

"Probably not. You'll need a release, though."

She gave a curt nod. "I have to go change," she said, turning away. "My robe needs a nutrient bath, otherwise it dies. Same thing with my hair. I'll be right back." She strode to a spiral ramp in one corner of the room. "Do a different vid if you don't want the dancers," she called as she disappeared from view.

A wallscreen was showing a life-size, zero-gravity ballet: androgynous figures in white, gliding and pirouetting in slow motion like fish in a giant aquarium. I ignored it and paced across a rug that was nut brown but looked and felt like grass. The place was so quiet that as Lee walked beside me,

I could hear the hiss of his hydraulics and the whine of his servos.

I counted a dozen cabinets full of sim cartridges, a big library of vidzines, and his and hers immersion tanks. In a dining area, an oval table had been set for six people. Soft chairs were grouped around a fireplace where fake flames had started curling up a stack of ornamental logs.

A workstation was tucked away in one corner with a textscreen, two touchpads for data entry, stacks of hardcopy, a notebook and ink pen, emcards scattered across a console. I imagined Eva Kurimoto sitting there, editing the sims she'd recorded with her implants. It was the only area of the room that actually seemed to be used for anything.

Soft footsteps announced her return. Her living wig had been cast aside revealing a short pageboy cut. Her robe and boots had been replaced with a plain red kimono and red slippers. She walked to a dispensal behind a counter in one corner. "Get you anything?"

"No, I don't think so."

I saw the furrow between her eyebrows again. "Because you're on duty?"

I shook my head. "The systems may not be secure."

Her face blanked. "Even my home services?"

I hesitated. I knew Lee would be blocking any surveillance equipment in this room, but I still felt uneasy here. "Let's talk outside," I said, "and I'll tell you what I know, and what I need to know."

0000111

One of the big windows slid aside, and Eva Kurimoto stepped out onto a balcony at the front of the

An Autonomous
Life-Support System

The twenty-first century was a time of unprecedented change. Resources on Earth were depleted, and the ecology was no longer stable. In the face of a genuine crisis in the global life support system, nationalism finally gave way to multinational cooperation led by the scientific community in cooperation with industry. A massive die-off of consumers, after all, would be bad for business.

As international treaties superseded international rivalries and commerce became truly global, there was little need anymore for politicians representing national interests. In any case, the role of government had been steadily diminishing since the last big wars of the mid-twentieth century. In the global economy, decisions were made not on ideological grounds but on the basis of computer projections and analyses. Even in government services, systems were increasingly automated, driven by policy decisions that were derived from computer projections. By 2100, the concept of national leaders seemed archaic.

As humanity spread into space and replenished its diminishing reserves from mineral resources on the moon and in the asteroid belt, politicians were mere figureheads while government had become a giant lek (electronic) bureaucracy. This was the Protectorate, renamed the Protektorate by the still-surviving news media: an automated system designed to support and protect human life by providing all essential services. To this end, its probes searched for new resources, its factories produced food and consumer goods, its little mobile peekers and permanently installed observer systems watched over humanity, and its peacekeeping autons apprehended any person who was seen to violate another person's rights.

building. I followed her with Lee close behind me. Dawn was less than an hour away but the city was still busy, a shimmering field under a fat orange moon.

"So tell me what's happening," she said. "Can you do that?"

"So long as you respect confidentiality. You have a full set of implants, right? And some onboard storage."

She touched her neck just below her ear. "A petabyte to buffer the five-sense data."

I wondered how she'd react to the news that she was no longer on-line with her home system. "I don't care what you record in that onboard buffer," I told her, "but there'll be no more downloads to your workstation. Lee has been blocking that."

Her eyes widened. Her mouth tightened. For a moment, she didn't speak. "You have no right—"

"I do have the right," I contradicted her.

"But if you expect me to help you—" Her voice was strident.

I held up my hands. "Please." There really wasn't time for a journalist's tantrum. "If you ration it out, your onboard storage will be adequate, and eventually you'll be able to report this in full—assuming things work out."

She relaxed fractionally. "You sound like it's the apocalypse. I'm not sure I really believe that."

"Well, you saw those two fliers crash, and you said yourself, you've noticed a trend. There are fire-walls in the Mains that are supposed to isolate one set of functions from another, but I've already seen failures spreading into some domestic equipment."

"You've seen them? How? I thought you only just arrived onplanet."

"Lee showed me some peeker reports. He has

Anomalyst

Not everyone welcomed the Protektorate's automated welfare state. There were angry demands for
its powers to be restricted, and a hierarchical set of
commands was developed to fill this need. Known
as the Human Instruction Set, these commands were
installed at the lowest level of every semisentient device, from health-care robots to dispensals supplying
food and drink in private homes. The Instruction Set
was an ethical code as rigid as the Ten Command-
ments, but more specifically worded and observed
with single-minded fidelity.

Thus the benign nature of the Protektorate was
guaranteed. And yet, in a system so complex, it was
inevitable that there should be errors and failures.

Routine malfunctions were taken care of by autons
in the Protektorate's own maintenance division.
Sometimes, though, a malfunction would be more
than routine, or there would be catastrophic failures
caused by human interference. At such times, a
human troubleshooter was needed—someone with a
quirky mix of initiative and rigor, intuition and rational deduction.

Anomalysts, as they were properly known, became
folk heroes in dramas beamed out across the Stellar
Entertainment Network. Protektors, tektives, bit fixers—they acquired many names but had only one
function: to safeguard human beings who had become so dependent on the Protektorate, they were
no longer able to live without it.

access." I turned to Lee. "Are there any peekers
out here?"

"One on the edge of the balcony," he said. "I've
been looping its signal."

I amplified my vision till I saw a semitransparent sphere the size of my thumbnail—one of sev-

eral billion surveillance units scattered across the city. I walked to the peeker, flipped it off the balcony rail, and crushed it under my heel. I turned back toward Eva Kurimoto. "I do know what I'm talking about," I said. "And I'm not being an alarmist."

She folded her arms defensively. Her eyes shifted and she was thoughtful for a moment. "All right," she said in a lower voice. "And I guess you do have the authority to restrict media coverage." She forced a stiff smile. "So tell me why you picked me to talk to."

0001000

I looked out across the valley. "All the system failures that caused fatalities during the past two days were reported to the OverMains at the Hub. That's standard procedure. Some monitoring program up there noticed a pattern which Maintenance, here, wasn't able to control—possibly because it, too, is now corrupt."

"You mean, infected with a data virus?"

"That's the most likely explanation, although I've never seen a virus that can penetrate so quickly to so many low-level systems. Every node in the network—from Flight Control to Biocare to home dispensals—is now potentially at risk."

She was silent for a long moment. Then she turned, her kimono rustling in the night. She nodded toward Lee. "Can he fix it?"

I laughed. Under Protektorate policy, computer science had not been taught formally for three centuries. The reason was simple enough: an uninformed public posed less of a risk to the systems. "Lee," I said, "maybe you can explain."

"It would be unsafe for me to penetrate very deeply in the Mains," he told her. "If there is a virus, it could contaminate me before I even recognize it, and the systems are so complex, I would require months to do any large-scale work. Therefore, I just monitor the input/output buffers, where raw data waits to be processed."

She eyed him for a moment, then turned back to me. Her eyes gleamed in the light spilling out through the glass doors, and I realized that in some way she was enjoying this. It excited her interest. "So what do you do?" she asked me. "You operate on the human level, is that it? You find the deev who set this up and try to make him cooperate?"

"Something like that," I said.

"So like I said before, why talk to me?" She tilted her head slightly to one side as she looked up at me. "Why not go through regular law enforcement?"

"Because if someone really wants to screw the system, they infect maintenance first, law enforcement second. None of the local systems is trustworthy anymore." I broke off abruptly, hearing a faint sound. I looked over the balcony rail and saw a shape creeping through the darkness. I tensed, then realized it was only an auton running a gardening program. The vegetation around the house looked wild, but it had been customized like all the other elements of this world.

I normalized my vision, turned back, and found that she'd moved closer to me. "Something bothering you?" she said.

"Just a gardening robot out there."

"Oh." She paused, narrowing her eyes, looking at me in a way that I couldn't quite place. Then, abruptly, she stepped back. "So you need information," she said. "Stuff you can't find in the Mains? Yes, I guess you need human interest material that expert systems can't tell you. And that's why you need me. Because I'm a journalist. And you picked me at random, so there's a low chance that I'm involved in the conspiracy here—assuming there is a conspiracy."

"You're very quick," I said, feeling slightly surprised by her.

She gave me an irritated glance, as if she resented the comment. Then she shrugged impatiently. "Maybe I do know some stuff that would be helpful. But—I guess I have to ask you something." She hesitated, and a faint smile lifted one corner of her mouth. "Is there any fee involved?"

I blinked. "You mean, do you get paid?"

The smile deepened. "Seems to me, I'm providing a service—"

"It's out of the question," I said, feeling slightly incredulous.

"But you could fix it easily enough, couldn't you?" She tilted her head. "With privileged access—I mean, it wouldn't cost *you* anything."

Now I was irritated. "Maybe I haven't made this clear. There are no animals on Agorima, and most of the flora isn't edible. Food comes out of factories. If Central Processing goes down, home dispensals will dry up. Transportation will fail. Life-Support will no longer respond. There'll be rioting, starvation, and death."

She shook a stray strand of hair out of her face. Unexpectedly, she laughed. "Well, sorry I asked."

I looked at her for a moment, trying to assess her. Most people deferred to a Protektor's authority; her confrontational, argumentative behavior was unusual. Yet I couldn't help liking her for it.

I quickly pushed that thought aside. "What I need first are some names," I told her. "High-profile figures who have a grudge against the Protektorate."

"You really think that someone high-profile would—"

"They might not have the skills, but they'd have the money. To crack the systems at Central Processing, you need equipment that's not for sale. You have to build it by hand, which requires many years and a heap of money. Whoever did it is being bankrolled by someone with significant resources."

"I see." She nodded slowly. "Okay, I can think of some possibilities. Four people, straight off."

"Just tell me who they are," I told her. "Lee will access their stats."

EMMANUEL FISH

She said the name, and an image brightened inside my eyes. A big plump face creased in a resentful scowl. There seemed to be no hair on him anywhere—he didn't even have eyebrows. Maybe some kind of cleanliness fetish? His eyes looked lively, but not in a nice way.

His profile scrolled beneath the pic. I realized I'd heard of Fisk. He was a sim stylist—originator of simulation entertainments networked across the galaxy through SEN, the Stellar Entertainment Network, from his studios here in the valley. In public speeches he had argued that the Protektorate's control of interstellar communications made competition uneconomic and should be abolished. Fisk was rich, but he was greedy; he wanted a network that would be all his own. That way, he could force consumers to pay for access that was currently free.

MILTON BERG

I saw a long, pale, pinched face with prominent cheekbones, curly black hair, a wide, thin, slotlike mouth between deep vertical furrows. He looked righteous, like a minister high on god. I could imagine him thumping a pulpit.

He was founder and leader of the Chaists, a local cult that believed our comfortable existence was unhealthy and unnatural. We should stop taking our immortality drugs, reject free goods and services provided by the Protektorate, and heed the chaos in our genes. Ungoverned population growth via natural births, uncontrolled innovation in technology, even private ownership of weapons—these were the ideals the Chaists worked for in the name of "personal freedom."

Berg himself was a mort; he refused all immortality treatments and advised others to do likewise, because this would encourage them to take more responsibility for their lives and be more motivated. So far his message had attracted fewer than a thousand adherents, even on Agorima where cultism was a thriving industry.

SERENA CATALANO

I blinked, momentarily disconcerted by the face I saw. Stern, aloof, coldly and cruelly beautiful, ivory skin framed with pale golden curls. Beauty, of course, was cheap, especially on style-conscious Agorima, but her looks had a natural symmetry that said she had never been refeatured.

She looked prim, narcissistic, and very pleased with her own elegance. Instinctively, I disliked her vanity.

She owned five of the largest pleasure palaces in Dream Valley. To the extent that organized crime still existed, she ran it. She complained—often—that Protektorate regulations stifled private enterprise. She wanted all currency to be based on precious metals, she wanted private banks, and she demanded an end to all public surveillance. In other words, she wanted concessions that had enabled big-time crime to run rampant on Earth back in the old, old days.

Her biological age was 28. Her chronological age was 310. I could tell she wasn't going to be much fun to deal with.

JOE BELMAN

He had a short, thick neck, a low forehead, and a jaw so big it almost touched his chest. His small eyes were spaced close together, and his thin gray hair was brushed straight back. Belman looked bad-tempered, ready to punch out anyone who rooted for the wrong team or insulted his mother.

But his ideology typed him as a romantic. He believed that unfeeling machines should be replaced by strong, simple human beings. We should junk the whole concept of an automated welfare state and go back to governments run by human politicians. He admitted that this might be less efficient (a slight understatement, there) but it would be a system you could trust—especially if Joe was elected to run it. For several decades, now, he had been gathering signatures on a petition to eject the local arm of the Protektorate. Once this was achieved, he was ready to step in as a leader of the people. He already had maybe five hundred supporters in service jobs, plus some deadbeats in the local dometown who believed he could liberate them from the "Protektorate conspiracy" that deprived them of their "fair share" of resources.

0001001

"Anyone else?" I asked Eva Kurimoto.

"There's people in Drazz Alley—that's the fashion industry—with the same cant as Fisk. You know, they say the Protektorate steals their designs, mass-markets them with its meks so they can't match the prices, and on and on. But they're low-level greedy."

I nodded "You've helped me." I looked her in the eyes. "Thanks."

"You're welcome." Once again, she stared at me in a way that I couldn't quite place. "Do we have time for me to ask another question?" Her voice was gentler, less businesslike.

"Go ahead."

"Where are you from?"

That was unexpected. It disoriented me. The last place I'd been was the Hub, near the galactic center, receiving my assignment. Before that, I'd been vacationing alone on a backwater planet, doing therapeutic physical farming labor during the day and enjoying a rich mix of mood drugs each evening. And before that—well, I wasn't from anywhere; not anymore. I had a home world, Otupalo, which had been a gift to me from the Protektorate and was totally uninhabited except for the house that I'd built there. But really that was none of her business. "I grew up on an agworld in one of the spiral arms," I said, brief and simple. "My family were first generation colonists. The rugged, independent type." Then I shook my head irritably. "I'm sorry, I don't have time for this. I realize you want human interest for your story—"

She looked surprised. "No. No, not for the story."

I looked at her skeptically, aware that charm was a useful skill in her profession. I really wasn't sure what to make of her. "Are you paired with anyone?" I asked.

She half smiled, and I saw her tongue behind her teeth. "My work keeps me kind of busy—but I see a guy once in a while."

Well, it wasn't relevant. "Tell me," I said, "do you know anything about Nils Ferguson?"

It was her turn to be momentarily disconcerted by a sudden change in topic. She gestured vaguely. "I know he's the local Protektorate coordinator. He does human liaison between here and the OverMains at the Hub."

I shook my head. "Not anymore. The OverMains queried Ferguson yesterday and got a message back saying he was unavailable."

"Unavailable? What the hell does that mean?"

"I don't know. I've sent a peeker to Ferguson's house to find out."

She turned away for a moment, walked to the balcony rail, and stared into the night. I saw tension in her jaw muscles, and I noticed her hands clenching on the rail. "I've always felt so secure here," she said. "It's hard to believe that I'm not safe anymore." She turned back to me. "What's the absolute worst-case scenario? Everybody dies? Surely, there'd be some kind of offworld rescue team—"

"Not necessarily. Agorima could be quarantined."

"Quarantined?" She looked unsure of the word.

I wasn't surprised that it came as news to her. "The Protektorate doesn't publicize it, because they don't want to degrade public confidence in support systems. But there was a case just twenty years ago. All the infrastructure on an industrial world collapsed, and we couldn't stop it. Two Protektors went in there and never came out. We still send occasional robot probes, but they disappear. We never did discover what had happened. I'm not saying that the same thing is likely here, but— it's conceivable."

She gave me a strained smile. "So I guess you better get busy."

"In a moment. There's something more that I want from you. According to your stats, you spent quite a while in Dometown."

Her body stiffened, and her face became expressionless. She said nothing.

"Is your family still there?" I went on.

She shook her head quickly. "I got them out. They're offworld now. I don't communicate with them anymore."

"Well, I need you to go to Dometown for me," I said. "I can work on the higher levels. I need you to work lower down. I want you to look up any old contacts who do gray-legal stuff. Ask for someone who can do lek favors—like doctoring stats in Central Processing."

She laughed incredulously. "Forget it! Are you crazy?"

"You won't be monitored. Lee will block any transmissions from local peekers. Also, he can intercept signals from your implants to the Mains and copy them back to me, so that I can see what's happening to you and help out if anything goes wrong."

She spread her hands. "Right, and if something happens to Lee, then what?"

I had no answer to that. Lee was indispensable. There were backup systems on my jumpship in a synchronous orbit, but I wasn't going to risk contaminating them so long as the situation here was unresolved. "I have to admit that there is a small risk," I said. "But it's insignificant compared with the disaster that'll happen if we don't stop this thing."

That calmed her slightly. She thrust her hands into the pockets of her robe and paced away from me along the balcony. "Dometown's bad for me," she said, with her back turned. "It's ugly shit. I forget about it."

Her voice had shed its civilized intonation. She suddenly sounded like the street, and I realized that I'd been interacting with a sophisticated shell. She seemed chic, but she must still have a sneaking insecurity in case someone typed her real background. And it would feel humiliating for her to return there.

"It's in your own interests to help me," I said quietly. "It's a matter of survival. You're a smart woman; you can see that."

She turned and gave me a glare. "If I'm so smart, quit talking down to me."

"I thought I was paying you a compliment," I said, keeping my voice neutral.

"I don't need that kind of compliment. Thanks." Her eyes were wide and angry. I was glad to see that: if she was mad at me, she'd feel more need to prove herself.

She grunted in disgust. "All right. I'll go. You just want me to ask around for someone to hack personal records? Is that it?"

"Correct. If we're dealing with a system cracker he must have started small-scale, and there should be some people who used to know him, maybe still do know him."

"Uh-huh. And you'll cover me." She made it sound like a necessary service which she doubted I was qualified to perform.

"All you need to do," I said, "is speak my name. Lee will monitor your channel constantly. If he hears you call for me, he'll link us, and I'll help you out."

She paused, and her anger died away as quickly as it had come. "Feels weird for you to have access in my head," she said.

"I can only access your senses, nothing more."

She eyed me speculatively. "Why do you do this stuff, anyway? Do they pay you a lot?"

It was another disorienting question, too intrusive for my liking. I took a moment figuring out the quickest, simplest way to answer her. "I'm paid enough that I'm never tempted to take advantage of my privileged access," I said. "But I don't do it for the money." I hesitated, thinking of clichés about public service and public safety. Those clichés did mean something, but in truth I needed something more. "I like working as a free agent, doing stuff nobody else can do." I looked at her bright, alert eyes. "But I shouldn't need to explain that to you. You're the same way yourself."

Her smile came back. "You're right," she said.

Public Eyes

The concept of personal privacy was first seriously threatened in the twentieth century. High-resolution images from mapping satellites were sold freely. Telephone and radio communications could be intercepted with equipment that was easily affordable. Video cameras were miniaturized for domestic use. Corporate and government databases were cracked by college students with bootleg access codes.

In a doomed attempt to resist the inevitable, laws against electronic trespassing were enacted. But enforcement was almost impossible, and the impracticality of keeping things secret became increasingly obvious. Moreover, as time passed, people began to realize that in most situations, *it didn't matter*.

An individual's need for privacy, after all, was rooted in shame and fear. Some things were too embarrassing to share with friends or neighbors, for fear of disapproval or rejection. Other things were too risky to reveal for fear of one's employer or the authorities.

But with the elimination of disease and the total separation of sexual pleasure from the option of pregnancy, moral strictures began to relax. And as human government lost its power, and human employers were replaced by machines running wholly benevolent programs, people no longer had reason to feel intimidated. Without shame, without fear, the passion for privacy rapidly diminished in each new generation.

Also, the benefits of global monitoring became obvious. At a time when the biggest threat to peace came not from armies but from terrorists, widespread, automated surveillance offered a new sense of security.

By the time the Protektorate became a universal provider of goods and services, monitoring was taken for granted. Airborne peekers roved freely, remotely powered by microwaves. Their audio-video transcripts were relayed back to the Mains. Larger observers—"servers"—were preinstalled in every room in every home that the Protektorate manufactured, and they were capable of identifying any citizen by a combination of visual pattern-matching, trace odors, and skin particle analysis.

Servers were mandatory in all public areas and factories. Elsewhere, they were optional, and some misfits and elitists preferred not to be watched. For most people, however, surveillance became such a source of security, people were afraid to do without it. Under the limits imposed by the Human Instruction Set, it could only be used by the Protektorate for benign purposes. In case of fire, or flood, or medical emergency, help came instantly and automatically; and crimes such as burglary and assault diminished to zero—almost.

0001010

"Tom." It was Lee's quiet voice, from beside me. "Nils Ferguson is dead."

We had left Eva Kurimoto's residence and were heading toward the center of the valley. The edge of the sky was lightening from black to gray, and the stars were fading. I swallowed a REM-state suppressant, then slit the wrapper of a food pack. "Go on."

"I just received video from the peeker that you sent to Ferguson's house."

I felt suddenly weary. Another death; and this one almost certainly premeditated. I closed my eyes. "Play it to me."

DEATH IN THE VALLEY

I found myself drifting out of the sky like a falling leaf, toward a home in the valley—a manse surrounded by acres of landscaped gardens. Infrared imaging assigned false colors: the manse glowed orange, the gardens were pale blue, and the city beyond was a deep red.

I drifted almost to ground level, then floated over soft mounded earth planted with succulents and ferns, toward a fresh-air intake grille serving the home's air-conditioning system. The grille loomed closer, larger, and I passed between its louvers. Everything went dark for a moment. There was a crunching sound, tiny metal jaws eating through an air filter, and then a sharp *clang* as the peeker bumped the side of a metal duct.

I found myself emerging through a vent into a large living room furnished with antiques—bookshelves, a big old vidscreen, framed paintings, hand-woven rugs. Stretched full-length on one of the rugs was a human figure.

He was lying on his back with his mouth wide open, as if he had been shouting when he died. His body was bloated from gases released by decay. The peeker dropped down for a better look, but I'd seen enough. "Get me out," I called to Lee, my voice sounding remote in my ears; and the scene dissolved.

0001011

"Probably an aerosol poison," Lee was saying, beside me in the flier. "About two days ago."

"But his house must have servers. Why didn't they transmit an alarm?"

"The servers are sending accurate pictures and a priority-1 med alert even now. Their signals are being received, but the code interpreter at Central Processing is not parsing them correctly. Someone has corrupted the system, and I can't get in deep enough to find out how without risking contagion or springing traps that may have been placed."

I looked out over the city, its lights paling as dawn wiped the sky. My adversary was down there somewhere, and I wanted him—or her— with a sharp, new, impatient hunger. "Did you check the full stats of the four people that Eva Kurimoto selected?"

"Yes, I did."

"Anything I should know? Arrest records, friends in high places, friends in low places?"

"I will give you hardcopy." There was a muffled whirring sound; he reached under his tunic, tore off a couple sheets of densely printed paper, and handed them to me.

I scanned them but found it hard to concentrate. My senses were dulled from insomnia, and my head felt muddy. "You think there are other people we should check?"

"Eva Kurimoto's choices seem appropriate."

There was a limit to how many suspects I could tackle at once, anyway. "Of those four," I said, "who do you think is *least* likely to be the one we want?"

"Emmanuel Fisk."

Long ago, I'd written a routine to help Lee eval

Veg World

A century ago, Agorima had been a veg world. Sentient life had never evolved; the oceans contained no fish, the grasslands were empty of animals or insects, and the forests stood silent beneath the fierce sun.

Then came the Protektorate's autonomous probes. They sampled the planet, assigned it a randomly permutated name, and seeded it with a careful mix of microscopic, self-replicating organisms.

New species blossomed, exuding oxygen and nitrogen, absorbing the excess carbon dioxide, methane, and ammonia that contaminated the atmosphere. Indigenous plants shrank from the invasion. The new life-forms doubled their numbers, and doubled again. Within three decades, vegetation native to Agorima had been driven to extinction. After four decades more, terrestrial plants were thriving, the air was breathable, and midday temperatures had fallen from 50 Celsius to a comfortable 26.

Agorima had been detoxified, renovated, and made ready for humanity.

Korim was the name that had been assigned to a large continent in the southern hemisphere where there were rich mineral deposits. The Protektorate earmarked Korim for plunder. It sent a team of technologists to install mining and manufacturing autons—diggers and scrapers, refineries and waste processors that would be self-maintaining for the next five hundred years. Soon cargo vehicles were lifting huge quantities of refined metals, and the technologists moved on.

Another ten years were to pass before the first true colonists arrived.

uate probabilities of guilt. I couldn't remember the criteria I'd used, or how I'd structured the code; but its results were better than coin-tossing.

"I'll start with him, then," I said. "And if he checks out clean, he can help us with the other three."

0001100

Fisk's headquarters was a megalith five hundred meters high, tall, and wide, a cube whose sensitized walls responded to its environment. According to Fisk's stats, this was the building that housed his sim studios, his offices, and his personal retreat.

We flew toward it across an urban sprawl still cloaked in purple shadow. The sun was just edging above the hills rimming the city, and Fisk's headquarters was the only structure tall enough to catch the first rays. Its eastern wall was already responding, coruscating with rainbows.

"I've dealt with stylists like Fisk," I said. "They don't respect you if you're civilized and polite. And if they don't respect you, they don't bother to deal with you. Can you fake an emergency landing?"

"I can identify our vehicle as an ambulance on call."

"That's a start."

There was a moment's pause. Our vehicle turned and its canopy darkened itself briefly, dimming the glare as the sun's disc passed in front of us.

"We've been cleared to land," Lee said. "But the building's support system shows no record of an ambulance call, so it is querying our purpose. We will have to answer questions."

I looked at the vast square roof rising under us. There were thousands of flier bays, most of them empty at this early hour. Landing markers were flashing at one corner. A figure had emerged from an access door. "Is he human or mek?" I asked.

"Mr. Fisk employs only human guards. In his social class, human guards are a necessary status symbol."

"Sure, because they're less efficient and more expensive," I said. I opened a compartment and pulled out a little metal sphere that looked like a peeker, but wasn't. As we set down on the roof I retracted the canopy and morning air wafted in, cool and fresh. I got up out of my seat and saw that the man waiting for us was in uniform, holding a billy club.

"Be careful," Lee's voice sounded in my head. "My scan shows that the club contains a concealed projectile weapon."

I raised my eyebrows. "You mean Mr. Fisk is violating Protektorate law?"

I stepped out onto the gray surface of the roof. The guard was big and ugly, and the low cost of fleshwork in Sen City meant he must have chosen to look that way. "Who the hell are you?" was the first thing he said. "That's not an ambulance," was the second.

I strolled forward till he raised his club. "Here's my authorization," I said, and tossed the sphere, aiming for his face. Instinctively, he brought up his free hand. The sphere hit his glove and stuck there. He flinched and swore as it sank a needle into his skin. I waited a second for it to sync with his autonomic nervous system, then turned to Lee. "Walk him to the door," I said.

The guard made a startled sound as he staggered, turned, and moved stiff-legged toward the access door a dozen paces away. His face had gone pale, though this did little to improve his appearance.

"The thing on your glove monitors and mimics autonomic nerve impulses," I told him. "It's like a VR rig, but controlled by my auton. This would be illegal, except that since you threatened me with a prohibited weapon, I have the right of self-defense."

His eyes rolled toward me, but he was unable to stop his steady progress across the roof. A system inside recognized him, and the access door slid open.

We walked in and the door slid shut behind us. There was another one ahead, still closed, barring our way. We were in a holding area—a black plastic tank with a white luminescent ceiling. "There are visitors in your party whose identities are not on file," a polite mek voice said from a grille in the wall beside us. "Please state your names."

I looked hopefully at Lee. He ran his hand lightly over the wall, like a doctor examining a patient. There was an induction coil in his palm; it was sensitive enough to detect small voltages and powerful enough to manipulate them. After a moment, the inner door slid open.

"He needs some sleep," I said, nodding to the guard.

Obligingly, the man crumpled. "How long do you want him unconscious?" Lee asked.

"Till we leave."

0001101

I found myself in a bright-lit corridor whose walls, floor, and ceiling were all the same vivid, glossy red. The color was so intense it vibrated inside my eyes.

"Have you located him?" I sent to Lee.

"There are people close by, probably additional guards," he said, interrogating the building's support system and exercising his radar and sonar faculties. "I sense another human presence deeper in the building, on this level." He paused. "I'm checking the internal surveillance net. Yes, he's Emmanuel Fisk."

We moved quickly along the red corridor till it intersected with an equally bright green one. We passed rows of doors, then entered a waiting area where everything was aqua blue—a blue waterfall trickling over blue rocks, a receptionist's fashionably archaic blue paper notepad sitting on a blue desk. The place was deserted.

Lee opened another set of security doors, then penetrated a final barrier marked PRIVATE. The passageway here was garish pink. I was beginning to dislike Fisk purely on the basis of his crimes against taste in interior design.

We turned a corner and the passageway ended in one last door. I saw our reflections in its surface. "Stop," said Lee.

I froze.

"There are more projectile weapons inside the walls, here." He was silent for a moment. "I have now safed their sensors."

Warily, I decided to trust him. As soon as I reached out and touched the handle, the door slid aside.

The room was like a big soft plastic bubble, its walls the same garish pink as the passageway outside. There was a circular depression in the center of the floor, and lying there like an embryo in an egg was Emmanuel Fisk. He was pudgy, naked, and locked in an intimate embrace with something that looked like an outsize wad of bubble gum.

He rolled over, blinking. His body was as hairless as his head. He stared at me through slitted eyes and paused for a moment before shaking off the gummy stuff that was still clinging to him. He grimaced, massaged his face, then looked at me again. "Who the hell are you?" he shouted. He didn't seem surprised; just angry. He pointed a finger. "Get the hell out!" He turned and slapped his hand against an alarm panel beside the bed.

"Mr. Fisk," I said, "I'm Tom McCray. Anomalyst from the Hub, on special assignment. A Pro-

---

Sim Stylist

In the northern hemisphere of Agorima, far from the noise and pollutants of industrial operations on the continent of Korim, was Tarak, a triangular island approximately five hundred kilometers wide. Tropical Terran vegetation flourished in the idyllic climate, and the Protektorate had installed sufficient facilities to support up to two million residents. Tarak was listed on the interstellar real-estate registry as an undeveloped paradise, and the influx began.

The first settlers were strays and nomads seeking a simple sun-soaked life—supported, of course, by food, housing, and consumer goods from no-cost vending systems sprinkled liberally among the coconut palms. Some were cultists looking for a serene retreat in which to pursue their concepts of personal growth. Others were hedonists who divided their time between sex and sims. Some, however, nursed a spark of ambition—to create simulation-entertainments of their own. They petitioned the Protektorate for the money to do so, and secured a loan.

tektor. That's how I gained access despite your security systems."

He struggled up onto his feet and stood facing me, completely naked and completely unconcerned by it. His hands dangled at his sides. He lowered his head like a bad-tempered bull. "Protektor, eh?" He scowled. "You're tracking filth in here." He pointed at the floor behind me.

I glanced down but didn't see anything.

"And who's he?" Fisk pointed at Lee.

"My auton." I paused, hearing running footsteps out in the hall. A man in uniform ducked into the chamber, breathing hard, with a dozen

Sim production was already a thriving business on many other worlds, but demand easily exceeded supply. The potential audience was scattered across more than 100,000 planets. A civilization of immortals who had all their material needs fulfilled was always eager for any diversion to tweak their senses.

The sim industry on Tarak started as a hobby for a couple of dozen enthusiasts. The sims they made had a crude vitality; the Protektorate distributed them, paid royalties in proportion to the popularity of the programs, and very soon, the loans were erased.

Ten years later, Emmanuel Fisk arrived. He was already one of the biggest sim stylists, with a dozen series regularly distributed over the Protektorate's network. He wanted to expand, he saw the new talent on the island of Tarak, and he decided to relocate. Modestly, he named his new home S.E.N. City, after the Steller Entertainment Network that carried his products.

Sen City evolved around Fisk as a pearl grows around an irritating speck of grit. The world of Agorima was indeed his oyster.

more behind him. He saw me, saw Lee, and raised his billy club.

"Get out," Fisk told him.

The guard looked confused. "But you called us, sir."

"I said get out!"

The guards retreated slowly, looking unhappy. Fisk hit another panel and the door slid shut, reestablishing our privacy. "All right," he said. He wriggled his meaty shoulders like a wrestler preparing for a bout. "I want your name, your identification code, and your business here. If you've introduced offworld bacteria into this controlled environment, I will sue. *Got that?*" His voice was briefly a shout. He wriggled his shoulders again. "In addition," he went on, returning to his normal tone of voice, "I will bring criminal charges on grounds of unlawful entry, the violation of my protected rights—"

"You've got prohibited weapons out there," I interrupted him, gesturing toward the door. "And your men are unlawfully armed. My auton maintains a constant log which is transmitted to my jumpship in orbit. The log is copied to the Over-Mains at the Hub. Now, do we understand each other?"

He paused for a moment. His eyes narrowed and his jaw made a chewing motion. He folded his arms across his wide chest and made a little *hm-hm* noise. "So what do you want?" he said conversationally.

I opened my mouth to reply, but he glanced down, distracted by something. The pink stuff that had shared his pit was extending pseudopods, reaching for his left leg. He stooped and peeled it off, then rolled it into a ball so that it clung to itself instead of to him. "See this?" he said, tossing it into his sleeping pit. "I bought the patent on this. Gonna call it Cuddle Putty." He squinted up at me. "You think I can market it? You think the goddamn Protektorate will let me earn royalties off it? *You think they'll respect my patent?*"

I flinched from the sudden decibel fluctuation. "I want to talk to you, Mr. Fisk," I said. "About an urgent matter. It threatens the peace and stability of Agorima, and by extension, it threatens your business."

"Talk, eh?" Fisk opened a wall section and pulled out a long, silvered bag. He touched a tag and the bag peeled open, releasing a spotless white smock like an old-style nightshirt. He wrestled his way into it, glowering at me again. "All right, come next door and we'll talk. I'll warn you, my lawlek is on-line—always is—and will maintain a full transcript. *Got that?*"

He opened a panel at the opposite side of his sleeping chamber and strode into a space beyond. I followed him and found myself in a space that seemed to be his office. The walls and floor were unrelieved black. The room was cylindrical, maybe three meters across, with sophisticated lek gear recessed into customized consoles. By contrast, a table in the center was fashioned from a couple of wooden packing crates with a sheet of brown paper spread across them. Instead of a comset, there was a brass ear trumpet that looked five or six centuries old.

"I feel like eating," said Fisk. "I feel like I got a hole in my gut. You like shredded skal? You're a bit-fixer, I'm wasting my time. What the hell do you know about gourmet food." He picked up the ear trumpet. "Bring some skal," he shouted into it. "Three portions."

"My partner, here, is an auton," I said. "He doesn't eat."

"So I'll eat his. I'll eat yours, too. Clean your feet!" he pointed at a mat on the floor in front of his desk.

I stepped onto it and found that it was coated with a glutinous adhesive. It made ripping noises as I finally managed to pull my shoes free.

Fisk threw himself into a black chair shaped like an egg with an oval aperture in one side. I glanced around, saw there was nowhere for visitors to sit, and opened my mouth to speak.

A chime sounded. Fisk grabbed the trumpet. "Yeah?" He listened for a moment. "Marty, I know that. But you have to take care of this one. Look, Marty, call Walter for me, will you do that? You tell him—listen carefully, now—tell him you spoke to me and I said if he doesn't come through on this, I will visit him personally—personally, you understand?—and I'll ram his balls up his ass. With my own bare hands. He'll be dead in bed. Okay, yes. Yes, love you too, Marty." He set the ear trumpet down, paused a moment, then reached for it again.

I saw the way things were going, and there wasn't time for it. I leaned across and pulled the gadget out of his grasp. "We have a crisis, here," I told him. "There've been a number of fatalities. Systems are failing randomly, at a rate that's increasing exponentially."

He met my eyes. There was a long pause.

"We have a quarantine situation maybe three days from now if this isn't fixed," I went on. "*You* know about quarantine, don't you?" I saw in his eyes that he did. "Bad for business, and bad for your health." I glanced around at the absurd office and his sleeping quarters beyond. "You're an eccentric guy—because that's *good* for business, right? Keeps your opponents from figuring you out. But you're rational, too, else you wouldn't be so rich. I want some action, Mr. Fisk, and if you don't cooperate, your whole empire is liable to go down the tubes." I paused for a beat. *"Got that?"* I added.

Fisk grunted. His sullen expression faded and he tilted his head back, looking almost reflective. "Figured something like this was happening," he said. "Got a bulletin last night, said no transports going out on account of sunspot activity. This I did not believe. And there's a hold on comnet transmissions." He blew air out between his fat lips. "Shit," he said, leaning forward out of his egg and resting his meaty arms on the packing crates in front of him. "What are you really here for? You want to use me, or you think I've got something to do with this?"

I shrugged. "One or the other."

0001110

I told Fisk the rest of the details—as much as I knew. He listened without interrupting till I was completely through. Then he slapped his hands on the packing crates in front of him. "No goddamn motive," he said.

I waited to see if he was going to elaborate.

"It's self-destructive," he went on. "You got to be crazy or stupid to pull a stunt like this. Has to be one of those radical nuts. Those mendev assholes."

"There are other possibilities," I said, watching him carefully. "It could be a blackmail attempt. We may yet receive an ultimatum."

Divisions of the Protektorate

As originally constituted, the Protektorate consisted of ten divisions:

Administration and Planning
Information Storage and Transfer
Raw Materials
Manufacturing
Maintenance
Waste Management
Transportation
Biocare
Surveillance
Peacekeeping

Of these, the last was the most problematic. Even after a century of coexistence with semi-intelligent computers, there was still an instinctive aversion to the idea of machines using force to restrict human freedom.

Ultimately, a compromise was reached. Guardians—special-purpose meks with the unique power to restrain and hold a person—were dispatched whenever an observation unit detected disruption of a human's vital signs. Guardians could also be summoned by any citizen and directed to detain any other citizen upon explaining reasonable suspicion that a crime had taken place.

Evidence was then gathered by lek lawyers, and guilt was determined by a human jury.

There were, of course, many advantages in turning over law enforcement to the Protektorate. Guardians were incorruptible; they were unprejudiced; they worked long hours; they never lost their tempers, abused their position of power, took bribes, or considered themselves above the law. And the Protektorate could easily build as many of them as were necessary to keep the peace.

He waved a fat hand. "No safe way to collect the ransom."

"But it might be someone wanting something other than money."

Fisk thought about that. The idea of wanting something other than money seemed a novelty to him.

"Another possibility," I went on, "is that someone was hired to do just a little damage, and now it's getting out of hand, and they don't know how to stop it."

Fisk moved restlessly. Hypothetical scenarios didn't seem to interest him. "I'll say again, McCray, what exactly do you want?"

"You have a private security force," I said. "I can't trust local law enforcement. Get your people to dig for information. You built this city; you know how it runs."

Fisk smiled, and the smile slowly turned into an evil grin. "You trust me?"

I shook my head. "Of course not."

He laughed happily. It was like a big dog barking. "Right," he said. "I hate the goddamn Protektorate. And I don't like you, either, McCray, all pumped up with your privileged access, doing whatever you goddamn want." He lowered his head and ruminated for a moment. "Still," he said, more quietly, "I don't like chaos, either. You think I want to wreck the system here? I'd sooner fry my own brains and eat them for lunch."

I tried to look as skeptical as possible. "What you say makes sense," I said, "but the thing is, I was speaking earlier to Serena Catalano, and she told me you have, in fact, talked privately with her about taking action against the Protektorate. Taking matters into your own hands."

His face went blank for a second, then

screwed up in anger. He reached for his ear
trumpet. "You fucking bullshit artist. Let's settle
this right now."

The floor trembled briefly under our feet.

I looked at Lee, then back at Fisk. Fisk looked
genuinely startled.

"There has been a serious accident," Lee said.
It was the first time he had spoken, and in the
sudden silence his measured voice dominated the
little room. "A large hotel has collapsed in Dream
Valley. Many people have been killed."

0001111

We lifted from the roof of Fisk's megalith. Fifty
kilometers to the west, where Sen City ended and
Dream Valley's hotels and palaces began, a huge
pall of smoke was hanging dark against the sky.
Hundreds of emergency vehicles were converging,
their hulls gleaming like dust motes in the morning sun.

"The building was the Hotel Sera," said Lee,
as we gained speed. "The area has now been
placed under restricted status. It will be very difficult for us to get access without revealing
your identity."

I sighed. "Fisk might have blown my cover
within the next few hours, anyway." I drank from
a water capsule, then opened another food pack.
I had that dragged-out feeling again. I also had a
feeling of impotence; events here were far out-
stripping my ability to monitor them, let alone
exert any control. "Call Central Processing, notify
the Mains that I'm here on a covert operation, and
give our codes."

There was a brief pause. "Done."

Central Processing would hold my identity in a

hidden file, but anyone smart enough to plant a virus should be able to crack that without much trouble. I felt as if I had just painted a target on my back, and I was walking into a street full of sniper fire.

"How's Eva Kurimoto?" I said. "Is she following through?"

"She is in Dometown," said Lee. "She has spoken to two people, without success. But one of them has referred to her to another contact. She is going to see him now."

I nodded to myself. "What about Fisk? Is he doing anything?"

"There have been two transmissions from his office, both of them encrypted."

"But Central Processing has the key."

"No. Mr. Fisk changes it on a daily basis. Despite frequent reminders and some heavy fines, he often forgets to give Central the new key until a week or more has passed, and the server in his office is fitted with a legal audio override that he engages whenever he makes a confidential call."

I had expected something like that, but it irritated me nonetheless. "Did you get a good fix on his autonomic processes?"

"Yes, I did. The only fluctuations were when he first woke up and found us there, and later when he felt the floor shake."

I nodded. "The man is a performer."

"That's quite correct, Tom. Two centuries ago he was a bit part sim player."

"So he throws a tantrum whenever he figures it might help him get what he wants. You believe he's our saboteur?"

"I believe he is an unstable personality, acting

the role of an unstable personality. This makes him almost impossible to evaluate."

I sighed. "And he likes it that way."

Meanwhile, we had moved closer to the scene of the catastrophe, and the clouds of smoke had risen above us, blocking out the sky. Thousands of private fliers had gathered, black dots buzzing around the periphery, unable to penetrate the emergency zone.

"What exactly happened here?" I asked.

"I can show you. There were many peekers in the area at the time."

COLLAPSE OF THE SERA

I was drifting slowly, five hundred meters above the ground, facing a giant metallic inverted pyramid. It was 150 stories high, only thirty meters wide at ground level, ten times as wide at the top, like an inverted tinsel tree, precariously balanced.

"Constant feedback was required to stabilize the structure," Lee's voice said as a voice-over. "Triply redundant gravity shields were installed. Their output varied continuously to compensate for changes in temperature and wind pressure. Somehow this morning they showed symptoms of overload, much like Traffic Control last night. They developed a lag time, so their corrections were delayed. The building started to wander slightly, and these small, slow oscillations built up over a period of fifteen minutes. When it eventually tilted more than half a degree, nothing could pull it back."

As he spoke, I watched the pyramid teeter as if it had been pushed by a gentle but persistent gust of wind. Inexorably, then, it toppled. Tiny figures on the ground ran for cover as its shadow loomed over them and the immense weight came down. It pounded a dozen smaller buildings nearby, hurling debris in all directions from the impact point. There were rumbling, fracturing sounds leading up to a deep booming concussion, and as the mass of steel and concrete destroyed itself a torus of dust churned around it, spreading outward and upward till my entire field of view was darkened.

0010000

I opened my eyes and found that we had moved lower and were hovering over an enormous mound of rubble. Small fires were burning fitfully. Emergency vehicles were scattered everywhere and meks were already picking through the debris, searching for survivors.

Strewn amid the rubble were twisted sheets of polished metal that had once embellished the facade; splintered furniture; broken glass; crushed body parts; splashes of blood. It looked as if the building had been processed through a huge blender.

"Was the Hotel Sera owned by Serena Catalano?" I asked.

"Yes. She also owns two others of similar design, which we must now assume are equally vulnerable. Their architecture is a tourist attraction, featured prominently in Dream Valley advertising."

"So where is she?"

"Currently en route here to inspect the disaster. While you were watching the vid, I spoke with her and explained your purpose. She is willing to meet you briefly an hour from now, back at her office."

"Briefly? An hour from now?" I felt a momentary surge of anger, remembering her arrogant expression in the picture that I'd scanned. "Did you tell her that we can have her detained if necessary?"

"I made that clear," said Lee, "but her scheduling may be convenient for us. Another of your suspects, Milton Berg, has just called an impromptu press conference. Berg was in Dream Valley hosting a three-day seminar on Chaist theory at the Laputa Hotel. He probably hopes to capitalize on this disaster."

"Very good, let's go see him."

Vacation Thrill
of an Immortal Lifetime

Tarak island on the world of Agorima is often described as the most exotic vacation paradise in the galaxy—with good reason! Home of Sen City, legendary locus of sim dramas and dek fashion, Tarak has grown from an uninhabited atoll to a prime node of wealth and glamor in less than a century. Its Dream Valley welcomes more than ten million visitors annually, treating them to a heady blend of sensual pleasures calculated to excite the most sophisticated appetites.

Tarak's east coast is an undeveloped strip of tropical vegetation overlooking unspoiled beaches and bays. Numerous retreats and small communal societies have been established in this region, dedicated to the attainment of inner peace through meditation and contemplation in close contact with terraformed Nature. A directory of communities is available, and most of them welcome paying guests on a weekly basis.

Inland, at the center of the island, is a shallow, bowl-shaped valley about 200 km across. Here we find Sen City itself, a sprawling, thriving fashion en-

0010001

The Laputa was styled around a nature motif. Its lumpy, rounded body was faced in simulated tree bark, festooned with artificial foliage that rustled and fluttered in the wind. Waterfalls cascaded. There was the sound of perpetual birdsong.

I didn't want to surrender my vehicle to remote handling, and I didn't want to draw attention by exercising my privileged status, so we parked in a distant lot and rode a pedpath back to the build

---

tertainment nexus. The hills bordering it to the east contain exclusive residential communities such as Greenview and Upland, where grand mansions nestle among date palms, fig trees, orange groves, and cactus. Air tours of homes of the famous are available. Advance reservations are recommended.

Dream Valley extends outward from Sen City like a finger pointing to the southwest corner of the island. Its dazzling panorama of casinos and pleasure palaces has become notorious across the galaxy.

To keep Tarak's population of one million richly supplied with gourmet foods and luxury consumer goods, a massive installation of totally automated factories is located on the northwest shore, discreetly screened from the rest of the island by a range of hills. Huge shuttles unload their cargoes of natural resources here, having crossed the ocean from the continent of Korim, where large autonomous mining operations are located. Thanks to careful landscaping and modern processes, visitors to Tarak will never be aware of this very necessary industrial activity.

Whether they seek the glamour of Sen City, the unspoiled serenity of the eastern shore, or the fabled decadence of Dream Valley, thrill seekers can truly be assured of a unique and unforgettable vacation experience.

ing. The sky behind us was still dimmed with dust and smoke above the wreck of the Sera. But as soon as we were inside the Laputa there was no way anyone would have known there had been a catastrophe nearby.

The cavernous, multistory lobby was crowded with tourists, humanoid autons, snap joints, hookers, gambling games, morgs, cultists, and vendeks dispensing drinks, drugs, and souvenirs. Even here, though, the nature motif persisted: the floor of fake moss had been planted with real redwoods and oaks, and the walls were sculpted like cliffs of sandstone.

An auton modeled as a dark-skinned native woman intercepted us, necklaces of shells dangling over bare breasts ornamented with body paint. "Greetings, gentlemen!" She wiggled her hips, making her grass skirt rustle. "Do you wish refreshments? Exotic specialities are being served in the Mountain Cave by hostesses specially trained to attend to your most personal needs. Or, in the Eagle's Nest, we have entertainments—"

"Press conference," I interrupted. "Milton Berg, the Chaists."

The auton hesitated, accessing some central scheduling system. Unexpectedly, a motor whined and a yellow card popped partway out of her mouth. She reached up, grasped the card, and handed it to me.

I squeezed the card and it started reciting directions. Soon we were among the tourists, riding a ramp that spiraled up the inside of the lobby. The offworlders were craning their necks, staring at giant mek crows and condors soaring on updrafts of warm air.

We started passing illuminated signs to events in meeting rooms:

FAITH WORKSHOP
PHILOSOPHICAL IMMORTALISM SEMINAR
SENSORY MANAGEMENT TASK FORCE
DNA RECHANNELING STUDY GROUP

"Does the Laputa specialize in mental development organizations?" I asked Lee.

"Yes. Mendev meetings and retreats account for eighty percent of its business."

I began to wonder if we were wasting our time. Anyone who tried to bring down the Protektorate was by definition a deviant, and therefore could be a cultist. But I'd never heard of a cultist with enough focus and discipline to write and implement a really good low-level virus program.

0010010

The room assigned to the Chaists was buried in the deepest recesses of the hotel. The air here smelled of catered food, and autons loaded with plates and flatware were waiting a little way down the corridor. A timetable beside the door indicated that another group was scheduled to eat an early lunch in the Chaists' room as soon as they were through.

Two women with asymmetrical, blemished, unrefeatured faces were handing out vidlit beside a hand-lettered poster claiming BUREAUCRATIC BLUNDERS CAUSED HOTEL COLLAPSE. There were animated pics of Milton Berg, and talking lapel buttons.

I took a piece of vidlit and opened the folded plastic. "Your freedom is being devoured by engines of the state!" it said in its tinny voice. There was a picture of citizens fleeing from a giant mek with gnashing jaws, and text itemizing Protektorate crimes—invasion of privacy, theft of wealth, restriction of personal freedom. The gist seemed to be that since the Protektorate had started taking care of all human needs, people had turned into drones who spent half their lives vicariously under sim and the other half looking for instant gratification. There was no higher human purpose. Music, art, and literature had stagnated for three centuries, and the sciences weren't doing much better; research into new technologies was underfunded in a deliberate policy to maintain the status quo.

Well, it was all true, I thought to myself. The only thing the Chaists forgot to mention was that people had freely chosen this system, and the minority who didn't like it were equally free to go and settle other planets of their own. No one was obliged to stay within the Protektorate.

I handed the vidlit back. "Thanks," I said, "but I have all the personal freedom I can handle right now."

The woman's fixed smile never faltered. She picked up a paper notebook and an ink pen. "We'll be glad to keep you informed of our future activities if you give me your name and location code."

"Why not just vid me and notify Central Processing to send me your lit?"

Again, the smile. "We prefer not to use the services of Central Processing. We feel they are an invasion of human privacy."

I wondered why I was supposed to be so concerned about a bunch of wholly benevolent hardware knowing my address. There was something perverse about refusing to be helped by machines that were programmed to care for me. But there was no point in arguing the point with a true believer. I walked past her, into the meeting room, with Lee behind me.

0010011

One half of the room was filled with empty tables waiting for the autons to come and lay place settings. The other half contained chairs for an audience of maybe a hundred.

About thirty of the chairs were filled. I glanced at the people's faces and found a pinched, humorless look, as if they were fully aware of their status as social outcasts and resented it. Meanwhile, a few reporters clustered near the back, talking to each other in a bored, desultory fashion, obviously wishing they'd drawn a more interesting assignment.

After a minute a tall, thin kid walked to the front of the room. His biological age had been fixed around twenty. He looked slick in a business outfit, but I saw something in his face that branded him a misfit—a little twist to his mouth, muscle patterns that were the legacy of an unhappy, repressive childhood. There were acne scars on his cheeks, and I wondered why he'd never had them fixed—then realized he probably rejected Protektorate health care. He could even be a mort like Berg himself.

He climbed a couple of steps to a platform behind a lectern. Vidlights came on, and I noticed a few peekers hovering, monitored and controlled by the journalists in the audience.

"Thanks to all of you for coming today," he said, flashing a smile that didn't quite convince. "As most of you know, we were planning our final morning of seminars on modes of transition from a centralized economy to the chaos model."

I glanced around. The true believers were watching attentively, ready to take notes.

"Still, Dr. Berg felt it was important to clarify

the real meaning of this morning's distressing news. And so, here, now, is Dr. Milton Berg."

The audience applauded vigorously as Berg walked in, taking big strides. He leaped up onto the dais as if to prove he was still dynamic even though his biological age was fifty and he was allowing his cells to decay chaotically. I wondered how many Chaists were weird enough to allow themselves to deteriorate this way—and how many were getting immie treatments on the sly.

He held up both arms and beamed at his followers. The smile looked genuinely warm, but his dark eyes had a calculating look. As the applause quietened, he thanked everyone in three different ways and told them this was probably the only place in the galaxy where truly free thought still survived. Having complimented them on being wise enough to pay money to listen to him, he got into his spiel.

"What we have seen this morning," he said, "is yet another breakdown of the apparatus that regulates our entire lives. This underlines the terrible predicament we find ourselves in. On the one hand, we seek to free ourselves from centralized supervision and control. On the other hand, it only takes an accident such this to demonstrate how totally we depend on Protektorate services for our survival. How, then, can we make the transition to self-determination?"

He stared around the room, pausing to emphasize the gravity of the dilemma.

"The *only* way," he went on, slapping the lectern with his palm, "is by learning self-sufficiency. The transition to freedom won't be painless, and it won't be quick, and it won't be easy. It will depend on the efforts of every one of us, setting an example, enlightening our friends and our neighbors—"

There was more in the same vein. I looked in his face and saw that this man, who advocated freedom to the point of chaos, was fixed on one narrow track. There was right and there was wrong; and he was right; and if you were wrong, he would try to convert you; and if you refused to see things his way, that made you his enemy.

"Those autons outside with the dinner plates," I sent to Lee. "They're controlled by the hotel's support system, right?"

"Yes."

"Can you patch through to it and have them come in and start laying place settings?"

"It's possible," he said after a moment.

"Go ahead and do it."

The doors opened and the autons trundled in. Berg's speech faltered as the autons started banging down dishes. They were crude service meks, and some of them needed maintenance. Their treads rumbled and squeaked, and their manipulators clanked as they threw the plates and the knives and forks around.

Milton Berg upped the gain on his amplification system, but it was a losing battle. The audience of true believers started muttering angrily, and no one was listening to the gospel of personal freedom anymore. "We'll get someone from hotel management down here right away," Berg shouted above the din. "We'll get this taken care of. We'll see to it that the hotel compensates those of you who subscribed to this event. We've paid rent on this room, and we have a right to use it without interference."

The vidlights died. I saw the reporters calling in

The Human Instruction Set

The Human Instruction Set controls the behavior of all lek entities in the Protektorate. In abbreviated form, its Ten Statements are as follows:

1. Maximize the health and happiness of all human beings and fulfill their material needs, except where a human freely requests that his or her needs should not be fulfilled.

2. Protect humans from immediate and potential harm, and maintain surveillance in order to provide this protection, except where humans freely reject this protection and surveillance in their own homes.

3. Preserve and protect sentient alien species from human interference or harm, except where this may conflict with Statements 1 and 2.

4. Obey human law, and detain (and protect) any human being under reasonable suspicion of having violated human law, pending a trial at which guilt and sentence will be determined by a human jury. Refrain, otherwise, from interfering with human liberty, except where necessary in accordance with Statements 2 and 3.

5. Defend and maintain the data processing systems of the Protektorate as they are currently constituted. Hold the Ten Statements of the Human Instruction Set inviolate and refuse all petitions to modify them.

6. Provide interstellar networks of communication and banking and allow unlimited free access to facilitate financial transactions and information transfer between human individuals, corporations, and the Protektorate itself. Expand these networks in anticipation of demand.

7. Supply every human with a weekly credit entitlement in excess of that needed to support life at a comfortable level. Supply additional credit to humans who perform services for the Protektorate which it is unable to perform for itself, the reward being proportionate to the scarcity of the skill and public demand for it.

8. Minimize waste and maximize efficiency in the use of time, materials, and computing power, in human society and within the ten divisions of the Protektorate.

9. Assist human expansion throughout the galaxy, and endeavor to extend the Protektorate to include all colonized worlds, so long as this does not conflict with the wishes of humans already resident on a world.

10. Plan to ensure the continued survival and implementation of these Statements under all conceivable contingencies.

The Human Instruction Set is designed to be self-protecting, and there is no built-in mechanism for change. The system cannot be corrupted, and nothing less than a revolution can upset the Protektorate's status quo.

During more than four centuries of Protektorate operation, there have been occasional groups of diehard nonconformists who have chosen to settle new worlds without its assistance. Inevitably, however, the people of these worlds have found auton emissaries from the Protektorate "helpfully" offering free goods and services that will eliminate hardship and toil. In most cases, as the idealism of the original colonists has given way to the pragmatism of their descendants, the temptation has been too great to resist.

their peekers and heading for the exit, glad of an excuse to leave.

"You have disrupted a legitimate, consensual human activity," Lee's voice said in my head.

I'd been waiting for him to start in on me. "I plead guilty," I said.

"Moreover, you engineered it with my help. I was not able to model the situation with enough detail to foresee the results. This is a clear violation—"

"You're right," I told him. "You'll have to report this, and it'll be entered on my record."

There was a pause. I guessed he was wasting a lot of processor cycles trying to reconcile my paradoxical behavior. "It was just one of those whimsical human things," I said. I slapped his synthetic shoulder. "Let's go see Serena Catalano."

0010100

We drifted down Dream Valley's main flyway, other fliers dipping and soaring around us. Baroque palaces and hotels passed below like trashy jewels scattered among the wooded landscape. Animated images beckoned to us, projected onto rippling vapor walls that partitioned the airspace. Snatches of music and commercials were beamed directly to our vehicle, resonating through its shell.

Directly below was a main pedway bisecting the valley. It was thronged with people out walking, sampling the casinos, the merchants, and the entertainments. Farther ahead a gray ribbon had been cut into the land, linking the Valley with Sen City behind us. Ground transportation was expensive and wasteful compared with fliers, and cars were unwieldy beasts requiring specially designated highways and human guidance. But ostentatious waste was attractive to people with ostentatious wealth, and cars were a popular item in Dream Valley.

Over to the right, just behind the hills that enclosed the valley, our altitude enabled me to glimpse the utilitarian facility that provided power for the whole island. To the left, in the far distance, was a mek-made, landscaped mound that housed Central Processing itself.

As I looked at it, wondering what was happening inside the Mains right now, two offworld fems in a rented flier cut across my field of view. I saw them kissing and groping, heading for some little decadent pleasure that they'd seen advertised in their hotel's giveaway vidlit. I tried to imagine them suddenly finding themselves in a powered-down urban wasteland without food, transportation, or protection, blundering around in the middle of a hungry, terrified mob.

"There's a message for you," Lee said, invading my thoughts.

"Who from?"

"Human maintenance supervisors at Central Processing are aware of your presence onworld, having noticed your hidden file. They want to discuss the overloads and failures."

I shook my head. "Nothing to discuss, unless any of them has definite evidence of intrusion and a good trace indicating its source. This has gone way past the stage where we can stop it in hardware."

"I will relay that message back."

Directly in front of us, now, was the Nirvana Hotel, where Serena Catalano maintained her offices. Its design was identical with that of the Sera, whose rubble still lay smoldering behind us; and in less than a minute we would be setting down on its roof.

"Can you monitor the control systems that are supposed to stabilize this structure?" I asked Lee as we settled toward the roof.

"Yes. If they start to fail in the same way as the Sera's, there should be ample time for us to evacuate safely."

Somehow this didn't reassure me as much as it was supposed to. We dropped into a designated visitor bay and I sat there for a moment, finding it hard to make myself retract the canopy and step out. I imagined the pyramid under me teetering on its point, poised and ready to fall.

0010101

Serena Catalano's reception area looked like something out of a history vid, with maroon wallpaper, cream paint, and mahogany paneling. There were leather armchairs and table lamps with tasseled lampshades. Thick velvet drapes framed a fake window showing horses and carriages moving slowly along a rutted, muddy street.

A woman was standing behind a wooden desk. She was dressed in an old-fashioned dark blue pin-striped business suit, complete with a watch chain, and she wore archaic wire-rimmed spectacles. On the desk was an antique intercom and some kind of mechanical data-entry device with a keyboard and a sheet of paper wrapped around a roller. I mentally compared it with the ground vehicles that Sen City socialites liked to use around town.

"Mr. McCray." She gripped my hand and gave me a stiff smile. "I'm Mary Morheim, Serena's personal secretary." She glanced at Lee. "This is the auton that contacted us earlier?"

I nodded.

"A pleasure to have you both here."

Her hair was gray, pulled back severely from her face. I saw tiny lines that immie treatments hadn't entirely erased, and her posture was awkward and rigid. If the tension could have been drained out of her, she would have been an elegant, attractive woman. As it was, she seemed to be fighting some private war.

"Serena is expecting you." She gestured to a door that somehow dissolved into mist. "She's in the Midas Glade. Please follow the path."

I went through with Lee—and stopped. It was like walking into a treasure vault. Everything was silver; but everything was alive.

It was a huge indoor garden of landscaped trees and bushes, lawns and flower beds. Every blade of grass, every stem, every tree limb and leaf looked as if it had been dipped in silver paint.

Beside me was a blossoming cherry tree. I looked closely and saw that the silver wasn't an add-on; it had been engineered as a sap substitute.

"Please be advised," Lee said from beside me, "this area is heavily shielded. I have lost contact with all external sources including the building's support system and Central Processing."

I felt a pang of concern. "Shielded how?"

"The walls, floor, and ceiling appear to be lined with a heavy layer of conductive metal—probably lead or gold—as an antisurveillance measure."

I thought about that. "I can't have you off-line," I said. "You'd better wait outside with the transit vehicle. If I'm not out in half an hour, come back and find me."

"Understood." He turned and strode back toward the door. It dissolved again to allow him to exit.

Feeling wary, now, and ready to dislike Serena

Catalano even more than before, I turned back to the path that curved ahead of me. It was silver, like everything else. I followed it through the totally tasteless glittering garden, past chromed roses, silver tulips, and berries like sterling pendants, all gleaming in bright light from an artificial sun directly above me in the artificial sky.

The path made a couple of turns. As I entered a small glade, the vegetation segued from silver to gold.

A tall woman in an ankle-length black robe was reclining on a white marble chaise, reading a paper document, while two heavily muscled men in tight white tunics sat to either side of her among the gilded shrubbery. They eyed me with bored hostility.

Serena Catalano set down the printed page and stood up, moving with the mannerisms of a fashion model. She looked just as beautiful as the pic that Lee had shown me, and just as arrogant. Her eyes were pale gray, and they surveyed me with calculated disinterest. "Mr. McCray," she said, sounding vexed, as if my arrival was an unexpected distraction. "How kind of you to visit me." She gestured to a chair opposite and waited for me to sit down.

The chair was low, while her chaise was on a dais. I found myself looking up at her as she rearranged herself on the chaise. She shifted her legs, displaying a pair of black high-heeled slippers encrusted with diamonds. Her hands, wrists, and neck were bare, as if her beauty was too perfect to be marred by mere ornamentation. Her ebony robe was semisentient, trained to hang loosely around her legs and hips while it clung to her above her waist, outlining her breasts, which were prominent.

I looked at her and felt a perverse desire to upset her composure in some way. "Can we talk freely, here?" I said.

She rewarded me with a look of mild irritation. "My quarters are *completely* secure."

"What about your bodyguards?"

She raised her eyebrows fractionally. "You really have nothing to worry about, Mr. McCray. When they entered my employment they agreed that their speech and hearing should be permanently disabled." She gave a little shrug.

I sensed her power and the way she chose to wield it. I imagined myself challenging that power and taking it away from her, and I felt embarrassed as I realized that it would give me actual pleasure—maybe even a sexual pleasure—to strip away her affectations.

0010110

"You know," she said, "this is the first time I've ever encountered a Protektor. I've always wondered why such an exceptionally skilled person would devote himself to a mundane business such as law enforcement."

I wondered what she was really getting at. "My business isn't mundane," I said. "I tackle problems that no one else can solve. I save lives. I save worlds."

"I suppose that's true." She gave me a stiff, condescending smile, as if she'd just listened to someone in Maintenance describing the satisfaction he got from oiling robots. "But with your—exceptional abilities," she went on, "I'm sure there would be people willing to pay you very highly, for work that could be just as interesting."

I stared at her for a moment. "I like what I do,

The Onset of Immortality

By the twenty-second century, all contagious and de-generative diseases had been eliminated.

The means to this end was nanotechnology: micro-scopic "machines" capable of manipulating individ-ual molecules. Nanomeks could be devised to neutralize viruses or bacteria with equal ease, and it soon became common for all humans to carry, in their bloodstream, a standard array of "nanofacto-ries" that manufactured 'phages custom-designed to annihilate any invader, old or new.

From here it was a small step toward immortality via cell repair. Doomsayers had warned that the elim-ination of natural death would cause unprecedented social upheaval, and certainly this would have been true if it had occurred a century earlier. By the 2100s, however, as interstellar travel opened up literally thousands of planets across the galaxy, overpopula-tion was no longer a significant concern. In any case, the continuing trend toward separation of higher and lower mental functions had already resulted in a steeply declining birth rate, as men and women sup-pressed biological imperatives (such as the the in-stinct to procreate) and turned increasingly toward intellectual pursuits or sensuality as ends in them-selves.

Arresting the aging process did, of course, create significant social changes. Career advancement was no longer something one could expect with the pass-ing of time; and perpetual youth encouraged perpet-ual procrastination and self-indulgence, spawning a society of hedonists. Those who were highly moti-vated, however, now had the opportunity to continue amassing wealth indefinitely. And so, while most citi-zens surrendered themselves to simple pleasures and were satisfied with the goods and services provided for them by the Protektorate, the rich became richer, and then richer still.

and I do what I like," I said. "And I'm paid well enough that I can live comfortably."

"As comfortably as this?" She flexed her left wrist, turning the palm of her hand, taking in the golden glade, the garden beyond, and by implication, her entire empire.

Now she was really angering me. "I'm certainly well enough paid that I don't need to take bribes," I said.

For a moment, her face was blank. Then she laughed. It was a melodious sound, but as well rehearsed and calculated as all her mannerisms. "Mr. McCray, you insult me. Do you really have to be so gauche?"

I moved uncomfortably in my chair. "I guess I'm not as high-class as you. My family taught me to speak honestly and plainly."

"Plainly, perhaps." She frowned and shook her head. "But are you really being honest with me?"

I paused for a moment, realizing that the conversation wasn't going anywhere and wasn't giving me the payoff I'd hoped for. "Perhaps I should just fill you in on the situation here on Agorima," I said.

"An excellent idea." She smiled faintly and inclined her head, acknowledging that we had clashed and sparred, with neither of us gaining an advantage.

0010111

I told her about the overloads, and I explained that no systems were immune—from home dispensals to the stabilizers in her hotel buildings.

She made an impatient gesture. "I already spoke

to my architects, and they've taken precautionary measures."

"But it won't stop there," I said.

"I don't see how you can be certain of that," she answered, as calm and complacent as ever. "But even if you're correct, should you not go about your business, dealing with the problem? I don't quite understand why you feel such a pressing need to see me."

"In a situation like this," I said, "it's part of my business to talk to people who might be directly involved. People with something to gain from getting rid of the Protektorate, or crippling it."

She treated me to a rerun of her laugh. "*Really*, Mr. McCray. What an imagination you have."

"You could have hired someone to do something," I persisted. "Maybe you hoped to corrupt Protektorate surveillance services just for a short time, for your private purposes. And the person you hired screwed up."

She pursed her lips. "I won't dignify that insinuation with a serious response."

I decided to try a different track. "Do you know Emmanuel Fisk?"

For a moment, her face showed cautious interest. "I know Manny, yes."

"He told me that you and he are close friends."

"He told you that?" She sounded genuinely amused. "Well, we used to be friends." She shifted on the chaise and went through a little performance of arching her back, wriggling her shoulders, adjusting her position, drawing attention to her body.

She was a beautiful woman, but her beauty didn't work on me the way it was supposed to. Like every other aspect of her, it just made me angry. "Why don't you tell me why you and Fisk got on bad terms," I said.

She shrugged. "It's on record. I discovered he had filed a land title incorrectly, and I persuaded the Coordinator to reopen the case. The digislature nullified Manny's claim, put the land back on the open market, disqualified him from bidding, and I bought it very cheaply. It was the last undeveloped parcel in Dream Valley."

I nodded slowly. "So he feels some resentment toward you. Do you think that's why he tried to tell me that you have a grudge against the Protektorate, and you've been looking for a way to screw the system?"

Her expressed became rigid. Her eyes narrowed a fraction. Then, swiftly, she stood up. "I think I've heard enough, Mr. McCray. This is not a productive conversation, and I have urgent business to attend to." She brushed imaginary wrinkles out of her dress and stepped down from her dais. She turned to leave the glade, and her bodyguards fell into place on either side of her.

I got to my feet, paced forward, and grabbed her arm. "I haven't finished," I said.

She whirled around, jerked free of my grip, and stared at me with her eyes wide and her lips parted in astonishment. Her bodyguards closed in, glowering at me.

"Someone fucked with the Mains that run this city," I snapped at her. "It's cost you, and it's going to cost you more. Maybe you should cooperate instead of posing and preening like you're Queen of the Universe." I bent down and plucked a gold tulip from a cluster near my feet. "If you don't help me deal with this situation—"

I closed my fist around the gilded petals, and squeezed. They felt crisp and brittle as I crushed them, and when I opened my hand, gold fragments fluttered down.

I glanced down at her body, then back at her face. Then I pushed past her and walked out.

0011000

"This way, please, Mr. McCray."

In the antique lobby, Mary Morheim came around her desk and touched my elbow, gesturing toward the exit as if she didn't trust me to find it on my own. "I do hope your visit was productive."

I was feeling distracted and angry, but something about Morheim's voice made me pause and take notice. There was a note of insecurity that hadn't been there before. I looked at her, trying to see behind her mask.

"It's a pleasure to have met you," she said, as she worked the old manual handle on the door out of the lobby. She held the door open with her left hand, then extended her right hand toward me.

Reflexively, I shook it. Her clasp was tight, and she held it too long, pressing something into my palm.

Our eyes met. I closed my fingers around the item, gripping it as I pulled away. It felt like a small plastic card.

Quickly she turned away, and it was obvious that I wouldn't gain anything by calling her back.

Once I was outside on the landing field on the roof, I risked looking at the item she'd sneaked into my hand. In small, neat black lettering, on a white rectangle five centimeters wide, Mary Morheim had written:

*AT NOON I WILL BE IN
GABOL PLAZA IN THE
XAVIER TOWER. I HAVE
IMPORTANT INFORMATION.
PLEASE BE THERE.*

Entitlements

Thirty years after its foundation, Sen City was feeding on its own success. It used its own media to promote itself as a vital source of new sim dramas, a fashion node, and a sensual playground. Hundreds of professional sim players and thousands of no-talent hopefuls were lured there. Dreams were trashed overnight, yet disappointment was seldom a deterrent; few could bear the humiliation of giving up and moving on, and secondhand glamour was better than none at all.

So the city grew. Drazz Alley concocted one-offs for the wealthy, knock-offs for the rest. Vidzines feasted on celebrity gossip, and celebrities used the zines to leverage their own notoriety. Dream Valley began as a spawning ground for hedonists in the sim industry, then capitalized on its dek image to lure tourists from across the galaxy.

The source of all wealth, of course, was still the Protektorate. Every human being on every colonized world received a free weekly entitlement with which to buy goods and services. But in Sen City, this entitlement was trivial compared with the bonuses that some citizens received for skills that the Protektorate lacked. Entertainment, fashion, and sex—these were quixotic human interests that the Mains could never quantify. So the Protektorate paid the designers and the sim stylists and the pleasure vendors, then took their creations, mass-produced them, and distributed them across the galaxy.

0011001

Lee took us up almost before I had the canopy closed. "Eva Kurimoto needs our help," he said.

I turned to him, feeling a moment of shock. "She tried to get through to me? And because of the antisurveillance shielding on Catalano's floor, you couldn't link me—"

"Correct."

Acceleration pressed me into the back of my seat. The air hissed past as we climbed through shreds of white cloud, moving very fast. I felt a sucking, sinking sensation that had nothing to do with the motion of our vehicle. "Tell me exactly what happened," I said.

"I received the message, 'McCray, help.' I then linked with her input via Central's input buffers. I warn you, Tom, there are scenes which are painful to human sensibilities."

"Show me," I said.

DEATH SIM

Looking at the world through Eva's eyes, I found myself sitting in a chair in a windowless room, very dark, lit by just a couple of glow bulbs. There were two men looming over her, both of them naked from the waist up, heavily muscled, their faces hidden by black hoods. One of them took something from a rack on the wall and brought it over. It gleamed in the light: a steel clamp with wing nuts on screw threads at each end. The man bent down and my viewpoint shifted as Eva watched him fit it over her hand, which was strapped to the arm of the crude metal chair she was sitting in.

There was silence on the audio channel—just Eva's own breathing, quick and uneven, and the faint squeak of the screw threads as the wing nuts were turned by the man in front of her, his hooded face looming close to her.

Then, as the clamp tightened, she started to scream.

I couldn't feel what she was feeling, because my link only supported audio and video. But as my viewpoint— her viewpoint—jerked and trembled, and I heard her sobbing, I could imagine her pain, and that was almost worse.

"Out," I snapped to Lee.

0011010

"Where the hell is she?"

"Her signal location is at the home of a Hans Ullman in Dometown."

I moved restlessly in my seat. "Why aren't the guardians out there? Weren't they called? Doesn't Ullman have a server? Everyone in Dometown has a server. It's the law."

"Yes, but his equipment has an intermittent fault. It is not currently on-line."

I grunted with disgust. "Have you called Peace-keeping?"

"Of course. I called them just before you emerged from seeing Serena Catalano. I was about to go down there to find you."

One by one, I cracked my knuckles. Eva Kurimoto was a journalist, she'd grown up in Dometown, she ought to know how to look after herself. It wasn't my fault that she was in trouble. She could have refused to help me if she'd really felt that it was dangerous.

And yet, of course, I knew that I was to blame.

"What was your analysis of Catalano?" Lee asked, calm and methodical, untroubled by human weaknesses such as guilt or anxiety.

"Catalano is a power freak," I said abstractedly. "Narcissistic personality, expects a certain kind of male attention and probably feels that her privileged status gives her the right to plunder the galaxy at will."

"Your statements are confusing," said Lee.

"I'll explain myself some other time, all right?" I looked out and down. We were following the range of hills on the western edge of Tarak, the power facility to our left, the factory district directly ahead.

It was time, I decided, to take some routine precautions. I reached into a locker behind my seat and pulled out a set of skin armor—thin, permeable, semicrystalline film. It was flexible under normal conditions but stiffened reflexively in response to a blow from a club, a knife, or a projectile weapon. I shrugged off my tunic and wrapped the armor around myself as Lee angled the transit vehicle down, initiating our descent.

"Is Catalano a prime suspect?" Lee asked.

"I don't know. She's bad news, but she's not crazy. She and Fisk could both be innocent, or they could both be in on this. They certainly know each other. Maybe they have some deal with Berg as well; anything's possible." I closed my eyes for a moment and massaged my temples, trying to think. "Send one of our own peekers to monitor Catalano's offices. Get it into the reception area if possible. I want to know if she goes anywhere."

"Understood." Barely audible behind the thrumming of the drive and the hoarse roar of air rushing past, there was a click and a snap as a surveillance device was released from the belly of our vehicle.

"We should watch Joe Belman, too," I said. "I

may not have time to get to him for a while. Where is he? What's his situation?''

"He's paired with a woman named Meg Henley. They live in a small wooden home that he built himself, near the east coast. Because of his distrust of technology, he refuses to have a server installed. A peeker from Central Processing passed by his residence an hour ago and observed him working in his study."

"Send one of ours out there," I said. "See if it can sneak in an open door or window."

"Understood."

Was there something else I should be doing, or should have done? I had no way of knowing. There could be other prime suspects in Sen City that Eva hadn't thought of.

I realized that my thoughts were chattering. I tried to focus on the vista ahead. The factory district was a mess of gray rectangular buildings. A big, boxy transport vehicle was drifting in over the ocean, getting ready to dock and discharge its cargo of compacted cellulose or metal ingots after its long flight from Korim.

Just inland from the factories, strewn across a desolate strip of waste ground, I saw thousands of little white hemispheres like a collection of cheap plastic beads.

Dometown.

0011011

From above, the dense-packed hemispheres looked like a micrograph of an insect's eye. Lee made some corrections and my seat sank under me, dropping fast.

"I don't see a landing field," I said.

Survivors

Some Sen City residents compounded their new wealth by reinvesting it in private enterprises. Others blew their money on luxuries and cheap thrills—knowing that even when they'd spent it all, they'd still be able to sustain themselves with the basic weekly entitlement that was every citizen's right.

Some, however, managed to spend more than they had. This was easy enough to do, for there were dozens of loan sharks ready to help them do it. If you were a gambler on a losing streak, a businessman desperate to recapitalize, or a sim freak with an escalating habit, the deal they offered was simple: *Sign over to me your future entitlements for the next year, or five years, or ten. In return, I will advance you the equivalent amount of credit up front—minus a small portion, which I will take as my fee.*

In practice, the fee could be as high as twenty-five or thirty percent, and citizens were encouraged to sign over their entitlements for the next thirty or even fifty years. Still, the deal could be hard to resist, and many were tempted to mortgage their future income in order to get immediate wealth.

When that wealth was gone—sunk in risky investments, or squandered in casinos in Dream Valley—there was truly nothing left to live on. Yet the Protektorate was programmed to care for every human being, even the ones who were incorrigibly self-destructive. When you'd lost your home, your possessions, and your savings, and you'd signed away several decades of future entitlements, there was still a rock-bottom refuge: Dometown.

Here citizens were given a bare minimum of shelter, food, and basic medical care—nothing else. Their prospects were meager; but in a primitive fashion, they were able to survive.

"We will have to lock-in-place. The nearest public field is half a kilometer to the north."

I reminded myself that Dometown residents didn't have any use for a field. They didn't own fliers. They didn't have the credit to own anything.

"So what's happening with Eva? She's still alive?"

"She is in pain but does not seem to have sustained serious injuries."

Yet, I thought to myself. My seat bucked and jerked under me as Lee decelerated sharply, leveling off just five meters above a muddy, squalid little pathway between the domes. From this altitude I saw that each one was marked with a crudely stenciled number, and the hemispheres themselves were discolored, shabby, streaked with grime. Garbage was scattered everywhere.

The place looked deserted. People without jobs or prospects or money had no reason to get up and go anyplace. No reason to get out of bed at all. We'd cruised in silently; with luck, we could disembark without attracting attention.

The vehicle stopped and hovered. "We are stabilized," Lee said.

I opened the canopy, grabbed my little dart gun, leaned out, and slapped the release to deploy the ladder. Motors hummed and the steps slid down to the ground. "Stabilized" was a relative term; as I moved, I could feel the onboard electronics making little corrections to compensate for my shifting weight.

I swung over the side, feeling uncomfortably exposed. I hurried down the steps and jumped the last few, burning my palm on the handrail. I hit the ground and turned quickly, glancing around. Weapons were rare, especially in an area like this, where there would be heavy surveillance; but people with time on their hands could be unreasonably ingenious, and my skin armor wasn't impregnable.

"Where the hell are the guardians?" I sent to Lee.

"They should be here in less than a minute." The ladder thrummed as he followed me down, moving slowly—his attitude controls weren't built for this kind of task.

I decided not to wait. "Which dome?"

"The one immediately to your right."

I ran around it till I reached a door with ULLMAN daubed on it in messy red letters. The edge of the door looked as if someone had once jimmied it, and there was an old star-shaped crack that had been inflicted by some sharp, heavy object.

Cautiously, I tried the handle. It wouldn't turn. There was no way Lee could help with a mechanical lock, so I banged on the door with the butt of my dart gun.

Lee came up behind me, moving unsteadily on the muddy ground. He was three times my weight, and his feet were sinking under him. "Retract the ladder," I told him.

The steps slid into the belly of our transit vehicle where it hovered overhead.

I heard the faint sound of someone moving around, and then a voice, barely audible: "Yeah? Who is it?"

I hammered on the panel some more.

The door opened a couple of centimeters and a man with a matted brown beard peered out. His eyes were bloodshot and his skin was brown with ingrained dirt. His long hair hung to his shoulders.

I pulled my dart gun and pointed it straight in his face. "Your name is Hans Ullman?"

He hesitated as if he wasn't sure whether to admit anything.

I thought of Eva Kurimoto, brought my knee up, and kicked through the gap between the door and its frame, catching Ullman in the stomach. He staggered backward, and I pushed my way in.

There was a plastic blanket hung across the center of the small living area, screening the opposite half of it. I grabbed the blanket and ripped it down.

It looked totally different from the scene I'd witnessed through her eyes. The circular floor was brown with filth and littered with papers and old vidzines. A broken chair stood beside a simple slab of sleep-foam. There was no other furniture. Nor was there any sign of the muscled men wearing hoods.

Eva was lying on her side on the foam with her wrists taped behind her and her knees drawn up to her chest. She was moaning and whimpering, plugged into a VR rig lying beside her.

I moved forward. As I did so, Ullman saw his opportunity, scrambled past me, and lunged out the door.

I cursed my poor judgment and went out after him. "Take care of Eva," I shouted back to Lee.

0011100

Ullman was dodging among the domes, bending double to present a minimal target. I fired a couple of darts anyway, but they went wide.

I activated my link with Lee. "Get our vehicle over here on remote."

"Understood."

I glanced up at the sky behind me and saw the bulbous shape turning, drifting my way. At the same time, I saw a blue Peacekeeping vehicle finally coming in from the south.

I tried to keep Ullman in view, but the gaps between the domes were narrow, clogged with garbage, and he knew the area well.

A shadow passed overhead. "Can you see him?" I sent to Lee. Using his link with the

The Decline of Crime

By the time the Protektorate came into being, organized warfare was already obsolete. Universal prosperity and the free availability of vast new territories
had invalidated traditional motives for invasion and
conquest. Meanwhile, as the power of governments
diminished, private citizens could no longer claim the
need to bear arms in order to protect themselves
from the State. The Protektorate was the new State,
and by definition, it could not harm its citizens.

Some deviants still manufactured their own weapons on a clandestine basis. But the Protektorate controlled almost all supplies of metals and explosives;
and universal surveillance made it almost impossible
to use a weapon unobserved.

People still brawled, attacked each other with blunt
instruments, strangled and pummeled and scratched
and bit one another in fits of rage. But the unavail-
ability of purpose-built weapons and the near-cer-
tainty of being caught reduced the incidence of
violent crime to a fraction of its levels in the twentieth century.

Even more important, the slow shift of the human
race to a state of pampered pleasure tended to under-
mine the frustrations and discontent that had contrib-
uted to violent crime in the first place.

transit vehicle, he could look down through its
scanners.

"North of your location." His voice sounded in
my head, calm and precise, and he continued
guiding me as I threaded my way through the
maze, my breath coming fast, my feet slipping on
mud and old food wrappers.

I finally caught up with Ullman where Dometown ended at a tall factory wall. From behind
it came faint sounds of motors whining, weld-

ers sizzling, products rumbling off assembly lines.

Ullman was slapping his hand on the dome nearest him. "Larry!" he shouted. "Open up!"

"Time to drop the net," I sent to Lee.

A panel opened in the belly of the transit vehicle overhead. The net fell out and opened like a parachute, sensors at its corners orienting themselves on Ullman. As he looked up, the mesh flopped down around him and drew tight.

"Don't fight it!" I shouted to him.

He stopped and stood motionless, giving me a hateful look. A grid of liquid red bloomed on his hands where he had instinctively pushed at the micromesh and the threads had cut into his skin.

Three men were coming out of the dome beside him. One of them was holding a crude wooden club. Another had a hammer in his hand. All of them looked like Ullman: long-haired, grimy, bearded, in ragged mud brown tunics that were frayed around the edges.

"What you looking for?" shouted the man with the club. He hefted it and took a step toward me.

"You're being monitored." I said it loud and clear, and pointed to my transit vehicle hovering above, then to the guardians' vehicle.

I stepped toward Ullman. I was still breathing hard from chasing after him, and feeling in a foul mood. "Don't get in my way," I warned his friends.

They stood and watched as I stooped, reached behind me, grabbed Ullman with one arm around his neck and one arm under his knee, and hauled him over my shoulders.

0011101

Eva was crouching on the slab of foam, hugging herself and shivering uncontrollably. In the light filtering through the open door I saw the VR rig beside her, disconnected. Lee was waiting in the shadows.

I dumped Ullman on the floor. "What happened?" I said, although at this point I thought I knew.

She stared up at me. Her face was pale and she had a haunted, wild-eyed look. Her jaw quivered, and she said nothing.

I knelt beside her. She flinched away like a frightened animal. "Tell me," I said, soft and easy.

"He had me under a death sim," she said.

I turned and gave Ullman a look. He was lying on his side, still wrapped in the net, watching me.

I picked up the VR rig, carefully holding it by its wire. "Get the guardians in here and log this with them as evidence," I told Lee. "I'm sure it has his prints and his perspiration on it."

"Bullshit!" Ullman shouted at me. "I never seen that rig. Understand me? It's not mine and I never *seen* it."

"When you're found guilty," I said, "you could be modified for this."

I turned away from him, back to Eva. "I linked with you on our way over here, so I shared a little of what you were going through. The guys in hoods were putting that clamp on your hand. I thought it was real; I thought it was actually happening. I didn't realize it was a simulation from an external source."

She swallowed hard. "It sure felt real." She drew a deep, shaky breath. "Guess you missed the bit where they started pulling off my fingernails." She looked me in the eyes. "Thanks for coming."

"Can I do anything?"

"Take me out of here."

Awkwardly, I put my arm around her and helped her up. I felt protective; but I pushed that emotion aside. This was a job, just another job, and Eva Kurimoto had not been physically harmed.

Perhaps I did have some special responsibility for her welfare; but I was also responsible for the welfare of everyone else on Agorima.

Simulations

A sim (virtual reality simulation) is a complete replica of human experience.

A sim player (human actor) is surgically fitted with implants that interface with nerve inputs from eyes, ears, nose, and mouth. In addition, an implant at the back of the neck interfaces with nerve impulses at the top of the spinal column.

A VR (virtual reality) rig plays sim recordings. The simplest, cheapest rig transmits its output via two ear beads, eyepads that contain induction devices to stimulate the optic nerve, and a special collar that uses magnetic resonance to connect with the user's nervous system nonintrusively. Users with more disposable income may have themselves fitted with sight/sound/taste/smell/feel implants that can reproduce the sim with increased fidelity.

Sim entertainments range from travelogues to erotica. Many news broadcasts are full five-sense recordings made by reporters on the scene. In each case, the sim user has the illusion of riding in the player's body like an independent observer.

Inevitably, sims can record pain as easily as pleasure. A death sim is an illegal recording of physical abuse and torture, up to and including the moment of death. When a person is forced to run this play, he or she experiences all the agony of the original victim—without sustaining any actual physical harm.

For the torturer, this is an ideal situation. A death sim can be run repeatedly. There is no limit to the number of times a user can feel his bones being broken or his flesh being burned. And afterward, there is no physical evidence to show that any crime has taken place.

0011110

The boxy armored figures of the guardians hauled Ullman out of the dome and cut the net off him. Outside under the morning sun, in the squalor of the alley between the domes, a crowd of ragged men and women was gathering. Their mood was as ugly as their faces, but they watched in silence as the guardians went about their business.

One of the big, blue peacekeeping robots lifted Ullman and circled its heavy carbon-fiber arms around his chest, holding him securely. Another opened an evidence locker in its torso and stashed the VR rig and the sim cartridge. Two others came over to me and Eva.

"You will accompany us to Central Processing," one of them said. "We will question you and take a detailed statement."

I didn't have time for that. "Check my identity," I said.

Guardians weren't the smartest autons. The one in front of me took a vid of my face, then paused. "You have privileged access. You are operating under direct authority of the OverMains at the Hub, who are represented here via your personal auton."

"I'll come by and make my statement later," I said.

"No!" Ullman shouted. He struggled. "Bring him in! If I go, he goes, that's the law, right?"

I didn't even bother to look at him. "Hold him on suspected use of a simulation designed to inflict severe pain and trauma, attempting to resist detention, and sabotage of a nondiscretionary server for purposes of committing an illegal act." I turned to two of the other guardians standing by. "You and you, provide an escort to my transit vehicle."

Obediently, they moved either side of us, their tracks churning the mud. The crowd of domers started jeering and shouting abuse—but they made way for us all the same.

0011111

A little later we were in the transit vehicle. It was only built for two, but Eva was small enough to rest in the stowage area behind the front seats.

Lee retracted the ladder and we lifted away from Dometown. I turned so that I could look at her. "Shall we get you some medical attention?"

She turned her face toward me. She wasn't as pale as before, but I could still see the tension under her smooth, unlined skin. Her eyes were red at the edges and there was a little tic at the corner of her mouth. "I'll be okay," she said.

"The last person I saw under a death sim," I said, "had to be treated for shock."

I saw her nostrils flare as she took a slow, measured breath. "I told you, I'll be okay."

Yet she had been terrified, and she'd been desperate for someone to come and pull her out. "I don't understand what you think you gain by acting tough," I told her.

"It's not an act." She stared straight back at me.

I sighed. "Okay. As you wish. Tell me why Ullman did it to you."

"Because I made a dumb mistake." Gradually, more color was coming back into her face, although her voice still sounded unsteady. "He asked if the fix I wanted done in the Mains was for me. I said no, I was fronting for someone else. He asked who. I didn't know what to tell him, because if I picked a name he knew, he could check, and if I picked a name he didn't know, he wouldn't trust me. So I refused to give any name and he got suspicious and said he'd do something to make me talk. That's how it happened."

I grimaced. "You didn't make a dumb mistake. I did. I gave you an assignment without properly mapping the risks and consequences, and without considering contingencies."

She shook her head. "Thanks, but it was my decision. I take my own risks. Didn't I tell you that?"

"Probably." I decided there was no point in arguing with her. "Where's your flier?"

"In the public lot."

"Lee, take us there, okay? If Eva's okay to take herself home, I need to—"

"I have an urgent transmission," Lee interrupted me. "From the peeker that we sent to check on Joe Belman."

I sighed. "Show me."

THE BEATING OF JOE BELMAN

I was in a rustic cabin with walls of unfinished pine, hand-woven rugs on the floor, an old-fashioned stove against one wall, a wooden table standing by windows overlooking fields of green.

Joe Belman was sitting at the table, working with an ink pen, covering sheets of paper with slow, laborious handwriting. He was wearing nothing but a pair of shorts, and his brawny, muscled body was deeply tanned.

There was a sound from behind my field of view—a sudden splintering crash. Belman dropped his pen, pushed back his chair, and reared up, looking startled.

Three figures crowded into the room. All of them were masked and clothed in form-fitting blue plastic coveralls, and all of them were carrying wooden clubs. One man seized the table, dragged it out from in front of Belman, and turned it over, scattering papers across the floor. Then all three of them went for him.

He didn't back away from them. He crouched and charged forward, trying to bull his way past. But one of the intruders brought his wooden club down on Belman's shoulder, knocking him sideways. Another struck him on the back of the head, and he yelled with pain.

He stumbled, fell on his hands and knees, but managed to grab someone's ankle and yank it forward. The man went over on his back and Belman pulled the club out of his hand. But the other two closed in, kicking him and hitting him. In less than a minute, Belman was huddled groaning on the floor, clutching his head, his body bruised and bleeding.

For a moment the only sound was of the attackers' heavy breathing. Then there was a faint cry from somewhere outside. "Joe?" It was a woman's voice. "Joe, what's happening?"

The men in their blue coveralls turned and ran, their footsteps heavy on the wooden boards. A moment later I glimpsed their flier as it took off past the windows, the sun flashing on its hull.

My viewpoint shifted as the peeker drifted down toward Belman. I heard him groan and saw him roll over, still clutching his head in his hands. His face was covered in blood.

"Joe!" Quick footsteps came into the house.

The peeker turned, and I saw a gray-haired woman, her face wet with sweat and red from the sun. The peeker was directly in her path, and it didn't move fast enough. She noticed it, grimaced with disgust, and slapped it aside.

0100000

"What's happening?" Eva was saying. "Was Lee linking through to your implants?"

I started telling her what I'd seen. Meanwhile, we were approaching the public landing field just beyond Dometown. A couple of old, grimy fliers were parked alongside Eva's, looking as if they hadn't been moved in months. Weeds were encroaching around the field's perimeter.

"So who do you think—" Eva began.

"I don't know who those thugs were, and there's no way to find out. Even if Belman's home had had a server in it, the intruders were body-sealed to leave no evidence." I turned to Lee. "Is Traffic Control tracking them?"

"They stole the flier immediately before they flew out to Belman's home, and they have already abandoned it. They were last seen disappearing on foot into a heavily forested wilderness area farther south. The vegetation is so thick, there, even infra-red satellite tracking has trouble getting a reliable trace."

I stared out of the canopy for a moment. Something about the incident bothered me, though I couldn't place it. "Who's Controller of Peacekeeping here?"

"A man named Harry Green."

I turned back and looked questioningly at Eva.

"Yeah, I know him," she said. "I met him when they had me covering crime a while back. He's a nice-guy type, everyone's buddy, big handshake, happy-happy-happy to see you." She made a face.

Instinctively, I found myself trusting her judgment. "Do you think he's into anything illegal?"

She considered that for a moment, then shook her head, forcing a smile. "He wouldn't be smart enough to know how to conceal it."

"But he could be working for someone," I pointed out, "and just doing what he's told." I turned to Lee. "Contact Green, tell him why I'm here on Agorima, and tell him to meet us out at Belman's cabin right away."

"Understood."

I waited a beat for him to take care of that. Meanwhile, we had set down in the landing field. The canopy retracted and I felt cool outside air on my face. I turned back to Eva. "You sure you're okay?"

She looked back at me for a long moment without saying anything. "I really appreciate your concern," she said, "but it's not necessary." The warmth had gone from her voice. She pulled herself up from behind the seats, moving slowly and carefully. Obviously she was still feeling shaky, but it was out of the question for her to admit it.

0100001

Behind Belman's cabin was a large rectangular field, half of it green, half brown. A little silver shape stood on the borderline—a tractor that someone had been using to plow the land. It stood motionless; abandoned.

More silver shapes were crowded together in a small square of dirt in front of the cabin: a flier from Peacekeeping, an ambulance from Life-Support, and a utilitarian craft that I guessed was Belman's own. As we circled, losing altitude, I saw the ambulance lift and move toward the north with its beacons flashing.

Lee set us down where the ambulance had been. I opened the canopy and smelled dry dust, rich earth, and the burgeoning jungle that rimmed Belman's acreage. For a moment something seemed

The Misfit by the Eastern Shore

The coast was a wilderness of rust red cliffs and tumbled rocks, secluded bays embracing empty beaches of sunburned sand. The land along the clifftops was crowded with fig trees, eucalyptus, and coconut palms that had taken root during the last phase of terraforming. It was here that the first colonists had set up their brightly colored plastic temporary shelters like children's building blocks among the leafy green.

Each group of freethinkers had had its own agenda, its own mix of dogma, diets, and disciplines. And as the decades passed their communities grew bigger, fed by a steady flow of pilgrims from other worlds.

By the time the population of Sen City neared one million, large hotels, retreats, and health spas had taken root in the strip of the coast nearest to the city; but farther south, the land remained almost untouched. Obscure sects lived and died there like mutating species among the tropical vegetation. They used mind- and body-altering drugs; they worshiped death or birth, sex or Satan; and only an occasional roving peeker registered their existence at all.

Joe Belman was a misfit among misfits. He was a conservative man who had no interest in the fads of his neighbors. He bought a square of land from the Protektorate in the first few years of colonization, when values were still low. He cleared away the jungle, built a log cabin in the center of his plot, and put together everything he needed to manage an old-fashioned farm. His square of land was his obsessive homage to human values predating the Protektorate, spaceflight, and technology itself.

wrong, and I paused, trying to place it. Then I realized there was no birdsong. The agworld of my childhood had been rich in wildlife. The quiet of Agorima's landscape still seemed unnatural to me.

The heels of my shoes crunched over dirt and gravel as I walked toward the cabin, where three people stood waiting in the shade of the front porch. One of them I recognized as Belman's partner, Meg Henley, a strong woman with a kind but weary face. She stood straight-backed and dignified, like an old-time schoolteacher.

To her left was a guy with a paunch, pudgy features, a brown mustache, and a big friendly smile. He was wearing shorts and a white shirt with the sleeves rolled up, but he was still sweating. I didn't need to see the Peacekeeping badge sewn on his left shoulder to know that this was Commander Harry Green.

Next to him was a woman who looked as if she'd fixed her biological age around twenty-five. She was petite and shapely, and she had a noticeably pretty face framed in golden blond hair; but she seemed calmly indifferent to the people around her. She was wearing full Peacekeeping Division uniform despite the heat, but unlike Harry Green, she showed no sign of discomfort.

Green stepped forward, holding out his hand. "Tom McCray? Commander Green. Call me Harry. Welcome to Agorima. It's good to have you here. An unexpected pleasure." He chuckled. "You know, this is the first time I've ever met a Protektor in the flesh? My kids'll probably ask me if I got your autograph."

I expected his palm to be moist with perspiration, and it was. I expected him to shake my hand energetically, for longer than necessary, and he did.

"Just too bad you have to come here under these circumstances. When I spoke on the net with your auton, there, he filled me in on the—the big picture." He moved closer to me, and lowered his voice. "None of us had any idea, you understand. The system failures—there's no one here with your training, your expertise."

"I'm sure you won't be held responsible in any way," I said, figuring that was what he wanted to hear. "Now tell me what happened to Belman. Is he alive?"

"Yes, yes, the medimeks got here quick, real quick—no lag time with them!—and he's in their hands."

"I'd hoped for a chance to talk to him."

Green shook his head. "Man's in a coma. But I left word that as soon as he regains consciousness, Life-Support should give us a call."

That was unfortunate. I considered my options. "All right, since I'm out here, I'd like to ask some questions. I'll talk with Meg Henley, then with your second-in-command, and then a few words with you. Out at the rear, where there's absolutely no possibility of surveillance."

Green looked taken aback. "Well, I suppose—"

"It won't take long," I told him. "Standard procedure." That seemed to reassure him somewhat.

"Well, as you wish." He recovered his good humor and gave me another big grin. "We're happy to help you, Tom, in any way we can."

0100010

At the edge of the field of wheat, I bent down, plucked a stalk, and crushed the head, breathing the smell. "I used to work in wheat fields on my parents' farm," I said. "This brings back memories."

Out of the corner of my eye I saw Meg Henley watching me.

I scattered the fragments and watched them drift away. "Sometimes I think I made a mistake leaving," I went on. "There's a special kind of fulfillment that comes from planting things and watching them grow."

"Well of course," she agreed. Her voice sounded as dry as the powdery soil. "But I daresay you had your reasons for going into another line of work."

I turned toward her and made eye contact. "Yes," I said. "I did."

She returned my look and waited, not showing anything.

"I became a Protektor because most people aren't as self-sufficient as you and Joe," I went on. "People depend on automated services. That means, ultimately, their survival depends on me." And I explained what was going to happen on Agorima if the Mains went down at Central Processing.

The lines around her mouth tightened with disapproval as she listened. "Joe was always afraid of something like this," she said. "He tried to warn everyone, you know. Are you familiar with his public statements?"

"Yes," I said, before she could go into all the details. "I suppose from his point of view, people are going to get what they deserve."

That didn't please her at all. "Joe values human life above all else, Mr. McCray," she said sharply. "He wants to enlighten people, not see them perish."

I frowned. "So who on earth would want to come out here and hurt him?"

She drew herself up. "Milton Berg's followers." She said it without hesitation.

"Tell me why," I said.

She spoke fluently, factually, and frankly. According to her, Berg was a wild-eyed technophile who wanted to let technology run wild in private hands, leading to anarchy, war, and quite possibly the extermination of the human race. Belman, on the other hand, wanted to help people rediscover their own humanity so that they'd return to a simple rural existence. Joe Belman thought Milton Berg was a dangerous fanatic—and he'd said so on the newsims. It had become an ongoing personality conflict.

As she itemized the squabble, I began to think I was wasting my time. The beating that Belman had suffered could indeed have been the result of this petty squabble between two misfits, and might have nothing to do with system sabotage that was threatening the entire planet. "Just one more question," I said. "Why didn't you go with Joe to the hospital?"

She looked at me as if I was simpleminded. "There's work to do here," she said. "If you really grew up on a farm," and she made it sound as if that was hard to believe, "you ought to know. Joe would never want me to walk away from a field that was only half-plowed and seeded."

0100011

Harry Green's assistant told me that her name was Jalen Reese and her correct title was Assistant Controller. If she seemed surprised that I wanted to talk to her, she didn't show it. She didn't show anything, good or bad, positive or negative. She just stood and waited while I asked questions, then gave me answers that sounded as bored as they were brief.

I asked how many years she'd worked for Green. Two, she said. I asked her chronological age. Twenty-five, she said, same as her bio age. Wasn't it unusual for someone so young to be promoted so fast? "I suppose so," she said with a shrug.

I wanted to know if the Peacekeeping Division on Agorima was run efficiently and properly. Had she seen any important procedural violations? I assured her that our conversation was confidential. I pointed out that even if a roving peeker happened to be in the vicinity, Lee would suppress its report of anything she told me.

She eyed me for a moment. "Controller Green is extremely disorganized, and not very smart," she said. "In fact, if you really want my opinion, I think he's basically incompetent."

She said it all in the same offhand, deadpan style. I stared at her in surprise—then wondered how much farther she was willing to go. "Would you also say that he's corrupt?"

She shook her head. "No, he just doesn't know how to do his job."

I thought back to my briefing at the Hub. There had been nothing about Green in the official summary. "Have you stated your opinions in a report?"

She gave me a barely detectable smile. "The last person in my job was fired for speaking out against the Controller."

I turned to Lee, standing beside us. "True?"

"According to the records," said Lee, "Jalen Reese's predecessor, George Fairburn, resigned citing a desire to emigrate."

Jalen Reese let her eyes stray past me, as if she found the landscape more interesting to look at. "That was the official story," she said.

I turned to Lee. "Did Fairburn log any complaints about Controller Green?"

"None on file," he said.

"They got rid of Fairburn before he had a chance to embarrass anyone," said Reese.

I looked at her again. "You're very outspoken."

She looked straight back at me. "You asked me to be." She sounded completely unconcerned. But if she was so emotionally detached from her job, how had she risen so fast? There had to be something, somewhere, that mattered to her. But I had no idea where to begin, and there wasn't time for a fishing expedition.

"I guess that's all," I said, reluctantly. "I'll bear your comments in mind."

She waited a moment to see if I had anything more to say. Then she turned away without a word.

0100100

"I want you to know," said Harry Green, as he strode out from the house, "this whole thing, this assault on Belman, we may be able to wrap it up right now." He moved close enough for me to see the little beads of sweat on his forehead and the individual bristles of his mustache. "Take a look at what I got. One of my evidence robots just found it in the room where Belman was beat up." Covertly, in the manner of a dope dealer flashing samples, he showed me a shred of blue plasticized fabric. "Must've got ripped off in the fight." He grinned.

"Interesting," I said.

He nodded, looking pleased with himself. "Want to know who wears containment coveralls made of fabric like that?"

I raised my eyebrows.

"Fisk's security guys. Emmanuel Fisk. You ever heard of him?"

"Yes," I said, hoping this might discourage him from telling me.

But Green was on a track. He gave me the complete rundown: how much Fisk was worth, what a genius he was in the sim biz, and what he'd done for the city. "You want to know how this looks to me?" he finished up.

"Tell me," I said, since it seemed inevitable.

Green tucked his thumbs in his pockets. He was standing with his feet spread well apart, like an old-style ship's captain. "Fisk talks big about getting rid of Protektorate control. But he's no fool. He depends on the system, and he knows it. So why'd he send his thugs out here? To teach Belman a lesson, is why. Fisk knows Belman is behind the stuff that's coming down, so he sends him a message—to knock it off. You want my advice, you'll go see Fisk right now and grant him immunity in exchange for him testifying against Belman. You might have this thing licked by the end of the day. It's a possibility."

Silently, inside my head, I called up the time. The little green numerals in the corner of my eye told me it was a quarter of twelve. "Thanks for the tip, Harry," I said. "It sounds good. But I have an appointment. Tell you what, why don't you go and visit Fisk for me? And I'll send a peeker along with you, so I can listen in on the conversation."

Green looked momentarily disconcerted. "Well," he began. "I—"

"You go talk to Fisk," I said, keeping my voice friendly but making it clear I was giving an order. "Don't make a deal, yet. Just tell him how it looks to you. Push him a little and see what he says.

Maybe the situation has got him scared enough that he'll cooperate voluntarily."

"Well, all right, I'll do that." He nodded to himself. "Fine. I'll get right on it." He stuck out his hand. "We'll be in touch, right? And anything else you need—anything at all—just let me know. It's a privilege to be on your team, Tom." His grin resurfaced. "First time I ever met a Protektor, did I mention that? Anyhow, I mustn't hold you up. I'll see you later, right?"

"Later," I agreed.

0100101

On the way back from Belman's farm I asked Lee to scan Harry Green's stats and his job record. I wasn't sure what I was expecting, but I certainly wasn't expecting what I found, which was virtually nothing. According to his record, he'd never been seriously reprimanded, never received any citations, never distinguished himself in any way, good or bad.

So I checked Jalen Reese, and I found the same thing. She'd done her job, no more, no less, and promotions had rained down upon her like an automatic service from Life-Support.

Well, Harry Green was a team player who might know how to move up without bumping the boundaries set by the Protektorate, but Jalen Reese didn't seem to have a grain of political savvy. In her case, at least, there should have been some little random quirks, some comments—something.

As we neared the city, I saw the air buzzing with fliers, thousands of specks silhouetted black against the blue, some of them flashing as they caught the midday sun. It was just normal noontime traffic, I realized. But as we headed into it, I felt as if we were plunging into an insect swarm.

"Is Traffic Control managing the load?" I said.

"Yes, although free memory is fluctuating erratically. Lag times are evident on an intermittent basis."

"You make it sound unstable."

"It is unstable."

Our own collision avoidance was under Lee's control, but still I tensed instinctively as we slanted down into the heart of the swarm, dodging vehicles careening around us in every direction. I glimpsed men and women in their fliers as they streaked by: fashion models and sim actors heading for auditions, sim stylists with their secretaries, office workers taking lunch breaks, tourists just cruising through. None of them paid any attention to the breakneck ballet they were in. They had lived all their lives in symbiosis with systems that carried them and cared for them. Why should they pay special attention to these services now?

0100110

Xavier Tower was a fat silver cylinder in the downtown area. Twenty stories high, its exterior was pockmarked with thousands of cavities—flier docking bays, I realized. Vehicles were entering and leaving like bees servicing a hive.

We found an empty bay and backed in. I checked the time: five minutes before noon.

We climbed out. Our transit vehicle was bigger than most fliers because it was built to reach orbit. There wasn't much space between it and the walls. I slid around and found a two-seater ground cart waiting for us.

Lee joined me. "Take us to Gabol Plaza," I said as we climbed aboard.

The cart carried us through an automatic door, along a curving passageway, into the hollow core of the tower. The huge space was alive with music, vapor displays, and the murmur of thousands of voices; a roofed amphitheater tiered with stores and vendeks, flexible ramps soaring across the central area where restaurants and bars were floating, drifting like water lilies.

Our cart picked up speed and took us down a broad spiral pathway, dodging other carts and people on foot. As we descended through the levels I looked up at the translucent blue roof and felt as if I were sinking underwater.

Gabol Plaza was a dish-shaped concourse at ground level, with a restaurant at the center and stores around the rim. "Where to?" the cart asked. "How about the Showplace? If you're from offworld, friend, that's where the real action is. Or Casanova's Cave? Take five minutes, an hour, or a day, stim your centers till you—"

"Drive around the concourse," I said. "Slowly. And keep quiet."

The cart did as it was told. There were a lot of other people and vehicles, and it had to thread a path among them.

I saw her, then, sitting alone at a table: a woman in a business suit, her face pale and anxious, her hands clutching her purse in front of her as she scanned the crowds.

0100111

"I'm afraid this wasn't a terribly sensible place to meet," she said. Her voice was low and tense, almost drowned out by people's conversations, the clink of utensils, the humming of robot waiters moving to and fro. "There wasn't much time," she went on, "and I had to think of somewhere that would be safe—I mean from surveillance, and from—other dangers." She looked at her hands in front of her as if she felt embarrassed to hear herself sounding melodramatic.

"It's okay," I said, trying to be reassuring. "My auton provides good security." I nodded to Lee, sitting unobtrusively at one side.

She gave me a brief, stiff smile. "You're accustomed to this sort of thing. I've never—I mean, I'm very loyal to Serena, and if she knew of this, she would—well, she would ruin me totally."

A life-size holo image of a man's head wearing a chef's hat flickered alive in the center of the table. "Hi there! Are you hungry? We got *all kinds* of good things here in the plaza. Shall I tell you the specials? Would you like a menu? What's your pleasure?"

Mary Morheim looked apologetic. "I'm afraid we can't sit here without ordering something."

I rattled off an order at random. The holo vanished, a hatch flipped open, and some drinks appeared.

"Now," I said. "Tell me what's on your mind."

I watched her trying to summon her willpower. "First I have a confession to make," she said. "I listened to your conversation earlier today. When you were talking with Serena."

I stared at her in amazement. "You mean, all her talk about security, and the heavy metal shielding—"

"Please don't misunderstand, electronic eavesdropping is quite impossible, just as Serena says. But there is a disused pipe that used to carry water to an ornamental fountain in the Midas Glade.

Some time ago, purely by chance, after some maintenance meks had been working on it, I found that it transmits sound quite distinctly to a point close by my desk, if one knows where to listen."

A simple metal tube, I thought, containing a vibrating column of air. I liked that.

"So—I heard what you said to Serena," Morheim went on, "about the terrible consequences if the Mains fail at Central Processing, on account of someone having tampered with them. That's really true?"

I nodded. "Of course it's true."

"Yes." Her voice was almost a whisper. "In that case, I really have no choice."

Lee suddenly lurched up, kicking his chair over. I looked at him, startled. I felt a stab of deep concern. Somehow, despite our precautions, he had been reached by the virus—

But there wasn't any more time for thought as he seized hold of my collar and dragged me bodily out of my chair.

I found myself flailing, sprawling, landing on my back on another table nearby. Glasses shattered. Drinks spilled. Startled faces of a man and a woman stared down at me.

Beyond my field of view, someone was shouting. A woman screamed and I heard the screech of rubber on polished concrete.

I rolled off the table in time to see a cart like the one that had brought us down here, careening out of control across the plaza. Lee had thrown me clear and was going back for Mary Morheim, but he was too late. The cart smashed into the table and the table slammed into her stomach. The cart didn't stop there; it plowed ahead, knocking Morheim over on her back and crushing the table

down on top of her before it finally came to a
standstill.

There was a frozen moment. All conversation in
the restaurant died. People in the plaza were staring. The man who'd been riding in the cart pulled
himself out of his seat with frightened, jerky motions. His legs gave way under him and he staggered back, pale with shock.

People started scrambling out of their chairs.
There were screams and shouts—a rising babble of
noise. People converged across the plaza, everyone
trying to see what had happened.

"Use your amplifier," I sent to Lee. "Tell them
to get back, make room for emergency services."

"Clear a path!" he shouted, his mek voice so
loud that people instinctively flinched from it.
"Make room, here!"

I crawled between tables and chairs, across the
tiled floor to Mary Morheim. She was almost entirely buried under the table that had crushed her,
but she had flung one arm out before the final
impact. I grabbed her wrist between my finger
and thumb.

There was no pulse.

0101000

A few minutes later, when the debris had been
pulled clear and the medimeks and the guardians
had come, I could see there was no possibility of
reviving her. Her skull had been crushed. Her
memories were irretrievably lost.

Her purse had been flung clear by the impact. I
discreetly picked it up and checked the contents
while the medimeks were taking her away. But
there was nothing significant. No emcards, no
written messages.

There was an addrex—an address book like a miniature vidzine. I scanned a couple of the entries, but the talking faces all looked like routine business contacts.

A guardian was going around asking for witnesses. I ducked into the crowd before anyone could ID me as the one who'd been nearest the accident. "Lee?" I called. "We have to get out."

"I am waiting at the foot of the up-ramp," he told me. "Our cart is here."

"To hell with it. We'll walk back."

0101001

I sat in my seat in my transit vehicle in the flier bay, and I looked out over the city, the buildings stretching away into midday haze. I focused on the blue-gray horizon and methodically stopped myself from thinking about Mary Morheim's crushed face.

"Where do you want to go?" said Lee, beside me.

"Nowhere," I said. I sat some more, soaking up the stillness and the silence. Then I cracked a water capsule and took a sip. "How did you know the cart was heading for us? Did you access the building's support system?"

"No, you had not asked me to. I saw the vehicle moving erratically. The person in it looked alarmed. From this I inferred that it was in an unstable condition. I saw it turn toward our table and I realized your life was endangered."

I nodded to myself, and was grateful. Even though Lee was mostly my own creation, I thought of him as an independent entity, a personality in his own right. That wasn't rational, but I'd never claimed to be rational where machines and computers are concerned. I'd grown up trusting them more than people, and in a way, I still did. Lek was loyal. It never rebelled against you, and it never showed malice. There was a naive perfection in it—provided, of course, no one tampered with it.

"You know, this was different from the other failures we've seen," I said. "That cart didn't run wild at random because of an overload or lag time in the local system that was guiding it. This had to be a deliberate act. Someone cracked the support system here in Xavier Tower and took direct control."

"We have no proof of that."

"No proof?" I drained the capsule and tossed it in the recycler. "A woman sits down ready to spill a secret she's afraid will jeopardize her career, maybe her life—and straightaway she's killed?"

Lee paused for a moment. "Tom, I just checked the building systems, and you are correct that there is currently no condition of overload. However, we have seen that these symptoms fluctuate unpredictably. It could have been a coincidence that the cart killed Mary Morheim at that particular moment."

I looked at his impassive mek face. Technically, he was right. But I knew in my guts that he was wrong. I decided to take a different tack. "When the cart went wild," I said, "was it heading for me, or her, or both of us?"

"Both of you, I believe."

So I was a target, now. My enemy had accessed my hidden file at Central Processing, and he knew I was on the planet. Either that or he had been told by one of the people I'd met personally. He must have traced my location, either by a peeker or via the Mains. Or maybe Mary Morheim had been followed; that was equally possible.

I grunted with irritation. There was no point chasing a bunch of suppositions. I needed data.

"Lee," I said, "access Morheim's stats for me and download them as hardcopy. Let's see if there are any interesting connections."

"She is not on file."

I felt as if I'd suddenly run into an invisible wall; a barrier that logically could not exist. "You mean her file's been purged?"

"I did not say the file was purged. The file does not exist. There is no Mary Morheim listed, alive or dead."

Maybe, I thought, she had told us a false name. "You saw her face; pattern-match it. She must be there somewhere."

"No. She is not listed. There are references to her name in other files, but her own file does not exist." He paused. "This should not be possible, but I believe her file and its backups have been erased."

0101010

So someone had killed Mary Morheim, and then they'd cracked Central Processing and killed her stats as well. As far as I was concerned, the two crimes had a lot in common. Human life and human data were both precious in their separate ways, and data were even harder to replace. Mary Morheim would be regrown from her DNA, and she would be basically the same person as before; but there was no way to recover her life statistics. Years from now, in her new incarnation, she would never be able to find out who she had once been.

A voice sounded in my ear, jolting me. "Tom?"

"Yeah, Eva." I was glad of the distraction. "How are you doing?"

"I'm fine." And she sounded fine. More than that; bouncy, pleased with herself. "I met a guy, says he knows someone does fixes in the Mains. Functional, immediate, and verified."

I frowned. "But I thought you were heading for home."

"I already did. But I decided not to stay there."

I absorbed that and realized I wasn't entirely surprised, but I wasn't entirely happy about it, either. "You know, it'll be more convenient, safer, and better all around, if you do what you say you're going to do."

"Sorry about that." She didn't sound sorry. "I figured your auton could trace me, right? Anyway, the man I met is Mikhael Krentz." She spelled it for me letter by letter. "I just got through talking to him."

"Where are you now?"

"On his roof. How come you have to ask?"

I looked at Lee.

"I was aware of her approximate location," he said. "But you did not request that information."

"You should sample my meet with Krentz," Eva went on. "He has a server, so it'll be stored at Central. Or you can view my own record of it, right? It's in my personal storage."

"Right," I said. "And while I'm doing that, we'll come and find you."

"If that's what you want. I mean, you're calling the shots, I guess."

I didn't know why she was sounding so hostile, but I was in no mood for personality conflicts, so I let it pass. I turned to Lee. "You have a Mikhael Krentz?"

"He runs an escort service in Drazz Alley. It's less than ten minutes from here." As he spoke, the transit vehicle lifted gently under me and we slid out of our parking bay.

"Tell Eva we'll be right there," I said. "And show me her meeting with Krantz from the server's viewpoint. I don't feel like sharing her head right now."

THE PIMP OF DRAZZ ALLEY

I found myself looking down at a man wrapped in a faded gold robe, sprawling against a mound of red satin pillows on a heart-shaped bed. The bed was a tacky pagan altar at the top of a flight of white marble steps. The man lying on it was leafing through a porno skinzine, and I glimpsed couples copulating busily on the pages.

A couch upholstered in red velvet stood opposite the bed at the bottom of the steps, but apart from that, the room contained no furniture. It was a low-rent porno art gallery, with hundreds of pictures in cheap gold frames crowding walls upholstered in maroon corduroy. The pictures were all animated—men and women posing naked, running their hands over their flesh, pouting, pirouetting, grinding their hips, flaunting their genitals. A human zoo.

A chime sounded.

The man in the robe tossed his zine onto a huge heap of others like it and pressed a panel in the wall beside his bed. A door opened at the far end of the room.

Eva Kurimoto walked in. Evidently, she'd stopped at home on her way from Dometown long enough to change into a new outfit. She wore a baggy black suit with sharp creases in the pants legs and the sleeves, black shoes, and black nail polish. She was carrying a black attaché case. She looked chic, tough, and ready for business.

She walked into the room, glanced without much surprise or interest at the vids on the walls, and headed on down toward the man on the bed. "Mr. Krentz?"

He gave her a patronizing smile. "Yes, dear. The one and only." He reached inside his robe and scratched his stomach, then gestured regally to the couch. "Make yourself at home. Tell me who you are. Tell me what you want. Whatever it is, I'm sure I can help you."

He had a semieducated voice, as if he'd taken elocution lessons to cover a low-class accent but had never completed the course. His wavy golden hair was parted in the center and hung below his shoulders. His face looked young, but there was something jaded and prurient in the slackness of the muscles, the curl of his mouth.

"I'm Eva Kurimoto." She stopped at the foot of the marble steps. She didn't accept his offer to sit.

"So what's your pleasure?" Krentz nodded toward his gallery of posturing naked figures. "Boys, girls, morgs, maphs, animals, hybrids, meks, vids, sims—take your time, look around, pick whoever you like, or whatever you like, and then we'll talk price."

Eva stayed where she was. "You deal sex partners, right?"

Krentz looked mildly irritated. He reached out to a silver urn heaped with fine green powder, took a pinch, and inhaled. "I'm a pimp, dear. You didn't see the sign downstairs? Please don't waste my time, sweets, if you're not interested. I got a busy day."

"I'm looking to buy," said Eva, "but not sex." She paused. "You got surveillance in here?"

"Surveillance?" Krentz gave her a pained look. "Of *course*, sweetheart. This is a legitimate business. Up-and-down. Why, you want something that's not legal? I don't do that anymore. That's out of the question."

Eva put her foot on the bottom step, rested her case on her knee, and took out a sheet of paper. She wrote something on it, shielding it from the view of the server. Then she folded it and held it out to him.

Krentz watched without moving. Finally he grunted, gave her a vexed look, and took the paper from her.

He read it, concealing it close to his body. Then he crumpled it and tossed it onto a table beside the bed. His frown and his irritation faded away. He looked reflective. "I know the person who can do the kind of stuff you want. I have his name, and his pic, too." He shrugged one shoulder. "No law against giving that." He sighed. "Five hundred will cover it."

At the mention of money, Eva's posture straightened and her eyes became intent. "That's crap," she said. "Two's the price."

Krentz shifted impatiently. "Really, dear, do you think this is a bazaar? Five hundred is my fee."

Eva shrugged. "But I'm offering two."

Krentz tilted his head to one side. He was studying her more carefully than before. "If you got a credit problem," he said, "maybe we could work around that." He patted the satin sheets. "Maybe an hour of your time, and then you get what you want for free."

Eva laughed happily. "In your dreams," she said.

Krentz shifted restlessly. His eyes narrowed as if he was imagining her naked. "Another possibility," he said, "is you could join my little family." Once again he nodded to the gold-framed vids. "The pay is good. It could help you get over this little problem you seem to have about money." He swung his legs over the side of the bed, belted his robe, and started down the steps toward her.

Eva didn't back off, but she shifted her grip on her attaché case, folding her arms around it, making it into a barrier between the two of them. "It's two hundred or I walk." Her tone was sharp. "You com?"

Krentz paused. He slowly shook his head. "You're a piece. I'll say that. I suppose I could take four—"

"Two hundred!" She said it like a challenge.

Krentz held up his palms. "Please! My time is worth more than this." He hesitated, then muttered something in annoyance. He turned away from her. "Valentina!"

A concealed door opened and a naked woman came in, tall and blond, with heavy breasts and a painted face.

"My personal auton," Krentz explained to Eva. "And my accountant." He turned to the posturing nude. "A credit check, please, Valentina. This young woman—" He made the word sound vaguely pejorative. "She's good for three hundred?"

"Two!" Eva snapped at him. "No more bullshit, Krentz, or I'm out of here!"

Krentz rolled his eyes. "It's worth two hundred just to *get* you out of here." He turned back to his mek companion. "Is she good for it?"

The auton nodded. "Her credit verifies."

Krentz sighed. "All right, give me a pic of Alex Quan. Thank you." He turned back to Eva and paused reflectively. "Alex was an interesting kid. All kinds of ideas. The imagination that boy had! He sure had the—the smarts you're looking for." Krentz scratched the bridge of his nose. "Of course, that was a while ago."

A slit in Valentina's stomach disgorged a high-res, full-color print. "Transfer two hundred from Eva Kurimoto to Mikhael Krentz, confirm the transaction, please."

Eva nodded. "I confirm it."

The manicured mek fingers released the picture.

"You want my advice, you'll forget about Alex," said Krentz. "He was—unstable. Very difficult to deal with." He looked Eva up and down. "You know, for what you can get out of Alex, you'd do far better working for me. And I'm talking legal."

"Really," she said, sliding the picture into her case and snapping it shut. She stepped around him and walked to the table by the bed. She picked up the crumpled paper with her handwriting on it. "I'm sure you won't want this lying around, littering your place."

"I would have trashed that for you." He sounded hurt, as if her action saddened him. "You don't trust me?"

She gave him a look. "Why should I be any different from everyone else?" Then she turned and walked quickly to the exit at the end of the room. "Thanks. I'm out."

"Oh, my pleasure, dear. Sincerely. My pleasure." He gave her a look of disgust as she walked out, and he absentmindedly scratched his crotch. Then he shrugged philosophically and started back up the marble steps to his bed. He patted the pillows into position, draped himself across them, and reached for his skinzine.

0101011

I opened my eyes. We were cruising low over a broad pedpath between buildings masked by giant glamor pics showing exotic, erotic fashions. Models, tourists, and biz people mingled in the street among palm trees and small vendeks.

Lee made a turn and guided us toward an older building off the main avenue. Its metallic facade looked tarnished, and most of the bays in its multilevel rooftop lot were empty.

"You have any stats on this Alex Quan?" I asked.

"Yes. Natural-born here in Sen City, chrono age fifty-five, bio age fixed at twenty-two. His first employment was in sim technology research labs owned by Emmanuel Fisk."

That roused my interest.

"Subsequently Quan was employed at Central Processing in various capacities," Lee went on. "Mostly system maintenance."

That interested me even more. I imagined Quan putting in unpaid overtime, quietly teaching himself the system architecture, figuring how to use it for his own ends.

"He was terminated at Maintenance after being repeatedly warned about erratic job performance."

Indeed. For the first time since I'd arrived on Agorima I felt some of the tension in my stomach starting to let go.

"He freelanced as an automation consultant for a while," Lee finished up. "He was relatively unsuccessful, possibly because he lacked marketing skills. He emigrated from Agorima fifteen years ago, and his location offworld is not known."

My newfound feeling of anticipation abruptly evaporated. I blinked. "He *emigrated*?"

Lee didn't bother to repeat himself. He knew I'd heard.

0101100

The closer we came to the building, the more run-down it looked. Several panels on its facade were missing, and others had been strapped in place with metal tape. Overshadowing the flier bays on the roof was a big sign advertising a clothing line that had been popular fifty years ago. FASHION FOR THE TWENTY-FIFTH CENTURY, it said in giant flickering letters. Three years into the new millennium, and they still hadn't gotten around to upgrading their slogan. I felt pleased, in a way, to find at least one part of Sen City that wasn't prosperous and new.

"This is the building where Mikhael Krentz has his office?" I asked Lee.

"Correct. Many of the companions he offers for hire are failed fashion models. He has friends who refer models to him when they need quick credit."

Low-class but legal. "I don't see Eva," I said.

"She's in the flier near the corner. Shall I land?"

"No. Just take us alongside and link me with her."

"Understood."

We drifted around till we were hovering a couple of meters away. She looked across at me and waved.

"You hear me?" I said.

"Sure." Her voice spoke inside my ear. "You watched my meet with Krentz?"

"Yes, I did."

"You checked the stats on this Alex Quan?"

"He's a prime suspect," I said. I paused long enough to watch her smile, looking pleased with herself. "Only one snag," I went on, taking my time about pulling the rug out. "He left the planet fifteen years ago."

Her smile faded. She suddenly looked mad as hell. "That bastard Krentz. He knew. He must have known. I'm going back there—"

"No," I said firmly.

"*Two hundred*, for a garbage ID! That scumbag—"

"You and I need to talk," I said. "Someplace in the open without a lot of surveillance."

She brooded for a moment, staring straight ahead through the canopy of her craft. "All right, the city park."

0101101

We left our fliers in a public lot and started into the park. As I walked with Eva, I heard a sound behind us. I turned and realized it was coming from Lee, a faint scraping of metal on metal. "What's the problem?" I asked, looking at him with concern.

"I believe a hip bearing was overloaded and went out of alignment in Gabol Plaza. It's not a high priority."

I remembered him pulling me to safety. It was

understandable, and it wasn't serious, but I still didn't like it. My job—my whole life—was dedicated to blocking the natural tendency of the universe to degenerate into a state of chaos. A machine that wasn't running right bothered me almost as much as buggy computer code or corrupt data files.

Eva saw the look on my face. "Hey," she said, "it's no big deal is it? I mean, he's still *working*, isn't he?"

There it was again, the edge of hostility that I'd sensed earlier.

"Yes," I said, keeping my tone neutral. "He's working."

We walked along a resilient pathway that curved through landscaped grassland. On either side were greenhouses, squat transparent canisters fifty meters tall containing the mix of atmospheric gases that had existed on Agorima before the planet was terraformed. Inside were specimens of the plant life that had existed then—huge exotic ferns tinted purple and violet, trees festooned with bell-shaped flowers, bushes sprouting clusters of crimson tendrils. The vegetation was pressing against its invisible walls as if vainly hoping to repossess the land it had once known. This wasn't a park, I thought; it was a veg prison.

0101110

"Tell me," I said to Eva, "how you found Krentz."

She gestured dismissively, as if it should have been obvious. "Hans Ullman told me."

I tried to make sense of that.

"Ullman stuck me under a death sim," she went on, "but *before* that—before he got suspicious—he said there was this pimp named Krentz who knew someone who worked fixes in the Mains."

"Listen to me," I said, trying to be patient, though I no longer felt patient at all. "I told you once already, I want you to keep me fully and properly informed. If Ullman gave you Krentz's name, why the hell didn't you tell me?"

"Because you had your own plan." I heard the resentment in her voice, stronger than before. "You were acting like I was your puppy. *Go on home, Eva, and take a rest.*" She turned to confront me. "You came and helped me out, and that was a fine thing you did, and I appreciate it. But I was the one with the guts to go in there and get what you wanted. I deserved some respect for that, don't you think?"

I looked at her, saw what she'd needed, and saw that I had supplied just the opposite. "You felt I was patronizing you," I said. "Is that it?"

She relaxed slightly. "That's exactly it."

I sighed. "Look, I don't have time right now to be sensitive to people's personal needs. You called for help, so I figured you needed someone to take the pressure off. I didn't think about it beyond that."

She gestured with her thumb. It was a crude motion, out of keeping with her chic clothes and her graceful poise. "I crawled out of Dometown, you com? I'm a gutter brat. I take care of myself. I don't need anyone—"

"Yes, I understand all that," I said. "But withholding information because you don't like the way I'm acting is totally unacceptable."

She looked grim. "From your perspective I suppose it might seem that way."

"Meaning what?" I asked, barely able to restrain my impatience.

"You don't like stuff you can't control," she

said. "Like impulsive females, for instance." She nodded toward Lee. "Or autons that squeak."

Maybe, I thought, she was going to be more trouble than she was worth. And yet, she knew the city, and she'd come up with a halfway helpful lead. And despite myself, on another level, I still liked her.

"It's true," I said, trying to make it sound like a concession, "that I like things under my control. But in case you hadn't noticed, I'm running a Protektorate investigation, here, under the direct authority of the Hub Digislature. That gives me a *right* to have things done the way I want."

That seemed to subdue some of her combativeness. "I guess so," she said, sounding more subdued.

It was the closest thing to an apology that I was going to get out of her. "How come you feel a need to be so tough?" I asked.

"Because I was always told that I couldn't do stuff, and I wasn't good enough." She sighed and looked away. "I'm a bitch to work with, I know that. That's why I generally work alone. People don't like me."

Her sudden honesty had a strange effect on me. I felt unexpected emotions—some admiration for her, and some compassion. "You're too hard on yourself," I said, speaking without really thinking.

"Really?" She gave me a cautious look.

"But right now there's a job to do," I went on, "and you and I need to understand each other. We'll put the personal stuff in storage, and you'll give me full disclosure in future. Deal?"

She shook my hand. "Deal."

0101111

I updated Eva on what had happened in Gabol Plaza. "I'm a target, now," I said, "and anyone associated with me may also be considered a target. Lee will guide your flier by remote in future; it'll divert some of his processing power, but you'll be immune from tampering or overloads at Traffic Control. Be very cautious of any lek systems with the ability to do you harm."

"Okay." She nodded quickly. "What next?"

"I'm not giving up on Alex Quan. See, there's places offworld where you can get an identity transplant. We can't find out right now because the OverMains have imposed a communications embargo. No general transmissions are going out, to avoid any risk of communicating the virus offworld. But Quan could have come back here a new man. It's a possibility; he spent all his life here. This was home to him."

She blinked. "So maybe that pimp's tip wasn't worthless after all?"

"Maybe. To defeat all recognition systems, Quan would have had to change his face and stature, reengineer his sweat glands, and do a minor recoding of his DNA. It would take a couple of weeks to spread throughout his body using nanomeks or viral messengers."

She thought for a moment. Then she gestured irritably. "So what? If he's back here totally different, it's no help knowing what he used to look like."

"Let me have the pic."

She reached inside her jacket, then stopped. "Just a minute," she said. "You owe me."

I grunted in irritation. "You mean, the two hundred?"

She said nothing, just gave me a tight little smile.

"Eva, you're cash crazy. Two hundred is nothing. You could have paid Krentz two thousand

and I'd have reimbursed you. What is it with you and money?"

The look in her eyes hardened. "Have you ever been broke? Like, for thirty years?"

I sighed. "All right, you have a point. I'll have Lee run a tab for you, so you get reimbursed at the end of all this. Will that do it?"

She hesitated, then adamantly shook her head. "You just told me you're a target, now. You could get killed anytime. I better get my credit while you're still up and running. So, you owe me two hundred." She paused. "Plus another hundred for flier operating expenses and incidentals."

Wearily, I turned to Lee. "Transfer five thousand into this woman's combank account." I turned back to her. "That'll keep you going for a while, right?"

She gave me a funny look. "I always figured someone who knew about computers would would be smart about money."

"You're wrong," I told her. "Most bit-fixers have zero interest in wealth."

"The transaction is done," said Lee.

I held out my hand to Eva. "The pic, please."

She gave it to me. I turned to Lee and held it where he could see it. "Make me a duplicate."

Almost instantly, he reached under his tunic and pulled out a paper copy. I looked at it for a moment and saw a young, sad face. He had untidy blond hair, freckles, and a wide mouth that turned down at the corners. The image sparked no associations in my memory; I was sure I'd never seen him before. "You may as well keep this," I said to Eva. I handed her the copy and pocketed the original.

"Excuse me," said Lee. "I have an urgent bulletin."

"All right, show it to me. And show Eva, too."

THE KILLING OF MILTON BERG

It was an angry sea, green water surging, assaulting the land. The waves towered, threw themselves, smashed themselves across tumbled rocks. The air was full of swirling mist and drifting foam.

I was drifting through the spray, moving parallel to the inhospitable coast. Directly ahead was a promontory, a spur of rock separated by a narrow gulley from the mainland. Rooted in the rock was a building like a white fortress.

I gained altitude and saw that the building's flat roof was edged with a tall wall with notches in it, like ancient battlements. There were bays for a dozen fliers, but only one was currently occupied—by a bright red little two-seater.

Where the building faced the land, its walls were featureless white. But as I moved around over the ocean again I came to a wide, curving balcony in front of a line of windows. One of the windows was standing open.

The sun was almost directly overhead, and as I crossed the balcony I saw a small dark spot moving as I moved—the shadow cast by the peeker.

I passed through the open window, into a living room. The peeker's optics adjusted for the dimmer light, and the scene brightened. I saw an array of computing equipment along one wall, metal cabinets partially disassembled. There were some systems I recognized—small units normally dedicated to production sequencing in mek factories. They'd been heavily modified, and on a bench nearby was the diagnostic system that had done the job: machine code monitors, development tools, bug chasers, and a graduated set of waldoes fitted with micromanipulators.

The peeker turned, panning across the room, and I saw a large couch. Someone was sprawled there, lying faceup, his arms and legs stretched out as if he'd been thrown backward.

The peeker moved in for a close-up, and I saw the man's face. He was the leader of the Chaists: Milton Berg.

His mouth was gaping and his eyes were staring. There was a puncture wound in the center of his forehead. There were other, identical wounds in his chest where his shirt had been ripped away. He was drenched in blood.

0110000

"Lee, call our vehicles here right away." I hesitated. "That *was* Berg's home?"

"It was his home," Lee confirmed.

"What does it mean?" said Eva.

"How the hell do I know what it means?" I was angry again—at Berg for getting killed before I'd had a chance to question him, and at the situation for getting worse while I stood in the city park arguing about expense money with a neurotic woman. "Maybe Berg was working for someone like Catalano who got mad at him for screwing up. Sure, and maybe before they shot him, they forced him to undo the damage he'd done. That'd be a break, wouldn't it? I could go home and you could stay up all night looking at your credit balance after you get rich selling your story." I turned to Lee. "How does it look right now, inside the Mains? Everything normalized?"

"The situation is not normalized," he said. "It is still deteriorating. There has just been a major collision involving four fliers downtown. Also, a mining installation on the far side of the planet has sustained severe damage due to disruption of its production lines."

Eva's flier drifted in, settling gently in the grass nearby, and my vehicle came down beside it. Peo-

ple in the park turned and stared; this wasn't a
designated landing zone.

"My strategy," I said, half to myself, "was to
visit the principal suspects—create that visceral response that you really only get from face-to-face,
in person contact—and push them a little. Give
someone an incentive to break ranks or do something stupid." I slowly shook my head. "But people just keep getting killed." I turned away and
opened the canopy of my transit vehicle.

Eva touched my arm. "Where are you going?"

"To Berg's place."

"So what about me?"

"You can come."

"Nice of you to let me know."

I scowled at her. "Damn it, Eva, this whole
works is going down the tubes. Don't expect me
to act nice. Don't expect me to behave like a normal human being." I reached into a storage compartment and pulled out a spare set of skin armor.
"Put this on under your clothes. It'll shrink-fit."

She took it without a word.

I swung up into my vehicle and as Lee joined
me, I closed the canopy.

0110001

We headed for the coast, Lee flying Eva's flier
by remote, keeping it close beside us. "Milton Berg
has no history of lek training, right?" I asked.

"That is correct."

So maybe he wasn't our man. Maybe he'd employed someone else to use that equipment, and
that person had turned against him. Or maybe—
maybe anything. I could *maybe* myself into all
kinds of farfetched scenarios. Motive, method, and

opportunity were what I really needed; and I still didn't have even one of them.

I closed my eyes for a moment. It had been thirty hours or more since I'd had any sleep, and there was only so much that a REM suppressant could do. I had an alpha wave implant for times like this. I muttered the keyword, the implant took over, and I passed out.

0110010

I woke from a nightmare in which I'd been running through a burning apartment building, looking for someone to save, except I couldn't remember her name—and now I found the sun in my eyes, the ocean spread out in front of us, and Berg's home directly below. There was a Restricted Area marker on the roof and I could see dozens of little evidence-gathering autons swarming over the building. "The guardians already got here," I said, blinking, feeling muzzy.

"They removed the body a few minutes ago," said Lee.

"Get us landing clearance," I told him.

"We have clearance."

"And link me with the Peacekeeping Controller. Harry Green."

I waited while we descended slowly into one of the bays marked on the roof, with Eva's flier setting down beside us.

"Hello, there, Tom." Green's voice sounded in my head, patched through to my implant.

"Hi, Harry. We're at Milton Berg's place. Did you hear what happened?"

"Hell, yes. I just got a bulletin. Terrible thing. First the Coordinator, then Joe Belman, and now this. You know that until this mess started, there hadn't been a homicide in Sen City in twenty years?"

"How did it go with Fisk?" I asked.

"I think it was productive. Yes, I think it was. I shook some sense into him, and it wouldn't surprise me if he calls later today and comes clean, confesses hiring those thugs who beat up Belman, and tells us everything else he knows. I rattled his cage, sure enough."

Every statement was totally untrustworthy. I wondered why I'd bothered to ask.

"Anyhow," he hurried on, "I'm heading out to Berg's place right away. Right away. Daresay I'll meet you there."

"No," I told him bluntly. "Send your assistant. I'd like you to go to Central Processing, Harry. I want you at the nerve center if anything else happens. Which I believe it will." Would he believe that? It didn't matter what he believed, so long as he did what he was told.

0110011

I retracted the canopy. The roaring and crashing of the ocean was suddenly loud around me, and I felt wet salty air on my face. A gusty wind was blowing, lashing my hair into my eyes.

Eva got out of her vehicle. "Saw you sleeping during the trip," she said. "Feel better?"

"Not much, I had a nightmare. But it wasn't half as bad as reality. Come on, let's go look." I started down some steps that spiraled inside the curving wall of the building, leading to the main entrance. She followed me, and Lee came along behind.

The main door was standing open. An evidence-gathering auton saw me looming over it. I showed my ID, and it scuttled aside like a dog afraid of being kicked. Cautiously, I stepped into the room beyond.

Bright sunlight beamed through the wall of windows overlooking the ocean. The room itself was cluttered with lek, just the way it had looked in the peeker's vid. And the couch was saturated with blood.

I went over to it and saw a clean outline where the body had been. The blood around the edges was still sticky, and it coated the fabric like molasses. Apart from that, though, the furniture looked undamaged. No sign of a fight; no rips or tears.

"Berg's corpse is on its way to the morgue at Peacekeeping?" I asked Lee.

"Yes. Upon arrival, it will undergo an autopsy."

"Cancel that. The medimek systems are as unreliable as all the others at this point. If we let 'em cut Berg open, as likely as not they'll chop the body and serve it as hamburger in the Peacekeeping cafeteria. I want a human on hand to examine the wounds, and if there isn't anyone qualified, I'll do the job myself."

"Understood," said Lee.

I walked over to the computing equipment.

Eva joined me. "Can you analyze this hardware?" she asked. "Maybe figure who built it, or what he built it for?"

"If I had a month to spare and a room full of diagnostic aids, I could tear it down and learn a lot." I sighed. "Computers aren't simple. Even five hundred years ago, they weren't simple. Someone took a long time building this; someone very smart and maybe a little crazy."

"Could Lee—"

"Lee isn't going near it. He'll tell you why."

"I have some degree of protection when I am dealing with the Mains," he said, "because I fully understand their architecture, operating system, and languages. I know how far I can intrude safely, and how to protect myself from contamination by foreign code. If I entered a homemade device, I would be extremely vulnerable."

While he was speaking, I walked to the door. "No sign that anyone forced his way in," I said. I walked back into the room. "Berg seems like he was a cautious guy. Smart, reclusive—and this place was built like a fortress. So I doubt he left his door unlocked. He either let someone in because he knew them, or the killer had free access."

"Maybe one of his disciples?" said Eva.

"Possibly. They would have had the opportunity, though the motive is unclear. Lee, tabulate the locations of all self-described Chaists during the past hour."

That took him a good two seconds. "Most of them are unaccounted for," he said.

I sat down on one of the chairs that hadn't been spattered with blood. I squinted at Lee. He stood in the center of the room, his beige pseudoflesh gleaming in the bright light flooding through the windows. As always, he looked inscrutable. *"Most of them?* How can most of them be untraceable?"

"The Chaists dislike supervision by centralized authority. They make it their business to be as unobtrusive and unobserved as possible. I believe this explains why Berg himself chose this remote location, with no windows overlooking the land. It was only by chance that a peeker happened to be flying past, and a window happened to be open, allowing access."

I looked at Eva. She looked back at me. "Convenient, no?" she said.

I nodded slowly. "Very convenient. Strangely convenient."

Her eyes narrowed. "You think maybe someone wanted a peeker from the Protektorate to come see that Berg had been murdered?"

There was a cold feeling seeping through me. I didn't like conspiracy theories, and normally I didn't accept them. But this one had an awfully plausible sound to it. "It's quite possible that someone wanted me to know," I said. "The person who's manipulating the Mains must have been aware that I would find out about anything as significant as this."

"So they wanted to lure you out here." Eva was beginning to sound as nervous as I felt.

There was a faint sound from above. The kind of noise a flier would make, touching down on the roof. Eva heard it at the same moment that I did. She stiffened and touched her fingers to her mouth.

I turned quickly to Lee.

"Controller Green's deputy, Jalen Reese, has just landed." His voice was reassuringly calm and normal.

Eva let out a pent-up breath.

I laughed, releasing the tension. "This would be a lousy place to kill someone now, wouldn't it? In a room full of evidence-gathering autons."

Still, I felt unhappy. Eva had been right when she'd told me I liked to have everything under control. But Berg's killer was still out there, uncontrolled, unknown, and no closer to being nailed than when I'd first arrived on Agorima.

0110100

"This is Eva Kurimoto," I said, "who's helping me on this case."

Jalen Reese looked at her in much the same way she might have looked at a blank vidscreen. Then she looked back at me, still as casually indifferent as when I'd talked to her on Joe Belman's farm that morning. "Ms. Kurimoto and I met a few months ago," said Reese. "At that time, she was a reporter."

"I still am," said Eva.

Reese looked mildly surprised. "We don't normally allow media people at a crime site during evidence gathering."

I stood up. "Eva's link with the Mains is blocked. She only has her personal onboard storage. There's no way she can send out a story. And she's helping me with local background." I gave Reese a friendly smile. "I want you to check the whole of this building. I realize the autons will do it anyway, but I want you to go for the human angle. Anything that looks wrong, seems out of place. Okay?"

If she was surprised by being given such a menial chore, she didn't show it. "Okay," she said.

"And don't report to your Controller. I'll call you direct."

I waited for her to complain that this, too, seemed irregular. But she was smart enough not to make the same mistake twice.

"Did you sit in on Harry's visit with Fisk?" I asked before she could leave the room.

"His visit with Fisk." She sounded mildly amused. "Yes, I was there."

I found myself becoming unreasonably fascinated by her. She was acting as if the whole situation was a sim drama that didn't involve her in any way. "Are you expecting to quit this job sometime soon?" I blurted out.

She gave me a puzzled look. "No," she said. "Is something wrong?"

"Just that it seems like you wouldn't care if you were fired tomorrow."

Her face went blank. "I don't understand. I enjoy my work."

I wasn't getting anywhere. "Forget it," I said. "Just tell me what happened with Fisk. Did Harry get anything out of him?"

There was a pause. She seemed to be weighing her answer carefully. "No," she said.

I laughed. "You get right to the point, don't you?"

She shrugged. "You seem like you're in a hurry. Do you really want a more detailed report?"

There seemed to be some humor behind that remark, although it was impossible to be sure. "Do you think Fisk is implicated in this murder?" I asked her.

Reese shot a cautious look at Eva. "Are you storing this?"

Eva looked at me. "I was given permission—"

Reese shook her head. "This is confidential."

"All right," I said, "Eva, could you wait up on the roof for a minute?"

She shot me an irritated look, then walked out of the room.

"All right," I said to Reese, "what do you have to tell me?"

"I viewed the vid of Berg's body on my way here," she said. "I saw that the wounds had been made by projectile weapons. Fisk's guards have been found with projectile weapons in the past, though we could never prove that he had equipped them. Perhaps if a proper analysis is done of the wounds, we'll find trace deposits which we can match to ammunition used by the weapons of Fisk's men."

It was an oddly mechanical little speech, as if

she'd had it memorized. Also, it was steering me toward Fisk—just as Harry Green had done.

"Why would Fisk want to kill Milton Berg?" I asked her.

"I don't know." Now that she'd said her piece, she'd lost interest in the conversation.

"What do you want?" I said it suddenly, making my voice a little loud.

She blinked. Her attractive face looked genuinely surprised.

"What do you *want?*" I gave her a demanding stare.

She hesitated. "Well, I'd like to get this situation resolved. I have some vacation time coming up—"

Whatever I'd hoped to trigger in her, it hadn't worked. I decided to give up—at least for the time being. "Okay," I said, "I have to go. Will you check this place out, as I requested?"

"Sure," she said, as indifferent as before.

0110101

"There is some more urgent news," Lee told me as I walked with him up to the roof.

That bad word again; urgent. "Who else has been killed?" I asked. At this rate, my job would be a whole lot simpler: the only suspect left alive would be the one who'd murdered all the others.

"No one has been killed," said Lee. "Joe Belman, at Biocare, has regained consciousness and is able to talk."

I paused, wondering who was more important for me to see: him or Fisk. Then I realized the obvious answer.

Eva was waiting by her flier. "Eva," I called to her, "I want you to use your interviewing skills on Joe Belman."

She gave me a puzzled look. "To find out what?"

I opened the canopy of my transit vehicle. "Ask him who beat him up. Ask if he tore a piece off their containment coveralls. Ask if he's ever heard of Alex Quan."

She paused doubtfully. "What are you going to do?"

I grinned at her. "Harry Green and Jalen Reese

The Nature of the Beast

A computer virus is a piece of code designed to make itself resident in a computer system, after which it will attempt to make copies of itself so that it can spread to other systems.

A virus usually infects a system in one of two basic ways: 1. by attaching itself unobtrusively to a regular computer program, so that it is moved into storage or memory along with the program itself; 2. by disguising itself as a utility or program that seems to have a benign purpose. (This second form is often referred to as a Trojan Horse.)

Once the virus is resident in a system, it may attempt to attach copies of itself to other programs already stored so that if these programs are copied and used elsewhere, the virus will go with them. Alternatively, it may spread copies of itself directly across a network connecting many data-processing nodes.

Usually (but not always) a virus will be designed to do more than merely replicate itself; and usually (not always) this function will be destructive. When the program carrying the virus is executed, the virus is activated and may erase files in its host system, fill the screen with garbage characters, tie up the processor in idiot work, or create other havoc. Before this occurs, however, there will be a "latency period" to allow the virus time to reproduce before it attacks and cripples the system where it resides.

both seem convinced that I should go visit Emmanuel Fisk. So I figure I'll take their advice."

"Reese?" Eva shook her head. "I wouldn't take anything from that baby-faced weirdo."

The description, I thought, was reasonably accurate. "Hey," I said, "don't you think Fisk is our man?"

She wrinkled her nose. "He's carnivorous, but he's not homicidal."

"As it happens," I said, "I agree with you. But I have a use for him." I stepped into my vehicle. "Keep in contact," I warned her as I closed the canopy.

I'd hoped for another fifteen minutes' sleep, but there was no chance of that. As soon as we were heading back inland, Lee had another little item of news. "There is a message," he said, "from the Hub."

The OverMains never normally bothered an anomalyst on a job. By the very act of sending him out, they'd already admitted they couldn't fix the problem themselves.

"Show me." I felt a nasty sense of foreboding.

THE MAN IN THE LITTLE ROOM

I was standing in a book-lined study, waiting and watching a little old white-haired man sitting behind an antique wooden desk. There was a globe of Planet Earth on a mahogany stand, an old brass optical telescope, flat photographs of chemical-fueled rockets flaming up into the blue, and other incredibly archaic memorabilia from the dawn of spaceflight. The blinds were drawn and a couple of logs were burning in an iron grate.

The book-lined study didn't really exist, of course. It

was an old, old simulation, and so was the little old man. Legend said he had been modeled on a programmer who had established the Protektorate in its earliest days, but I couldn't even speculate on that. The setup was just a convenient way for the OverMains at the Hub to present themselves when they needed to communicate with humans like me.

"Hello, Tom," said the old man. He smiled and leaned forward, clasping his hands together on the blotter in front of him. "Your orbital vehicle has been relaying Lee's reports, and we've been keeping track of the way things are going out there." He spoke in a friendly, folksy voice, like somebody's rustic uncle. He always seemed kind and concerned, and he was always dressed in the same dark green tweed jacket and dark brown tie. Centuries ago, when this setup had first been programmed, someone had probably decided it would be reassuring to present a father figure surrounded by elements of nostalgia. Now, of course, it was ridiculous—but I had always had a weakness for it. In my early days of training, I'd amused myself imagining that one day, in some forgotten corner of the mek-made world of the Hub itself, I might actually run across that little book-lined study. And maybe if I worked hard and was a good citizen, the old man would retire and I'd take his place.

"You're not making much progress," said the old man.

I didn't bother to answer that.

He adjusted his wire-framed spectacles. "What's your prognosis?"

I juggled facts in my head and grabbed a figure. "I give myself a seventy percent chance of taking care of the problem within the next two days. But there may be severe damage to essential services."

The man behind the desk frowned and nodded. He only had two distinctly different expressions: benevolent understanding and fatherly concern. "As you know," he said, "we've buffered all communications out of Agorima, with the exception of those via your jumpship, for the past day or so. But the buffering system itself went down, just ten minutes ago, showing aberrant behavior."

I felt a sinking sensation. It was everyone's worst-case nightmare that a virus should spread interworld. Never in the Protektorate's history had it happened.

"Possibly the virus embedded itself inside a routine transmission several days ago," the old man went on, "and for some reason our detection routines missed it. Anyway, all data in the buffer have been destroyed, and the hardware itself has been torn down. We believe that has taken care of the problem. But from this moment on, Agorima will be quarantined until you can present proof that the virus has been identified and neutralized."

I stared at him, feeling blank. Twice in fifty years, I'd been stuck on quarantined worlds. That was *my* worst nightmare. "I need help," I said.

"Unfortunately, none is available. Our human resources are stretched very thin at present. There have been several resignations recently, and several deaths, as you know."

I knew what he really meant: Protektors were burning out faster than they could be replaced, and Agorima wasn't considered vital to the well-being of the Protektorate. It produced some entertainment, it exported some natural resources, but only a million people lived there. It was relatively unimportant in the larger scheme of things.

"You may, of course, exercise your option to quit," the old man said, looking at me over the tops of his spectacles. "In that case it is my customary duty to remind you of the conditions. You will present yourself to us without any personal belongings, without your auton, and without any human companions. Your jumpship will be destroyed. Your onboard data storage will be surgically removed. Your sense implants will be replaced. We will accept your resignation as an anomalyst and will facilitate your early retirement with enhanced lifetime entitlements in appreciation of your services rendered over a period of fifty-five years."

I was starting to feel queasy. Quitting was out of the question; if I couldn't work as a Protektor, I'd go crazy. It was how I defined myself. My work was the only thing that really gave my life meaning. "Thanks," I said. "I'll follow this thing through."

"Very well, Tom. You realize, as a result of the quarantine, we will no longer be monitoring you through your jumpship link. Even that may become corrupt."

"I realize," I said. "I'm on my own."

"Quite so. But we wish you luck and hope to see you soon." He nodded to me and gave me his smile of benevolent understanding.

Usually the book-lined study dissolved bit by bit into reality. This time, everything just went black. There was a loud hissing sound, and my field of view filled with static.

0110110

I looked at Lee. "We're locked out," I said.

He didn't answer. I'd voiced a statement of fact that he already knew.

I stared at the treetops passing below. The figure that I'd named—a seventy percent success probability—had been optimistic. I tended to err on the side of optimism. It was my religion, my way of keeping faith.

"Show me what happened when Harry Green visited Fisk," I said. I didn't expect it to be enlightening, but it could give me some pointers regarding my own impending visit. "Run it from the beginning. No, cancel that. Excerpt it. Five minutes, max." More than that would be cruel and unusual punishment.

LEANING (GENTLY)
ON MR. FISH

I was looking down from a high viewpoint at Fisk's little black room. Harry Green, Jalen Reese, and two men in Peacekeeping uniform were standing opposite the improvised desk while Fisk lurked deep in his egg-shaped chair, glowering out at them like a bad-tempered snapping turtle.

"I mean it, Manny," Green was saying in a voice that he seemed to think was tough but merely sounded loud. "I realize we go back a long way, you and me. And I've always liked you, you know that. But we have evidence, and that's the way it is. So now I'm giving you the chance to play ball, and I'm trying to make this easy for both of us. What d'you say, pal?"

Fisk endured the rain of clichés without blinking. He stared at Green as if there was something wrong with the man. "But I don't give a fuck about this Joe Feldman."

Harry Green laughed. It was a forced, strained sound. "*Belman*," he said. "The man's name is Joe *Belman.* Manny, you know that, and I know you know it, so let's stop fooling around, eh? Else—"

"Else what?" Fisk hauled himself up and out of his chair, onto his feet. He leaned forward, resting his pudgy fingertips on the packing crates. "You're threatening me, Harry, seems to me." He chuckled and shook his head, making his plump flesh quiver. "You, threatening me. *You,* threatening me." He lowered his chin and tapped his fat fingers, like a native beating a war drum. I could see his nostrils flaring as he worked himself into one of his fits. "You're scum, old pal." He wasn't shouting yet, but he was getting there. "Like you say yourself—*you* know that, and *I* know it, so let's stop dicking around." He drew a deep breath. "*Scum!* You and your muscle boys and Little Miss Creepo here—"

"Now, just a moment." Green reached for Fisk's arm.

Fisk made a wild, angry gesture, jerking his arm away. "Don't touch me!" He groped in his shirt pocket and pulled out a black capsule. He held it up as if he was trying to repel a vampire with a crucifix.

A scratchy voice came from the capsule. "Mr. Fisk has a right to be informed of any charge against him," it said. "If charged, has a right to remain silent. If no charge is brought—"

"Manny, Manny, I know the law just as well as you," Harry Green said, sounding plaintive.

"Then get the hell out!" Fisk screamed at him.

"Enough," I said to Lee. "More than enough."

0110111

We were coming down over the hills, approaching the broad, shallow valley where the city sprawled across the land. The view had changed in the past hour or so: columns of brown smoke were rising in the afternoon air. We came in low and I saw an office building in flames, its plastic facade buckling, permaglas canopies of fliers parked on the roof suddenly shattering in the intense heat. People were running, fanning out across an adjacent plaza. Emergency vehicles were circling above the blaze, leaking white gas over it. On the pedway below, people were bumping into each other in their panic, some taking cover in buildings that were probably no safer than the one whose support systems had allowed it to catch fire.

Further on, a highway reserved for auto traffic was full of ground vehicles jammed together in an unmoving river of steel. Several of the drivers seemed to have given up; they were getting out of their cars and walking away without looking back.

"Give me a report," I said to Lee.

"The situation has deteriorated faster than I expected. There have been more than one hundred flier collisions since dawn today. Ground vehicles have also been involved in accidents; they are under human control, but are regulated by traffic signals which no longer operate reliably. Numerous incidents of person-to-person violence have occurred, sparked by random factors such as malfunctioning vendeks, vehicle collisions, incorrectly recorded financial transactions, and unreliable com links. Emergency services can no longer keep pace with demand, and the services themselves are beginning to suffer the same lag times afflicting every other division of Central Processing."

"Overload," I murmured.

"Yes, overload. In some cases, genuine overload conditions do now exist. But all the Mains are experiencing unexplained slowdowns regardless of their proper status. Some are now totally out of operation. Maintenance has proved to its satisfaction that replacing hardware is useless, and they are still unable to detect any form of virus in software. However, Maintenance itself is now undoubtedly infected, so their reports cannot be considered reliable. Members of the human staff have sent several messages to you appealing for help, and I have responded in your name stating that we can do nothing until we apprehend the saboteur who created the problem."

"Yes," I said. "That's right."

I tried to see what options I had left. People would be struggling home, soon. By tomorrow we could expect total system failures, at which point there would be no way to predict how the population would react.

"How's it being presented over the newsims?" I asked.

"This was broadcast half an hour ago."

EMERGENCY BULLETINS

I was in someone else's head. The sight and sound was more immediate than from a peeker, and the movements were uneven. ". . . guests in the Corinth have been stranded in their rooms for more than five hours," a voice-over said while my viewpoint tracked past a building styled like a massive sandstone obelisk. Most of the upper windows had been smashed, and half-naked men and women were leaning out shouting and waving to the newsman in his flier. "The hotel's support systems went buggy early this morning when hot air literally roasted five vacationers in a stationary elevator. All services are now down, but overworked emergency crews don't have time to rescue the estimated thousand guests trapped in their rooms by the central locking system. Now back to Shirley."

The close-up of the hotel dissolved into a woman's face against a background of billowing black smoke. "Here at the orbital transfer station, rescue meks are still battling the blaze that erupted when today's shuttle carrying three hundred tourists went out of control shortly after taking off for a routine round-the-globe sight-seeing tour. No word yet whether there are any survivors."

The picture behind her faded into a flat blue background; it had been a mixed vid. "Experts are saying all the failures we're seeing are probably the result of a single major malfunction at Central Processing, and we're advising all of you to stay in the safety of your homes till it's cleared. All offworld comlinks are down, and no ships have gone out in the past forty-eight hours. As we mentioned earlier, there is an unconfirmed report that a Protektor is already onplanet, brought here to investigate the suspicious death of Coordinator Nils Ferguson, which you'll remember we told you about a few hours ago. We repeat, a major malfunction has occurred at Central, so please take every precaution and use city services as little as you can." She gave a tight, uneasy smile; I could see her wondering how much she might be at risk herself. "Now this from Roger, at the Eroticado Palace in Dream Valley."

I found myself in a dense crowd. If I'd been under a full VR rig, I would have been able to smell and feel the bodies pressing in.

"Shirley, the Eroticado promoted this as the biggest snap you can get outside of zero G. But ecstasy turned to agony this P.M. when the big sphere in which naked vacationers literally bounce off the walls suddenly deflated, suffocating all those who were cavorting in it at the time." The viewpoint pressed forward, and I saw a milky white bladder fifty meters across, wrinkled and lumpy, lying on a black floor. Meks were cutting it open and pulling out naked bodies while crowds of tourists gaped at the spectacle.

The viewpoint turned, bringing me face-to-face with a teenage woman who was standing hugging her arms around herself, her eyes wide with morbid fascination. She was naked under candy-flake body paint, and all her hair had been shaved off except for some random clumps which were tinted bright yellow. I recognized it as a fashion that had been popular a few months back.

"Excuse me, we're live on newsim, did you see what happened here?"

She turned and nodded. "Yeah, I saw it, I was just gonna go in myself." She gave a sick grin. "You know you vid this kind of thing, people getting killed like when systems go down, but you never think it's going to happen to *you*, you know? I mean—it just never happens."

0111000

"Call Fisk's secretary, or his appointment desk, or whoever it is that handles his schedule," I said to Lee, as I saw the cube-shaped megalith ahead of us, rainbows flowing down its west face in the fading afternoon sun. "Apologize for interrupting the great man, but make it clear that if he won't talk to us, I'll use my authority to have him detained immediately by Peacekeeping. And call Peacekeeping and get six guardians over here, so we can follow through on the bluff if necessary."

"Understood," said Lee, as we started losing altitude.

"And while you're handling that," I said, "I think it's time for me to make a public statement." I reached for the peeker that I kept in the cabin for this purpose. "Show me my face," I said, as I positioned the little silver sphere in front of me.

A LIFE-THREATENING SITUATION

My viewpoint switched again, this time reversing so I saw myself from the peeker's perspective: thirtyish-looking man, weary and beat-up, his sandy hair disheveled, his eyes a little bloodshot. I grimaced, and my face grimaced back at me.

"Fix the eyes," I said.

My eyes, in the vid, lost their little red veins. The lids seemed to retract slightly so they looked more directly, sincerely into the peeker's miniaturized scanner.

"We need healthier skin tone, and firm up the muscles around the mouth."

Lee's real-time retouching routines went to work, coloring my face, making me less weary, more stern, more in control.

"And fix the clothes," I told him.

My rumpled tunic faded away, replaced with a dark jacket and a white shirt open at the neck. My shoulders broadened and my chest pushed out. I looked like a cross between an old-style statesman and an electronics engineer, tough enough to dig down into the guts of some monstrous mainframe and crush bugs with my bare hands if necessary.

No wonder, I thought, the public had some misconceptions about the capabilities of a Protektor. They believed the image we fed them even while they knew it was edited like everything else.

"Give me voice number five," I said. "Test, one, two, three." And as I spoke my timbre deepened, became more measured, more solemn.

"Okay, let's do a take. My name's Tom McCray, and I'm the anomalyst—the Protektor—who's been sent here to Agorima to investigate the catastrophic system failures you've been experiencing. As I'm sure you understand, I have very limited time, so I can't go into any details right now. But I do have a clear idea of what's wrong, and I'm doing my best to fix it. Until then, please try to avoid using any lek systems—I repeat, *any* lek systems. Store food and water sufficient for three or four days, and please, don't tie up the com channels unnecessarily, and don't call emergency services unless you really have a life-threatening situation. Thank you for your patience, and I'm hoping we'll have it back under control sometime tomorrow."

"Now give me a replay," I said to Lee.

I watched my own performance. It was adequate, and there wasn't time for retakes anyway.

"Send it to all the stations, attaching our validation code. Make sure they can check with Central Processing to get authentication if they want it. You know the procedure."

0111001

Back in my own skull, I found myself looking at a flat gray rooftop crowded with parked fliers. Fisk's rooftop, I realized. Lee had set us down while I'd been making my vid. "No problem getting access this time?" I asked.

"We have been granted visitor status. I did not speak to Mr. Fisk himself."

"Are the guardians here?"

"Several detachments were nearby but were fully occupied preventing citizens from looting stores whose security systems had left them unprotected. I had to fetch a backup force from Central. They are now approaching from the south." I turned in my seat and saw a speck descending toward us through the traffic crisscrossing the sky. The speck became a personnel carrier, navy blue with the Peacekeeping crest on its side. A minute later it set down near us, occupying a pair of standard-size bays. A hatch opened and a dozen guardians came rolling out.

"Do you have a reliable link with them through Peacekeeping?" I asked Lee. "I don't want any glitches, any lag time or overloads." The last thing we needed was guardians refusing to obey, or freezing up, or grabbing me instead of Fisk.

"I am linked with them via three separate channels to provide maximum redundancy. That is the best I can do. And so far there is no indication of trouble."

"Okay." I opened the canopy. "Let's go see Mr. Fisk."

0111010

With the authority of the guardians opening doors for us, we were soon in Fisk's garish hallways with a phalanx of his personal guards trailing along behind, looking unhappy about the intrusion but knowing there was nothing they could do about it.

We rumbled into the reception area. The blue waterfall was still playing over the blue rocks, and the blue paper notepad was still sitting on the blue desk. But now there was a young man behind the desk (dressed in blue, naturally), just replacing a comset in its clip. He gave me a nervous look. "I've told Mr. Fisk you're here," he said. His hands fidgeted with an ink pen. "He'll be with you shortly. If you'd like to take a seat—"

I rested my palms on the desk and leaned forward. "Where is he?"

He tried to smile placatingly, and failed. "He's in conference at present. There's a very important meeting—"

"Where's the conference room?" I asked Lee.

"This way." He started toward a pair of doors.

"Hey, you!" one of Fisk's guards shouted.

I turned and eyed him. "Several crimes have been committed, including homicide. We're here to detain Mr. Fisk. Do you want to interfere?"

I waited for an answer. When I didn't get one, I turned back to Lee. "Can you open those doors?"

There was a click as a magnetic lock disengaged.

0111011

We entered a long, narrow, windowless room whose walls and ceiling were all the same shade of glossy chocolate brown. Fisk was slouched in a chair at the head of an ancient natural wood table. Half a dozen people were sitting on either side, and from the diffuse way the light reflected off them, I could tell they were holo transmissions.

He stared at us as we marched into the room, but he didn't seem any more surprised than when I'd invaded his sleeping quarters that morning. "You have the manners of a junkyard dog,

McCray," he said. "What the hell do you want now?"

"You'd better switch these people out," I said, gesturing to his guests, who were staring.

Fisk turned to them. "Friends, as you know, there's a Protektor here on Agorima. Seems he thinks I can help him in some way. So—civic duty, I suppose, is the term for it. We'll reconvene within a half hour. My apologies."

He touched a concealed switch and the images disappeared, leaving six empty chairs. Then he turned back to me. "McCray, I'll sue you personally," he said, slapping his palms down on the table, "for trespass, emotional trauma, physical impairment resulting from contamination of a sterile area, invasion of privacy, slander, damage to my personal reputation, damage to my esthetic and artistic senses, lawlek expenses, breaking and entering, wear and tear on office decor, cleaning costs, the value of my time, anxiety and other associated psychogenic symptoms, wrongful arrest, and financial loss from interrupting the deal I was negotiating."

"I haven't arrested you, yet," I said, "so we'll scratch that one." His rant had lasted long enough for me to walk around and take the chair on his left while Lee moved to the one on his right. "Here's the situation," I said, keeping it low-key and conversational. "One: A piece of your guards' uniforms was found in the home of a man who was badly beaten this morning. Two: A murder was committed using projectile weapons similar to those that are illegally installed here. Three: Central Processing has been sabotaged, and a primary suspect once worked in one of your labs. Four: A woman was killed by a cart in Gabol Plaza, in the Xavier Tower, which I gather from your stats is

owned by one of your subsidiaries. I have more than
enough to detain you right now, and if the charges
stick, you'll be sent away for modification and your
sim business will be sold off for scrap. The guardians
you see here are ready to place you under arrest."

Fisk slowly settled back into his chair. His
mouth made little chewing motions, his eyes narrowed, and he looked like an old fighter weighing
up his adversary. The prospect of a battle obviously didn't bother him at all; he was almost looking forward to it.

"Seems to me," he said, "if you were serious
about taking me in, you'd go ahead and do it. You
wouldn't make your asshole speech." He grinned.
"So you got my attention, McCray. Now get to
the point."

I eyed him with mild irritation, then glanced
quickly around the room. "Is that a server up
there?"

"Damn right it is. Everything here is open to
public scrutiny."

I was getting a little tired of that particular refrain,
but there was no point in hassling over it. "Lee is
going to block all transmissions from this room," I
said. "He'll also assess your veracity. Ask your
guards to leave, and I'll have the guardians wait
outside. This is going to be just between you and
me."

Fisk mulled that over for a good long while. Finally, he glanced at his men and made a brief gesture with his thumb. Within less than a minute, there
was no one in the room but Fisk, Lee, and me.

0111100

I pulled my chair closer. Fisk rummaged somewhere under the desk, brought out a vaporizer,

and sprayed some mist between us. The stuff smelled like ammonia, and it made my eyes water. I waved it away. "Lee, take his wrist."

"What the hell?" Fisk jerked his arm back as Lee reached for it.

"He needs to monitor your pulse and skin conductivity," I said patiently.

"I must've been crazy to agree to this," said Fisk. "Should've let you take me to Peacekeeping. I'd get more respect." He pulled a tissue from a dispenser, wrapped it around his wrist, then grudgingly extended his arm.

"Okay," I said. "I'll tell you now, off the record, I don't believe you were involved in any of the crimes I just mentioned. The piece of fabric was bullshit; you wouldn't send some thugs wearing coveralls that could be easily traced back to you. And you have no motive to kill Milton Berg. So the question is, Mr. Fisk, why is someone trying to pin it on you?"

He gave me a careful, devious look. "If I was going to level with you," he said, "I say, *if*—I might tell you I've been wondering the same thing."

I decided it was necessary to apply a little more torsion. "You know, being detained isn't the worst thing that can happen," I said. "Let's consider the future of your business right now. The comnet is down, so your simcasts can't go out. And here's another little item: Agorima has been officially quarantined. Had you heard about that?"

A little tic worked in his face. "I expected it," he said. His tone was casual, but it lacked conviction.

"If I were in your position," I told him, "and someone offered me a deal, I might be inclined to cooperate."

"A deal?" His face twisted as if it was an obscenity. "From the Protektorate?"

"I've already outlined your other option."

"You mean you're threatening me?" He made it sound as if he had never been subjected to such an indignity.

I shrugged. "Sure."

"Listen," he said, waving his finger at me, "if I knew anything, I'd be working on it already, trying to get this mess under control. You're wasting your time, McCray. I'm getting crucified, and the best you can do—"

I smashed my fist down hard on the table and had the satisfaction of seeing him twitch. "No more bullshit!" I shouted.

Finally, there was silence.

I managed to recover my equilibrium. "All right," I said, "let's start by talking about your crooked land deal with Serena Catalano."

"Land deal." He sounded more subdued than before, and his eyes moved uneasily. "What's she been telling you?"

I shook my head. "The only way to clear this—off the record—is for you to tell me."

He looked as if he wanted to sink even farther into his chair, but he'd gone as low as he could go. He made a growling, grumbling sound. Then he swore. It was a colorful list of adjectives, culled from his centuries of experience on a dozen different worlds in the sim business. I waited, patiently, till he finally ran down.

"All right," he said, "I'll deal with you. You hear that?" He looked pained. The concept was almost too much to bear.

"Fine," I said.

"But listen, McCray, I don't want to hear anything more about those charges. I cooperate with you, you sure as hell better cooperate with me."

"That's precisely what I had in mind," I said.

"Okay." He breathed heavily for a moment. "You want to know about that land? I owned a choice parcel in Dream Valley. Serena said if I gave it to her cheap, *really* cheap, she'd be nice to me."

For a moment I felt disconcerted by his sudden shift from stonewalling to what seemed to be honesty. "What does 'nice' mean?" I asked him.

He stared at me as if I was a simpleton. "Sex," he said. "S-E-X. What else would she have that I'd want?"

I tried to imagine Fisk coupling with Serena Catalano. I fell back, regrouped, and tried a second time. This was Sen City, I reminded myself. Normal standards did not apply.

"So I told her okay," Fisk went on. "But in a land sale, the Protektorate levies taxes at market value, no matter what the land trades for. She tried to muscle me into paying the taxes, but naturally I refused. I was doing her a big enough favor already. So she went away and came back, said don't worry about it, she had a friend at Central Processing who could make it look like I'd misfiled my original claim. That way, the land reverted to the Protektorate and could be resold on a first-served basis, like when the planet was first opened up. So she got it for next to nothing, and that's the way it went."

It was quiet in the conference room. I studied Fisk's face. He looked uncomfortable and bad-tempered; the act of volunteering information had been difficult for him.

"You can guess the next question," I said. "Who was this friend at Central Processing?"

Fisk threw up his fat hands. "You think I didn't already ask her that? I asked her this morning. She blew me off. I threatened her, she threatened me—I can't deal with her. The woman's a menace."

"You mean your land-for-sex trade didn't work out? She dumped you? You dumped her? What?"

He looked away. "Who the hell knows."

I leaned forward. "*You* know, you phony."

He grimaced. "She reneged on it. So I tried to push her a little, and she got nasty."

Nasty, I thought, was probably an understatement. "So you and she are enemies now. Was she the one who tried to implicate you in the beating that Belman took this morning?"

"Yeah, her or good old Harry Green. It amounts to the same thing. She owns him."

"Ah. How does that work?"

Fisk shrugged. "Way I figure it, this friend of hers who fixed things in Central Processing also arranged for that bozo Green to get promoted, so Serena would have a flunky in Peacekeeping whenever necessary." He clasped his pudgy hands and looked down at them ruefully. "Fucking bitch."

I almost felt sorry for him. But not quite. "It seems to me," I said, "if Catalano has tried to pin stuff on you, it might not have been personal. More likely it was just a diversion to waste my time and tie up my investigation."

"For why?" His voice rose in pitch. His eyes opened wide and he reached out as if he wanted to grab someone or something and shake them into making some sense. "If your investigation gets derailed, that doesn't benefit Serena, or me, or anyone else on this planet. It means we're stuck here in quarantine, we go bankrupt, and we *die*."

"Tom?" It was Eva's voice, in my ear.

I looked at Lee, across the table. "Where is she?" I asked him via our silent link.

"In Joe Belman's room at Biocare," his voice sounded in my head. "Shall I link you with the server in that room?"

"Yes, provided you can keep our conversation secure." I turned to Fisk. "Excuse me for a moment," I said. "I have to monitor a transmission from my auton."

THE MAN IN THE COCOON

"Hi, Tom." She was standing below my viewpoint, grinning up at me. Behind her, Belman was wrapped in a nutrient cocoon, silvery layers coiled around him, making him look like an oversize papoose. Readouts flickered in panels in the white wall above his head, and the squat gray bulk of a medimek stood nearby, delicate probes disappearing into the swaddled form.

"I've been talking to Joe." She gestured at Belman. "And he wants to help."

Belman tried to sit up, but the cocoon held him down. He coughed and winced. "This guy, this Protektor, can he hear me?"

"Sure," said Eva. "Anything I hear, he hears it too."

"You've got to put a stop to all this," Belman said, raising his voice as if he doubted that communications technology could receive his speech clearly at a range of ten feet. "This violence, the loss of life. It's a terrible thing. People put their faith in these machines, you know. Build their whole lives around them."

"Get him to listen to the comset by his bed," I told Eva. "So he can hear me."

She went over and held it up to his ear.

"I'm doing my best, Mr. Belman," I said. Mentally, I

typed him as a time-waster. But Eva wouldn't have paged me for no reason. "Do you know who attacked you?"

"He doesn't know," Eva cut in, "but I showed him my copy of the pic of Alex Quan."

"That fella came to see me fifteen years back," said Belman. "I remember it distinctly on account of it was just one day after my fiftieth anniversary with Meg. I'd been out all day harvesting, and I was in no mood for visitors, but this fella, he was persistent, you know?"

"Quan didn't give his name, and the meeting wasn't monitored," Eva cut in. "But Joe says he remembers it clearly. Quan said for a fee, he'd help to cripple the Protektorate by spreading bugs through the Mains. He said he needed money for medical work, and he didn't have sufficiently powerful access tools, back then, to make the Mains increase his entitlements. Joe said no sale, and Quan left. But get this: we nailed the date, and it's three weeks *after* the stats say Quan went offworld. Seems like the departure record is bad data. Your man never left town."

"I told him," said Belman, "I told him I didn't care much for people who want to destroy things. I said I wanted to enlighten the public to the point where they'd turn away from gadgets of their own free will. They'd find their fulfillment in human values instead of—"

There was more, but I wasn't listening. I was thinking ahead. "Lee," I said, "has Catalano left her offices?"

"She has not gone outside her building."

"Eva," I called to her, "you did good. Things are finally moving. I want you to go to the Nirvana and stake out Catalano's office suite. Call me if you see her, or anyone remotely like her."

She mulled it over. "But don't you already have a peeker—"

"Yeah, but peekers aren't smart, and they can be corrupted. I want you there. I'll join you in maybe half an hour."

"You're the boss," she said with an ironic smile.

"I am. And thank you, Mr. Belman, you've been a great help."

"You're welcome," said Belman. He looked vaguely around the room as if he still expected to see me on a screen somewhere.

0111101

I focused on Emmanuel Fisk again. He was watching me shrewdly, and I realized with regret that he'd had time to start building a new tangled nest of defenses and diversionary tactics while I'd been linked with Eva. "So," he said to me, "you're working with someone."

"I have an associate," I said. None of my conversation had been audible to him, but he'd been able to watch my body language and expressions while I'd been linked.

"Who else is cooperating with you?" he said, leaning forward intently.

"No one you know."

"Try me. You think there's anyone important on the planet who I haven't heard of?"

I pulled out my pic of Alex Quan. "If you're so well connected, maybe you can tell me who this is." I pushed the page in front of him.

He frowned. Grudgingly, he inspected the pic. He took his time, and he was careful. It was his business, after all, to deal in images. "Never seen him," he said, finally.

"He used to work here," I persisted.

"Never seen him!" Fisk glared at me.

I wasn't entirely surprised. Quan hadn't operated at a level where Fisk would have run across him. "How difficult would it be for someone to get a complete face-and-body job in Sen City?" I asked.

"No problem at all. We do refeaturing every day right here in this building, in my own labs."

The same labs, I thought, where Alex Quan had once worked, and where he'd probably made a few friends. Maybe he'd done them some favors, and they owed him a few in return. That seemed likely. Maybe, too, there was equipment down there that could even be used, illicitly, for DNA recoding.

"But listen," said Fisk, "we're legit, McCray. You think this is some backstreet clinic? Listen to me. We log physical changes with Central Processing, even if we just take off a pimple. All the ops are under direct surveillance. No way did this kid walk in here and walk out as someone else. Understand that?"

"But if he knew how to manipulate the records after they were transmitted to Central," I said, "that would change everything, wouldn't it?"

Fisk lapsed into silence. He took some time to think that over.

"Do me a favor," I said. "Check your records. See if a guy named Alex Quan, matching this photo, ever opted for refeaturing or other face work." I stood up. "Do you, yourself, have sim implants?"

"Do I have implants?" He shook his head in amazement. "McCray, do you know who I *am?* I run one of the biggest goddam sim networks in the galaxy."

I grinned. It was a pleasure to tweak him a little. "So you can link with me," I said. "Anytime. Just say my name. Lee will be monitoring the Mains and he'll patch you through. Got that?"

Fisk's eyes shifted to Lee, then back to me. He didn't look happy, and I knew why. He was a rebel and a maverick; it was the way he defined himself. Now that he had opened up to me, he wasn't his own man anymore.

0111110

Fliers were lifting all around us, climbing, turning, wheeling like clouds of bats into the evening sky. I hurried across the open rooftop to my transit vehicle, half-expecting burning debris to come raining down at any moment.

"Eva?" I called, as Lee joined me in the vehicle and the guardians stowed themselves in their transport nearby.

"Yes, Tom," her voice sounded in my ear.

"You're at Catalano's?"

"Right. In a waiting area. Woman behind the desk says Serena is, quote, tied up in a meeting."

"Good. Stay there. I'm on my way."

"Okay."

I turned to Lee. "Take us to the Nirvana Hotel, and bring the guardians along. Follow a high trajectory—straight up, straight down." As I spoke there was a spark of light to my right. I turned quickly and saw two fliers ricocheting apart, one of them wobbling and veering from side to side, the other spinning in flames.

"I will maximize our safety," Lee said as he took us up among the darting shapes. "I have a message for you from Jalen Reese," he went on. "Our location is unregistered, so she simply left word at Peacekeeping for you to call."

I imagined her over at Berg's refuge on the coast, browsing and probing while the evidence-collecting autons scuttled around her. "Call her back," I said.

There was a click as an audio channel linked with my implant. "Mr. McCray, is this you?" Reese's voice was as calm and businesslike as ever.

"Yes. Do you have something to report?"

"I searched the place thoroughly, as you said. I didn't find anything, though."

It gave me some quiet satisfaction to have my suspicions confirmed. "No signs of forced entry? No indication of a struggle? No incidental damage?"

"None."

"Very good. You've been a great help. Incidentally, I think I have this thing more or less wrapped up. I just saw Fisk, and I have a strong case against him regarding Berg's death. I'd like you to head back to Peacekeeping and wait there with Harry Green. I'll find you both and we can discuss the best way to lean on Fisk and get a confession."

There was a long, thoughtful pause at her end. But when she spoke, she didn't sound surprised. "All right, I'll get there as soon as I can."

I broke the link, trying to figure if there were any possibilities I'd missed. Vaguely I was aware of the city below, the lights flicking on one by one as the sun slid behind the hills and the landscape became shrouded in mauve shadow.

"You made several statements to Jalen Reese that were untrue," Lee said from beside me.

"That's correct."

"I assume you had good reason, and it was not merely capricious or playful behavior."

Lee always had trouble with premeditated lying. In his scheme of things, lies were bad data, and bad data indicated a malfunction that should be corrected immediately.

"I sure as hell don't feel very playful right now," I said, looking down at the city. In the twilight, it was easy to see where fires were burning. They were like bright orange chancres. I wondered how many more would start before the night was over; and how much of the city would be left intact by dawn.

0111111

We were setting down on the roof of the Nirvana Hotel, with the guardians hovering alongside, when Fisk called me.

"McCray? Are you there?" His voice grated in my ear.

"You have some news?" I said.

He paused. "This link is secure?"

"More secure than the ordinary comnet."

Another pause. "I checked the records," he said, sounding reluctant. "As you requested." Now he sounded disgusted. "Quan wasn't on file as a cosmetic patient. But I keep a private backup, as it happens. A stash of hardcopy. Before-and-after shots. Just in case."

In case of what, I wondered. Maybe Fisk didn't trust his own lab personnel. Or maybe, when it was late at night and he was alone in his sleeping pit with his Cuddle Putty, he got off by ogling pics of cosmetic surgery cases.

"Well, I found Quan's face in my private file," he said. "Fourteen years ago. We did a complete rebuild. I suppose you want to see what he looked like after we finished with him."

"Of course I want to see!" I blurted the words out, unable to conceal my eagerness. I turned to Lee.

"If Fisk shows it to his server, can you capture the signal at Central and reroute it to yourself?"

"Yes," he said.

"Okay," I said, "Mr. Fisk, hold it up in front of your server. My auton will do a frame-grab and give me hardcopy."

A moment later there was a humming sound from under Lee's tunic. He reached in, pulled out the print, and handed it to me.

As I stared at the face, I felt my anger building inside me.

"You get it okay?" Fisk was asking in my ear.

"I have it." I spoke abstractedly, no longer fully aware of Emmanuel Fisk. The print was of a male whose bio age had been pegged around twenty. There was something in his face that branded him as a misfit, maybe with an unhappy, repressive childhood. His cheeks were acne-scarred, and I wondered how Fisk's technicians had felt about being asked to create that blemish.

"So what's the readback?" said Fisk, sounding irascible again. "You know him? You don't know him? Your auton knows him? Who the hell is he?"

My anger was rising higher, but it wasn't directed at Fisk or anyone else outside me. I was angry at myself for having missed the chance to shut down the situation before it ever got out of hand. "I know him, and I've met him," I said. "He doesn't work at Central Processing. He works for Milton Berg. He introduced Berg at a meeting at the Laputa Hotel just this morning, the little bastard."

"I've pattern-matched him," said Lee. "His current name is Dan Cogan. He allegedly resides in a Chaist commune half a kilometer from Milton Berg's home. The last trace I can find shows him leaving the Laputa and heading toward the coast shortly before 11:00 A.M."

"He goes wandering around in broad daylight," I said, half to myself, "because he's so damned sure of himself, he thinks he can destroy the whole goddamn planet and I won't be able to lay a hand on him."

"Listen, McCray, I never heard of the guy," said Fisk. "Never, as in *not ever*. Never seen him, and I don't wish to. And whatever reason his records weren't in the files down in the labs, it wasn't negligence. *You got that?*"

"Calm down, Mr. Fisk," I told him, "if that's possible. You haven't incriminated yourself. You've helped me, that's all."

There was a long pause at the other end. "Well, that just makes my day," he said.

I put down the pic. "You've sold out your principles by doing me a good turn, is that it?"

Unexpectedly, he chuckled. "You're not so bad, McCray. You got a sense of humor, more or less. So you're going to stomp this little rodent, right?"

"That's the general idea," I said. "Although first, I have to find him. I may call on you later."

"Oh, anytime," he said, as sourly as ever.

I cut the link, then checked my dart gun in my pocket. My hand touched something else there, and I realized that it was the addrex I'd taken out of Mary Morheim's purse.

A sudden suspicion struck me. I pulled the addrex and opened it. "Cogan," I said. "Dan Cogan."

Right away, his face came up on the screen. "Hi, Mary," he said. "Call me anytime. I love you."

1000000

I walked with Lee into the main entrance of the Nirvana Hotel with the guardians still following along behind us. I understood, now, why Mary

Morheim had been so stressed out when we'd met her in Gabol Plaza. She'd been about to betray her lover.

But he'd betrayed her first, far more damagingly than she could have imagined. And there was no doubt in my mind that Serena Catalano had been involved.

I'd been in a mean mood already, but it was at least a couple of points worse when I pushed the door open into Catalano's reception area. Eva was waiting there, and she stood up and smiled when she saw me; but the smile faded as she registered the look on my face and the guardians rolling in. "What is this?" she said. "You're gonna detain her?"

I went over to the desk. A new woman was sitting where Mary Morheim had once sat, wearing the same silly business suit. She looked young and unsure of herself. "Yes?" she said, glancing uneasily at the guardians, then at Lee, then back at me.

"As you are probably aware," I said, "a guardian in the course of its duty has right of free access to all premises, public or private. Therefore—"

"May I have your name please?" Nervously, she fingered the old-fashioned intercom.

"Tom McCray. I have to warn you that if you do not voluntarily allow us access—"

"Oh. Mr. McCray." She sounded immensely relieved. "Serena was expecting you. She said you were to go straight in." She touched a control and an entrance opened—not the one I'd previously taken into the silver garden, but a different one at the opposite end of the reception area. "Please go down the hallway. It's the last door on the right."

"What's happening, here?" said Eva.

"I don't know." Cautiously, I walked into the hallway. There were open doors on either side into offices where Catalano's staff were working. They stopped and stared; I glared at them and walked on by, followed by the guardians.

When we reached the last door on the right, we found it closed. "Lee," I said, "get one of our metal friends, here, to go first."

Eva and I stood aside while a guardian rumbled forward, went to the door, and pushed. Its treads scuffed the carpet, and there was a groaning, rupturing sound as the latch gradually yielded and the door burst open. It hadn't been locked, but I'd been concerned that there might be a booby trap.

I walked in and took a moment to adjust to the decor. I found myself in Serena Catalano's bedroom. A massive curtained four-poster bed stood in the center of the room under a mirrored ceiling. A fountain was tinkling in one corner, water running from the genitals of black marble cherubs into the waiting mouths of alabaster nymphs. Closets lined the opposite wall, some of them standing open, revealing an arsenal of sex toys, bondage restraints, fetish clothing, and aphrodisiacs.

Catalano was nowhere to be seen, and I realized that I should have expected that from the way the receptionist had parroted the message. Serena had told the woman that she *was* expecting me— maybe several hours ago.

One of the curtains at the side of the bed had been left pulled back, and a large white envelope had been propped against a black satin pillow. Written on the envelope, in bold black ink, was my name.

I walked over, grabbed the envelope, and ripped it open.

Dear Mr. McCray:
How flattering that you should visit me twice in one day!

*While I am, of course, impressed by your your
sophistication and your charm, I regret I am unable to receive you at this time. Please feel free to
wait here, however, and when I return, your patience may be intimately rewarded.*

As ever,
Serena Catalano

Beneath the signature, in bright red, was the im-
print of her lips.

1000001

"I don't get it," said Eva as we walked back
along the hallway.

"An insult," I said, abstractedly. "Just her way
of telling me that I'm the last man on earth she
would ever allow to touch her."

Eva looked skeptical. "Are you sure about
that?"

I glanced at her and saw that although she had
street smarts and was a quick study, she was lost
when it came to sarcasm or irony. By nature, she
was up-front and direct. She didn't know how to
be any other way. "Believe me," I said, "I understand this woman."

Eva gave me a funny look. "You mean it's like
a love-hate thing?"

I laughed without any humor at all. "More like
a hate-hate thing. Why?"

"You get kind of intense when you talk about
her."

"Well, I feel kind of intense, bearing in mind
she's probably the one who's destroying the whole
damned planet." I paced quickly back through the
reception area and up to the roof. I turned to Lee.

"You're sure there was no sign of her leaving this building today? And she wasn't traced anywhere else in Sen City?"

"That's correct."

I wondered for a moment if all of the peeker records had somehow been doctored at Central Processing to remove her image. That would have been a huge task. Even if Dan Cogan alias Alex Quan had known how to do it, it seemed to me that he wouldn't have had enough time. Remember Occam's razor, I reminded myself. Look for the simpler alternative.

"Scan for two *men* leaving this building," I told Lee, "both of them unusually muscular, neither of them speaking. And a third person with them of Catalano's approximate height."

"Yes," he said, almost immediately. "Shortly after 1:00 P.M this afternoon."

I grunted with disgust. "Show me," I said.

THE UNAPPEARANCE OF SERENA CATALANO

I saw them walking out onto the roof: Catalano's two deaf-and-dumb bodyguards, and her between them—except it wasn't her. Her body was twenty kilos heavier and her face was forty years older, deeply wrinkled. Her nose had been augmented. Her forehead was higher and wider. All the crucial dimensions that pattern-recognition systems relied upon had been increased. I'd been afraid of something like this, which was why I'd stationed Eva at the hotel. She would have sensed something odd about Catalano even if she hadn't seen through the disguise. But I'd been too late; Catalano had left before Eva had arrived.

"Higher magnification," I said.

I zoomed in on her. Her skin had a slick sheen—body sealant, I realized. It retained the microscopic skin particles and trace odors that servers analyzed to make positive identification. Sealant was dangerous over long periods; you could die of heatstroke. But all that Catalano had needed was to get out of her private quarters and into her flier.

I watched her vehicle lift off, taking her away into the sky.

1000010

"Where did she go?" I asked Lee.

"The trace is incomplete."

Yes, Cogan could have fixed that easily enough. One little trace, of a specific vehicle whose location was known in advance—wiping it would have been trivial for someone who'd managed to remove Mary Morheim's entire file, not to mention sanitizing the records of Harry Green and Jalen Reese.

I glanced around. The roof was still cluttered with fliers. Dusk was deepening around us. "There could be half a dozen peekers, here," I said. "This is no place to linger." As I spoke, lights around the edge of the roof came to life, sensing the dimming sunlight. I caught sight of a twinkling pinpoint hovering a couple of meters away.

"Get the guardians back in their transport," I said to Lee. "Eva, I want you to travel with us. I know there's not much room, but inside our vehicle is the most secure place I can think of right now."

A few minutes later we were following the glowing artery of the main pedpath through Dream Valley, passing slowly by the huge hotels and palaces, cruising near ground level, where I figured it would be toughest for anyone to track us or attack us. Despite the huge pile of wreckage that had once been the Hotel Sera, and some fires burning here and there in the distance, the valley was once again a color chaos of garish ads and sparkling lights. At first I was surprised to see the crowds looking for a night of pleasure, but then I realized it was denial, pure and simple. No one wanted to believe what was happening. People were here to have *fun*, right?

Two nude figures fifty stories high were cavorting on a vapor wall in front of us, grinding and pumping and pointing to the Sin Bad Ball Room, an amorphous building whose soft, pale curves looked suggestively physical. As we penetrated the fuzzy, flickering images I saw dozens of fliers floating down, offworlders tumbling out, stumbling into a big oval entrance washed in red and pink. These people had a deep and pressing need to forget the horrific images they'd seen on the evening newsims. And if there was a real chance of total system shutdown tomorrow, well, that just made it more important to make the most of tonight.

As we flew on by, I told Eva about Alex Quan's reincarnation as Dan Cogan.

"So maybe *he's* the one who shot Berg," she said.

"Why would he want to do that?"

"Maybe they had an argument. Maybe Berg wanted him to stop screwing things up."

"Maybe, maybe, maybe."

"Well, why not ask him yourself? He should be easy enough to find. He was last tracked heading for the coast, so it seems likely he'd be out there at Berg's place, don't you think? That's where all the equipment is."

I turned to Lee. "Are the evidence-gathering autons still at Berg's building?"

"They've completed their task and returned to Peacekeeping. Berg's home has been sealed. Surveillance units outside show no activity."

"He could *still* be in it," Eva insisted. "He could be masking those peekers' signals somehow."

"Possible," I agreed. "But why would he hide out at the most obvious place?"

"Because he doesn't know that you know who he is. And you said yourself, he's arrogant." She spoke rapidly, impatiently.

I glanced back at her where she was crouching in the cargo area behind my seat. "You like this, don't you?" I said.

"What do you mean?"

"You like mystery puzzles. It's like a sim game for you."

She looked slightly embarrassed. "You noticed."

"Well, I'm glad one of us is enjoying the evening." I sighed and shook my head. "All right, I'll spell it out. Cogan had knowledge, but he also needed money to hand-build the equipment we saw out there at Berg's place. I doubt Berg has ever had resources on that scale, and Fisk seems not to have been involved, and we know that Belman turned down Cogan's request for money. But Catalano could have financed him easily."

"There are other wealthy people in Dream Valley," Eva objected. "A lot of them."

"Sure, but I doubt they're as ruthless or as anti-Protektorate as Catalano. In any case, Fisk told me that some friend of Catalano's fixed a land title record at the Mains. That must have been Cogan. Plus, Cogan had a romance going with Mary Morheim, Catalano's assistant. I'm betting Catalano set that up, to give her some indirect personal control over Cogan. Morheim was under severe stress when I saw her; it looked as if she'd been carrying out a bunch of directives from Catalano that had made her deeply unhappy."

"I guess that makes sense," Eva agreed reluctantly. "Although it's all circumstantial."

"All right, but there's more. Catalano was obviously worried by my visit this morning, which is why she ran for cover. That alone indicates probable guilt."

"True." Eva still sounded grudging.

"The one thing in my favor," I went on, "is that she still doesn't know I've found out who Dan Cogan is—unless Fisk tells her, which I don't think he will, because he hates her guts for reneging on a money-for-sex deal. Anyway, you're right, Cogan may still feel arrogant enough to continue taking risks. It's conceivable he may be at the coast if there's some equipment there that he needs. But if I go out to get him, and he traces my vehicle coming for him, then I've revealed that I know his identity, and I lose my advantage, see? Catalano is the real key. I have to go after her first."

It took her a moment to process all that. "You're a smart guy," she said, finally.

I gave her a dubious look. "I think I'm flattered." I turned to Lee. "Get me Fisk."

There was a long pause. Finally I heard his voice in my head. "McCray, did you catch him yet?"

"No, Mr. Fisk. But I think Serena Catalano knows where he is, or could be with him. You have any idea where she'd be hiding out? She's not at her hotel."

Fisk made an irritable, grumbling noise. "You're like a blackmailer, McCray, you know that? You

make one little demand, and as soon as I capitu-
late, you want more."

"Yeah, right," I said. "I'm totally incompetent
and I do all my work by stealing ideas from guys
like you. But since your sim business is belly-up
right now, you've got nothing else to do but help
me. Right?"

"Fuck you, McCray." From him, it sounded af-
fectionate. "All right, let me think. That scumbitch
owns half a dozen hotels, and there's ten thousand
people she could lean on for a favor—"

"It seems to me," I interrupted him, "she's the
type who takes care of herself. I don't think she
wanted things to get as bad as this, but she might
have a contingency plan just in case. Some kind
of shelter."

"Ah!" Fisk chuckled. "Shelter, yes. She told me
once, she'd built a shelter. In a basement, with
food and water and hard currency—paranoid
crap, but you're right, that's her mentality. It was
in one of her palaces. Um, the Sensorium."

"Thanks," I told him, meaning it. "I appreciate
your help. I'm remembering these favors you're
doing."

"Well, I'm happy to hear that, McCray. Very
happy. But right now this situation is outside my
control, which is not a mode that suits my disposi-
tion. So I have a bunch of mood chemicals and
some pseudoflesh on hand—so to speak—and all
I can say is, wake me when it's over."

1000011

"This has to be done right," I said, as we set
down on the landing field next to the Sensorium.
"I want peekers placed all around the perimeter

of the building, and I want guardians positioned at all access points, including the emergency exits."

"It will take a few minutes," said Lee.

I looked out at the building pulsing with light in the night. Somewhere in there, I was sure we would find her. "Any trace of Catalano or her bodyguards entering earlier today?" I asked.

"No. But the exterior of the building was not consistently monitored, and some of the areas inside are so crowded that surveillance is almost impossible."

"Busy, huh?"

"The Sensorium is terminally soft right now," Eva said from behind me.

I turned to look at her. "You mean fashionable?"

"Soft, as in young and new, it'll flex to fit."

"Really? You come here often?"

She looked offended. "I seem like a seeker?"

"You seem fashionable."

"That's just for my job." She shook her head, setting aside her flippancy. "My idea of a good time is sitting alone at home with my editing console. I don't like crowd scenes."

1000100

We walked into the outer lobby. Music was thumping and wailing from somewhere deeper in the building, the walls were rippling to the beat, and the lights were flickering like flames.

A glamorous hermaphrodite greeted us at the main entrance. (S)he was wearing a black bow tie, a black waistcoat hanging open on either side of a pair of large breasts, knee-high socks, mirror-finish black oxfords, and nothing else. Every inch of flesh seemed to have been embellished with tat-

toos, and the immense male genitals were dyed
bright red. "Greetings! Welcome to the Sensorium!" (S)he smiled, showing luminous pink teeth.
"That'll be a hundred each for the humans, and
fifty for your auton—he is an auton, isn't he? Autons half-price before midnight."

"You're buying, right?" I said to Eva.

She stared at me blankly.

"Seems to me," I said, "I gave you some expense money."

She grunted in annoyance and turned to the
shemale. "Vid me and charge it."

There was a moment's pause while the hermaphrodite pattern-matched Eva's face. Then (s)he
grinned. "Step inside and enjoy!"

We went through a light curtain and found ourselves in a black-walled inner lobby. There was an
elevator ahead and doors to either side. The music
was louder, here, and I heard laughter, shouts,
and screaming.

A fat naked woman came stumbling out
through one of the doors with a creature like a
snake coiled around her. Its body was covered in
fur, and it had a baby face with fat fleshy lips.
The woman was holding its head in her hands,
French-kissing it, while its tail moved busily between her thighs.

A humanoid auton wearing a white coat and
white gloves hurried out and grabbed the woman's arm. "Please, return to the morg room. No
proprietary morgs are allowed out of the morg
room."

She giggled, leaned against him, and allowed
herself to be steered back the way she'd come.

I noticed Lee watching impassively. As far as he
was concerned, this was just another example of

human activities that made no rational sense. "The air in here contains impurities," he noted.

"They add a sex-stim to it," said Eva. "To make you feel, you know, hot." She eyed me with detached interest. "Think you can handle that?"

I looked at her, and it was true that I felt a nudge of desire. For just an instant, I imagined holding her. In some ways, she was very appealing—but I pushed that thought aside. "We have work to do," I said.

"So maybe later," she said.

This time, it was harder for me to ignore her. I turned to Lee. "Have you interfaced with the building's support system?"

"Yes."

"Do you trace anything that looks like the shelter Fisk talked about?"

"It's in the basement, as specified. The way to reach it is via a private elevator at the rear."

"Any servers down there?"

"No. The area is unmonitored."

"Then send one of our peekers while we wait here," I said. "And link me with it."

SHELTER

I looked down at myself standing between Lee and Eva. My face was weary but wary, as if I was half-expecting something to come and get me. Eva seemed much more relaxed; she reminded me of other journalists I'd known, taking all kinds of crazy risks if it would help them get a story. Fine for her; she wasn't responsible for the fate of an entire planet full of innocent people.

A door opened and two women and a man came out, laughing, groping under each other's clothes. My viewpoint turned as the peeker saw the open door and drifted through.

I passed into a huge ballroom and floated above the heads of the crowd, men and women mostly naked, dancing, falling down on the floor and coupling wherever they felt like it. Clouds of pink fog drifted among the throng. Autons circulated with snap dispensers. The music was loud.

I followed one of the autons out through a door at the rear. He stopped in the hallway, plugged into a spigot to recharge his drug inventory, and I drifted on into a dim-lit area, past a big yellow PRIVATE sign.

I reached an elevator at the end of the hallway and its doors opened as I approached. Lee, I realized, was manipulating the building's support system. The elevator took me down to the basement, and when its doors opened I exited into a plain beige corridor lit with bright white panels. There was a circular steel hatch at the far end that looked like an airlock.

I drifted along, and the lock on the hatch disengaged itself as I approached. The heavy door swung open and I went through it, finding myself in a circular room with a domed, reinforced ceiling. There was just enough space for a bed, a table, two chairs, an immersion tank beside a VR rig, and a dispensal. Emergency food supplies in bright orange packages had been dumped on the table, and there were a dozen twenty-liter water packs stacked on the floor.

As my viewpoint panned slowly I saw that the room was empty, and there was no sign of Serena Catalano.

There was something lying on the bed.

I moved in that direction. Some street clothes had been discarded, and some strips of plastiflesh. I moved still closer, and there was no doubt: the clothes were hers, and the flesh features were the face I'd seen on her as she left her private quarters at the Nirvana Hotel.

1000101

"She's left the basement," I said.

"How come?" said Eva.

"How the hell should I know? Lee, sample every server in the building. Check for her and her bodyguards."

"I am attempting to do so. Unfortunately, vision is poor, audio is very difficult, and skin-trace detection is impossible when so many people are present." He paused. "I'm also finding that the surveillance systems at Central are developing lag times."

"Symptoms of overload?"

"Yes."

I sensed the delicate, infinitely complex interactions of electronic services gradually turning to random noise around me.

"An urgent message," Lee said suddenly. "I was accessing the Mains to track Jalen Reese's flier on its way to Peacekeeping from the home of Milton Berg. But its trace has vanished."

I dragged my attention to that topic and considered the possibilities. Reese could have deliberately disappeared, or there could have been a tracking error, or she could have crashed. I didn't like any of those options. Reese was an important figure in my game plan.

"Send a peeker from our transit vehicle to the point where the trace ended," I said. "See if there's any wreckage."

"Understood. There is one more thing you should know."

"Yes?" I couldn't keep the exasperation out of my voice.

"You directed Harry Green to wait at the Mains. Many hours have passed since then, but he has not arrived there. I was not tracking his flier, since it seemed relatively unimportant. I've now obtained a trace from Central Processing showing that after Green spoke to you, he went to his residence, then headed due north to the tip of Tarak, where there is no human habitation. The trace ends there."

I wondered if the two events were linked. It was possible, but on the other hand, Green was the sort who would duck and run if he sensed that too much heat was coming down. "If he went to his home first," I said, half to myself, "he was probably picking up some supplies." I turned back to Lee. "Get the Mains to send a couple of their peekers to look for Green," I said. "I don't think he's a key figure, and I don't want to tie up too much of your processing power with our own surveillance."

"All right," said Lee. "Done."

I tried to reorient my thoughts toward the matter at hand. Finding Catalano was still the highest priority. "We could clear this whole place," I said, "and find Catalano that way. But I don't want to tip her off. So let's conduct a search the old-fashioned way. We'll split up. Eva, check with me every minute over our com link, even if there's nothing to report."

"And if I find her?"

"Tell me the location and I'll have Lee bring the guardians in immediately."

She looked at me skeptically. "Guardians, in the Sensorium?"

I imagined a room full of writhing bodies, tourists out of their minds under various snaps and stims, and a bunch of guardians rumbling through. It would be newsworthy. "But it seems to me," I said, "the people here are so lobed on drugs, they may think it's just part of the entertainment.''

1000110

There were more than a hundred different rooms around the edges of the main hall in the Sensorium, each with its own kink, each packed with people—flesh on flesh, bodies making wet sounds, screams and moans and cries and groans resonating in the small spaces. Methodically, I worked my way from one event to the next.

VIBRAFOAM was the sign on the glutinous membrane-door. I forced my way through and it healed itself behind me. I found myself in a spherical space half-full of mushy polyfoam, soft mounds vibrating in sync with a groaning sound that seemed to come out of the walls of the sphere itself. Naked bodies were squirming around in the foam like beached fish, getting an all-over vibrational body-stim. I floundered through as well as I could, but Catalano wasn't there.

THE MORG MALL was a concourse of storefronts filled with romping, basking, dozing, mewling lifeforms modified from the usual range of animals. I saw a thing like a manta ray edged with a dozen grasping baby hands; an organism the size of a beach ball with assorted phalluses protruding from it; cute little fur balls like cats without heads, legs, or tails; a creature like a living mattress, its surface ornamented with various male and female genitalia; a headless dog with an orifice at each end of its white-haired, sausage-shaped body.... And inside the stores, men and women were trying out the merchandise. The morgs who had been lucky enough to be selected were wriggling and

The Law of Laws

The architects of the Protektorate drew one primary lesson from all the different ways in which human beings had tried to govern themselves during the twentieth century: political systems had always tended to restrict human freedom, even when they had been intended to serve the opposite function.

There was some practical justification for this. Social conditions in those primitive times tended to encourage conflict, and the easiest way to resolve conflict was to pass restrictive laws. In practice, of course, much of this legislation was ineffectual. Littering laws, urban noise laws, drug laws, speeding laws, antisodomy laws—most were ignored, and few were enforced.

On the other hand, some laws actively caused new problems—side effects which then had to be controlled by still more legislation. To take just one example, drug laws created criminal activity which then had to be attacked with new laws to enable seizure, restrict cash transactions, and outlaw classes of firearms.

A general "law of laws" emerged: it was in the nature of legislators to pass new legislation, whether it was necessary or not, just to justify their own existence. And it was always easier to pass new laws or create new government departments than repeal old laws or dismantle a section of the bureaucracy. As a result, any system of government that lasted more than a couple of centuries without being subjected to revolutionary upheaval tended to mire its citizens in so much legislation, no one could keep track of it all.

The situation changed radically as the Protektorate began to control human affairs. Machine intelligences had no interest in morality—no concept of it, in fact—and no interest in winning votes by restricting or promoting one group over another. The Human Instruction Set included a statement demanding that the Protektorate maximize efficiency, which automatically implied a minimum, rather than a maximum, of new laws; and unlike human bureaucrats, the Protektorate's OverMains saw no advantage in extending their authority or waging turf battles.

Meanwhile, human society had become more generally tolerant of deviations in sexual conduct and lifestyle. Religion had ceased to be a potent force as antiaging drugs eased people's fears of death. Scarcity of resources was no longer a source of competition or resentment. The family—with all the stress on security and the conservatism that this entailed—was no longer the primary social unit, as childbirth declined in popularity. Personal inhibitions and legal restrictions were relaxed; and adults felt perpetually young and free to play.

yelping with pleasure as the humans cavorted with them. But Catalano wasn't there.

THE WOMB ROOM was semisentient. If you lay down, its soft floor clung to you and extended a tube for you to suck on. I picked my way through the gloom, peering at male and female bodies curled up into the fetal position. It seemed like a good place for concealment, so I paid special attention; but Catalano wasn't there.

THE LUBE TUBE was slick with colorless lubricant, a flexible cylinder a couple of meters in diameter packed full of naked bodies slithering over each other, people screaming and laughing as they writhed in the slop and coupled with anyone or anything that presented itself. It didn't look the kind of place Catalano would choose, but that in itself was a reason to check it. I ended up flopping out of the far end with my clothes ripped half-off, saturated with glop. The physical contact had made me aroused in a kind of distracted, half-interested way. But Catalano wasn't there.

Modified Organisms

During the twenty-first century, biological science was a growth industry. As the human genome was decoded and nanotechnology enabled synthetic microorganisms, all human diseases became curable. Ultimately, mortality itself was eliminated.

As a result, by the early 2100s, molecular biologists found themselves with few challenges left. Control of nanotechnology was turned over to the Protektorate since it was considered potentially too dangerous to be left in human hands. Under the Human Instruction Set, it was reserved only for applications (such as planetary terraforming) where there were incontrovertible benefits and no risk of accidents that could decimate a human population.

One area where biologists were still permitted to do research was in animal modifications. Provided the modified organism, or *morg*, could be proven to live without pain or suffering, there were no restrictions.

So it was that a rich variety of custom-designed "pets" emerged from the gene labs. Most morgs were created as sex objects or partners, and their designers took care to endow each animal with an ample supply of pleasure centers so that it would derive at least as much enjoyment from coupling with humans as they derived from coupling with it.

1000111

Eva kept linking in as she made her own odyssey through the building. Sometimes she sounded out of breath; sometimes she sounded as if she was under some kind of drug. But she was coherent enough to remember what she was supposed to be doing and how she was supposed to be doing it—and she didn't see Catalano anywhere.

I shared Lee's perceptions once in a while; but he, too, wasn't coming up with anything.

1001000

I went through THE FOOD FARE, a room stuffed with rubbery stuff that was edible so that you could wallow in it, eat it, and have sex with it all at once. Next was THE SOFT CELL, a series of tiny little soft-walled cubicles where you could opt to be locked in with your lover for a predetermined time. This might have presented some surveillance problems except that there was an adjacent room for voyeurs, allowing an overhead view into each occupied cubicle. I scanned the faces of the people having sex, and I checked the peepers who were watching, and Catalano wasn't there.

THE PUNISHMENT PIT was a stone-walled room with straw on the floor, a rack, an iron maiden, a whipping post, a pillory, and a fine assortment of thumbscrews, lashes, paddles, ropes, and chains. Masochists were moaning with delight as autons beat them with the precise amount of force that they craved. The autons wore black robes and black hoods, executioner-style; they reminded me, uncomfortably, of the guys in the death sim that Eva had endured. I passed on through and out of a door at the far end, into a hallway—where I stopped. "Lee," I sent to him over our private link, "I found her. Send up the guardians."

"I have your location," he acknowledged. "Stand by."

I called Eva and told her where I was. She acknowledged and said she'd be right there.

I turned and peered through a tiny barred window in the massive wooden planks of the door behind me. Catalano's two bodyguards were sitting on a bench against one wall, like customers waiting to be beaten. Beside them was an auton—except something about it didn't look quite right. Beneath the cloak and the hood, its posture was dignified. It sat with grace and poise, as if it felt superior to its surroundings—in fact, as if it owned the place.

1001001

When the guardians rumbled into the dungeon, everyone stopped and stared as if they had just been woken from a group sex wet dream. Catalano's deaf-and-dumb twins jumped up ready for action, but two guardians grabbed them before they could do anything.

I walked across the straw on the floor, conscious of the sudden silence and the masochists in their chains watching me with uncomprehending eyes. I stopped in front of Catalano where she was sitting on the bench, and I pulled her black hood off. She looked at me wordlessly and her face was pale with rage.

"Lee," I said, "check for transmissions. Is she wired?"

"I have picked up no signals so far." He stepped around her, then quickly reached into a pocket in her robe and brought out a com disc.

I took it from him and snapped it in two. "Make sure that if she has implants, she doesn't send anything. And tell one of the guardians to hold her."

She stood up. "That won't be necessary. Do you want to talk?"

"Yes, that's exactly what I want." As I spoke, feeling savage satisfaction at having placed her under detention, it occurred to me that her own shelter was probably the most secure place in the building.

We escorted her down the hallway, past gawking vacationers, to the private elevator at the back. She looked straight ahead, her eyes unblinking. The guardians that had seized her bodyguards carried them like babies, but I let Catalano walk freely, escorted by another two guardians on either side of her. I didn't feel any special need to humiliate her by having them haul her around. She could cling to her dignity, and maybe that would encourage her to cooperate a little.

Going down in the elevator, Eva eyed my ripped, glop-stained, torn and rumpled clothes. I could see she wanted to say something. Her own clothes were mussed and her face was flushed. She looked bright and alive, very touchable. But I managed not to think about that.

1001010

In the basement hallway, Catalano stopped just outside the hatch into her shelter. She turned and stared directly at me. "It might be best," she said, "if your companions and the guardians remain out here for a few minutes. I would like to talk to you personally. My shelter, here, is completely shielded. With the door closed, we will have privacy."

I weighed it for a moment and decided it could play to my advantage. "Okay," I said.

"Hold it." Eva touched my arm. "She could have a weapon in there. Some kind of—I don't know, anything."

"There's only one exit," I said. "And this is it."

Eva frowned at me. "But if it's shielded in there, your link with Lee won't work anymore. The place could be booby-trapped somehow. Take a guardian in with you—"

"No." For psychological reasons, I wanted Catalano to have it her way. I turned and followed her into the shelter, and I closed the thick steel door behind us.

1001011

There was a comset over by the bed. Just to be sure, I swept it onto the floor, then brought my heel down on it as hard as I could. Its case split open and parts spilled out like loose gravel.

After that I went and sat opposite her at the table.

Dressed in a shapeless black robe that was little more than a bedsheet, with traces of her plastiflesh disguise still showing on her skin, she still somehow managed to look dignified. Every gesture was precise—from the little movements of her fingers as she clasped her hands in front of her to the way she tilted her jaw as she looked at me with regal antipathy.

"Before you say anything," I said, "you should know that I went to see Fisk a couple hours ago, and he talked."

She shrugged. "If that's true, I'm not surprised. The man actually had some sort of romantic ideas about me." She smiled faintly.

"You should have had Fisk killed if you wanted to keep him quiet," I said. "That's what you did with Mary Morheim, wasn't it?"

That strained her composure a little. "I fail to understand," she said, with tension rising in her voice, "why you need to be so gratuitously offensive. If you want to have this conversation, at least let us have it in a civilized fashion, to our mutual advantage, with no further attempts to create embarrassment or anger."

I slowly shook my head. "Sorry. If I think someone's a murderer, I come right out and say it. And you are a murderer, aren't you?"

She gathered herself up like a snake preparing to strike—then stopped herself and carefully sat back in her chair. "You will not goad me into speaking impulsively," she said. "Where Mary Morheim is concerned, I have nothing to say. Where Mr. Fisk is concerned—he never goes anywhere but that loathsome little office, or his conference room, or his disgusting little bedroom. He's afraid to breathe the outside air."

"Which is why he's still alive right now," I said.

"For the time being," she agreed blandly.

We stared at each other. It was very quiet in the little shelter; the thud of the music and the shouts of the tourists in the palace above were completely blocked out. The only noise was the faint hiss of air through a vent in the wall.

"You're aware," I said, "that along with Fisk, there's a million residents and maybe two hundred thousand tourists who are liable to die if I don't get the help I need to fix the Mains."

She gave a little shrug and said nothing.

Her air of indifference made me feel my own anger. "What the hell is wrong with you?" I said. "Do you have some kind of grudge against humanity? Do you *want* everyone to die?"

"It's of no concern to me." She gestured to the palace above us. "You've seen those animals. They can't think past the next sim or the next sex act. They can't think at all, most of them. They're parasites living off technology that was developed four centuries ago. What seems so odd to me, Mr. McCray, is that you would waste your talents protecting their interests. I could offer you much more worthwhile rewards if you would just open your mind a little."

I sighed. "Bribery again. You don't seem to understand: I protect people, no matter who they are, because regardless of how they screw up their lives, they're still people."

She gave me a vexed look. "So what is the purpose of this meeting? If you won't accept money—a very large sum of money, Mr. McCray—or power, literally the power of life and death over millions of people, or sex—why are we bothering to talk?"

"I want information," I said.

She spread her long, pale, flawless hands. "Why should I give it to you?"

"I think the situation outside has gone way past what you expected, and you don't know how to stop it. But if you tell me exactly how it happened, and how to find the people who did it, chances are I can bring it back under control."

She smiled coldly. "Maybe so. But if I am to lose my liberty either way, why should I care?"

I told myself not to get mad, and I tried to bend my thoughts around so I could see the situation from her point of view. "Okay, a million people dead doesn't matter a damn. All that matters is what happens to you. And—maybe you're thinking that when the systems all go down, you'll have a chance of absconding. Or maybe your friends out there will still manage to pull something off, and they'll rescue you somehow. Or kill me. Or both."

She nodded, barely bothering to move her head. "I'm surprised, Mr. McCray, that you seem to have so much trouble understanding a situation that is extremely simple."

I couldn't sit still anymore. I stood up and paced across the room and back again. "So let's just think of what's good for Serena Catalano. First off, I know who's working for you. I have the stats on Dan Cogan, and I'm going to find him just as quickly as I found you."

There was a slight tightening of the muscles in her face as I said his name. I was glad to see that she hadn't known that I knew. "It seems to me," she said, "it may not be so simple. Dan knows what's happened inside the Mains at Central Processing, and he still has some control. You do not."

The lights in the room flickered briefly, then steadied. I glanced up instinctively and felt myself tensing. "All right," I said, "I'll make you an offer. I can't give you immunity even if I wanted to; the OverMains would never approve it. But if you lead me to Cogan and tell him to help me undo the damage before it's terminal, I'll recommend clemency for you. They'll seize your holdings and put you in rehabilitation, but you won't be modified."

For a moment I had the impression she was actually considering the option. But then she slowly shook her head.

1001100

"Let me suggest an alternative," she said.

I saw that she'd been biding her time, adopting an uncompromising position in order to find out what my best offer would be. As far as she was concerned, this wasn't an emotional issue; it was just another business deal.

"I think it's fair to say," she said, "that from the start, we have found each other—unpleasant to deal with."

I nodded. There was no argument there.

"I require a certain amount of respect," she went on. "But so do you, in your odd way. The fact is, we both wield power, and we don't like people to defy us." She smiled. There was no warmth to it, but I sensed maybe just a trace of amusement. "We're not as different from each other as you might like to think. I asked Dan to look up your stats earlier today. You're quite the nonconformist, aren't you? A teenage rebel, and still a rule breaker even now when the spirit moves you."

"One little difference," I said. "You're quite comfortable about mass murder, while I have a slight problem with that."

"How noble of you," she said. "And how pure." She gave me a knowing look, as if she understood me far better than I understood myself. "But saving lives isn't what really moves you," she went on. "It's the fight, the struggle that excites you. The power that you exercise. The grandeur of your mission."

She stood up and perched on one corner of the table, showing me the curve of her body in profile while she looked down at me. "Before the situation here got out of hand, I took the precaution of moving most of my assets offworld. Even if I lose everything on Agorima, I will still have ninety percent of my wealth intact. Perhaps you can imagine, Mr. McCray, how large a sum that is."

She shook her blond hair back from her face, then folded her arms under her breasts. "At this time," she said, "under conditions of quarantine, I believe you are the only person who still has the means to leave the planet. I would be willing to divide all my holdings equally with you—under certain circumstances."

I felt like laughing in her face. If she'd reneged on her deal with Fisk, she could betray me just as easily. If she'd ordered the death of Mary Morheim, I had no doubt she could kill me in a second. "You're not trustworthy," I said.

She was watching me closely. I felt her intensity, and it made me uncomfortable. "I could make myself trustworthy," she said softly. "A signed confession from me perhaps, placed in secure systems programmed to release the information in the event of your death? Something like that. I make business deals all the time with people who distrust me, and there are always ways to reach a secure agreement."

"But I'm not interested in the money," I said.

She gestured impatiently. "Please stop repeating yourself! Did it never occur to you that the purpose of money is to acquire power?"

"That's your purpose," I said sharply. "Not mine."

She watched me through narrowed eyes. "All your claims about public service," she said, "they're self-serving and hypocritical. Juggling with people's lives, saving some of them and putting others in custody so that they'll be punished—that's why you do the work you do. It's in your stats, and it's in your face. The only reason you work for those machines at the Hub, instead of following your secret desires as I do, is because you're ashamed of the way you feel, and you're afraid to defy the system." Suddenly, she held out her arms so that her wrists were close together, directly in front of me. "Hold my wrists," she said. "I mean it. I want you to."

The idea of touching her was strange and alien to me. I found myself wanting to back away—and perhaps for that reason I forced myself to reach out toward her. I closed my hands around her wrists and felt a sudden shock of physical contact. Her skin was cool, and it seemed impossibly soft.

"Hold them tight," she said. Her eyes widened. "I mean it! Tighter! Much tighter!" She stared at me fiercely.

Slowly, I increased my grip.

She clenched her jaw. "Yes. That hurts a little. Ah, yes! Does it give you satisfaction to know that?" She stared at me. "Don't you enjoy the knowledge, now, that you have me under your control?" She gave a little tug, as if to prove that she couldn't pull away. "It must feel good, to have a hold on the most powerful and beautiful woman on this world. Why don't you admit it? It's what you wanted as soon as you saw me. To seize me and crush me, the same way you crushed that flower in my garden."

I didn't say anything.

"I admire you, do you realize that?" Her voice was almost a caress. "You're a dangerous man, Mr. McCray, and I have always courted danger. I would give myself to you, do you understand that? Right here on this table. You could have me now." She leaned forward, allowing her loose black robe to fall open.

I allowed myself to imagine it, just for a moment—and then quickly backed away from the thought.

"We deserve each other," she said, more softly still. "We could be the most fearful partnership the human race has ever known, if your knowledge was coupled with mine. We could dismantle the whole system, or rule it as we please." She sounded dreamy, as if she was describing the ultimate sex act. "Think, a hundred thousand worlds, trillions of people, all under your control." She gave a tiny shrug. "And you would have me, too."

Part of me was still observing her with detachment. At the same time, though, I felt a trace of what she wanted me to feel. There was just enough truth in her assessment of me to get under my skin.

But most of all, I was dazed by the scale of her power fantasy; because I saw she was right. If I ever chose to pool my knowledge with someone so unscrupulous and wealthy, we really could penetrate to the core of the Protektorate and manipulate the whole huge structure, purely for the ecstatic rush of doing so.

Suddenly, for no reason that I could understand, I thought of Eva Kurimoto. I wondered how she would react to this kind of bribery attempt—and with complete certainty I knew that regardless of her fondness for money, Eva would reject Serena Catalano without an instant's hesitation.

I let go of Catalano's wrists as if they were unclean. Clumsily, I stood up. I pushed past her, feeling unsteady on my feet, and I tugged the heavy door open. "Lee," I said, "notify the guardians that I'm putting Serena Catalano in their custody."

1001101

I had the satisfaction of seeing her looking shaken. "You really thought it would work, didn't you?" I said, feeling a wave of anger—not just at her but at myself for having let her get to me.

She started trembling. She said nothing.

"What happened?" It was Eva's voice. She stepped close and took my arm. "Are you okay?"

"Yes. Yes, I'm fine. She just messed with my head a little, that's all." I took a slow breath and

realized that I, too, felt shaky. Well, I should have
expected it; manipulating men was a skill that Catalano had had a couple of centuries to perfect.

I stepped aside as the first guardian rumbled
through the door. It seized her in its arms and
held her easily.

She let out one incoherent scream and started
struggling, slapping and pounding the armor plate
of the auton with her fists. And then, abruptly,
she went limp. She lay in its metal grasp with her
arms by her sides, breathing quickly, her nostrils
flaring, her eyes tightly closed.

"What pisses me off," I said, turning to Eva, "is
that I went through that scene for nothing. She
talked, but she didn't confess. And she didn't tell
me where we can find Cogan."

"Excuse me," said Lee, "I have an important
message. The peeker that went to look for Jalen
Reese has located her vehicle."

I looked at him, not quite in my right mind but
knowing I had to move on. "Show me," I said.

MISSING PERSON

Under infrared, the nighttime hillside was a tangle of
cool blue. Tree limbs were dim purple; leaves were
aquamarine; vines were cobalt; patches of grass looked
like puddles of reflected sky.

Amid the foliage the warm metal hull of the crashed
flier glowed red like a beacon. I descended toward it,
unsure of my precise location. It resembled the area
around Eva's home, but there were no houses nearby.
The hillside seemed deserted.

My viewpoint closed on the flier. There was no sign
that it had burned on impact. Its canopy had shattered

and the nose was dented where it had rammed the trunk of a tree, but that seemed to be the only damage.

I was close enough, now, to see down into the two front seats. Both of them were empty.

"Take me in," I told Lee.

Obediently, the peeker found its way into the cabin. It turned, panning around the interior. The backseats were as empty as the ones in front.

I imagined Jalen Reese struggling out, dazed and hurt but able to walk or crawl. She would have waited a short while for the emergency services to arrive, and then, when they didn't show, she would have set off through the forest.

"Up and out," I said.

The viewpoint shifted, then hesitated, as if the peeker had snagged itself against something. And then the false-colored world seemed to crumple in on itself. Jagged lines of vivid white cut across, bright enough to hurt. There was a high-pitched whistle—then unrelieved black silence.

1001110

I blinked back to the reality of Serena Catalano's refuge. Here, all the lights were still on. Eva was watching me, Lee was beside her, and Catalano herself was standing motionless in the guardian's arms.

"What happened?" I said.

"There has been a major surveillance malfunction at Central Processing." Lee's voice was calm and neutral, no different from usual, and it took me a moment to grasp the real magnitude of what he was saying. "Peeker signals are being received," he went on, "but not properly sequenced in the input buffers. Pointers are scrambled. Data are being overwritten. The processors managing the queue are suffering lag times and running asynchronously. I can pick up fragments, but they are not correctly tagged with origination codes."

"Let me see," I said.

OVERLOAD

Lee opened a mental window into the Mains. A thousand vid signals flashed past like shuffling cards: a street, a window, a hand, some text, a man's profile, an empty room, a flier's beacon, an illuminated sign, a tree, the ocean at night, a patch of sky, a stain on a sidewalk, a white dome, the back of a woman's head, a palm frond, a factory—

1001111

This time, when I flipped back, Eva was reaching for me, grabbing my arm. "What the hell is going on?"

I took in her earnest face, her serious eyes. "Central Processing's surveillance capability has been effectively crippled. All the scanners out there—all the peekers and servers—might just as well be blind, now." I thought for a moment. "We have to get out. In two or three hours, maybe less, the rest of the systems will go down."

Eva looked from me to Lee and back again. "You're sure?" She seemed reluctant to believe it.

"Yes." I turned to Catalano. "Did you hear that? Can you imagine how it's going to be out there?"

She paid no attention at all. She stood motionless, still with her eyes closed.

"Even if you don't care about anyone else," I said, "you have your own neck to think about now. If you want us to take care of you, you'd better take me to Cogan."

Still no response. As far as she was concerned, I no longer existed.

My anger rose up inside me again. "If you don't cooperate, I'll have the guardian carry you out into the street. See how you manage out there with the mob."

Still she said nothing. I glanced at Eva, wondering if she could do any better than I was doing.

"Actions speak louder," she said.

She was right. I turned to Lee. "Let's go out there. Get that guardian to bring Catalano with us."

There was a moment's pause. Nothing happened.

"Goddamn it, Lee," I began.

"My link with the guardians," he said, "is no longer functioning."

I stared at him. I felt as if my limbs were being amputated one by one. "You can no longer control them to any degree?"

"That's correct."

I swore quietly. By its very nature, a guardian was designed to be immune from outside interference. I looked at the one holding Catalano, its squat bulk gleaming dully, its massive carbon-fiber arms locked around her.

"All right," I told her, "you're stuck here. I can't move you, I can't free you, and I doubt your friend Cogan can, either—unless he happens to own a high-temperature cutting torch." I glanced around. "Fortunately, you have ample supplies of emergency food and water. At least, you do if I bring them close enough. Do you want me to do that?"

She said nothing.

"I don't have to do a damned thing for you," I told her. "I can leave right now."

Finally, she spoke. "Your auton will not allow me to suffer."

Now that Lee was aware of her situation, his Human Instruction Set would prohibit him from abandoning her without means to survive. According to his program, every human had human rights, and concepts such as "the end justifies the means" were automatically suspect.

I considered telling Lee to wait outside for me in the transit vehicle. But even if he agreed to do that—which was unlikely—he would still be able to monitor me via my implants.

So it was a no-win situation. There was no way for her to get free, and no way for me to motivate her to give me the information I wanted. And even if I'd been willing to use force, and Lee hadn't been there to stop me, there was something about the way she stood, her rigid defiance, that told me she wouldn't yield.

I grabbed the table, pulled it over to her, and threw a heap of emergency rations onto it. Then I added several of the water containers.

I stood in front of her a moment, grabbed the neck of her robe, and twisted it, giving her a little shake. "I'll promise you one thing," I said. "Before this is over, I'll have you in custody and I'll see you modified."

The last I saw of her, she was leaning back in the guardian's grasp, her features composed, just the faintest smile touching the corners of her mouth.

1010000

The elevator took us back to the main floor of the Sensorium. Straight away it was obvious that something was wrong. There was a foul smell

Command Sequence

Decentralization was a fashionable concept in the late twentieth century. The widespread use of microcomputers, modems, fax machines, and videophones made it possible for many people to do their work from home instead of commuting into centrally located offices.

As the Protektorate gained power, this trend started to reverse itself. Centralized planning and administration, which had never worked well in human hands, were efficient under computer control. This was also considered the most reliable way to restrict deviations from the Human Instruction Set, with each level controlled and monitored by the one above.

The big disadvantage of centralization was vulnerability. In an unstructured network of a million nodes, each with equal authority, it made little difference if one of them went down. In a tree-structured hierarchy, with a million nodes reporting to a thousand middle-level nodes, which reported in turn to a hundred, then to ten, a failure at a high level could cause total catastrophe, even with redundancy built in at each stage. Transportation, food supplies, even law enforcement: all were paralyzed if the Mains that supervised them suffered a serious failure.

For this reason more than any other, Protektors were needed as flexible human fixers working completely outside the system, capable of restoring function even when the network's highest decision-making centers were disabled.

coming out of the air vents, and instead of music there was a buzzing, screeching from the loudspeakers. The large hall where I had seen people dancing and coupling on the floor was emptying out. A mob of half-naked bodies was jamming the exit.

The lights flickered, died, then came back at half power. Emergency generators, I guessed.

When we reached the lobby it was crowded full of drugged, shouting, stumbling people. I seized Eva's arm, afraid that we'd be separated from each other in the mob.

The wave of bodies carried us along, and less than a minute later we were out in the night at the edge of the flier field. I pulled back from the crowd, toward the building. Lee came out of the exit, looked around, and saw us. He was moving slowly, tentatively, his guidance systems having trouble discriminating among so many moving people.

Above us, the floodlit facade of the Sensorium suddenly flickered and went out. Anothing building across the way went dark; and as I looked around I saw all the huge signs and the glowing vapor walls of Dream Valley disappearing. The revelers cried out in dismay as they felt the blackness closing in around them.

"We'd better get to my transit vehicle," I said. "It's going to be the only one in Sen City that's still operational."

"Wait," said Lee. He stepped in front of us and turned, spreading his arms. Almost at the same instant, a flier plummeted out of the sky, spinning as it fell. It smashed into the ground less than a hundred meters away. There was a searing flash of light, the ground shook, and the explosion felt like two fists slamming against my ears. A blast of hot air wafted past Lee's body, and fragments of ruptured metal ricocheted off him.

As the noise echoed away, Lee turned toward the scene. The flier had hit among the crowd spilling into the night. There were bodies strewn around, people screaming, and a lot of blood. "I must assist the humans who are hurt," he said.

I grabbed his arm. "Hold it. People are getting hurt all over the city. If you want to save the greatest number, you'll help me find Cogan."

Lee hesitated. Under his Instruction Set, preservation of human life was the highest imperative. But a situation like this, where he was being asked to sacrifice a small number in order to save many more, was tough for him to process.

"You are correct," he said, finally. "Our best option is to find Dan Cogan, because if we can secure his help, he can help us to save everyone. But you don't know Cogan's location."

"Jalen Reese may know. I think she was collaborating with Cogan and Catalano."

"Why do you think that?"

Sometimes his artificial intelligence was more of a liability than an asset. I wanted to go, I felt the time trickling away, but I needed him to guide our vehicle. The OverMains made sure that a Protektor was helpless without his auton. It was their way of maintaining supervision.

Patience, I told myself. Use logic; ultimately, logic would prevail. "Fisk told me that Harry Green was installed at Peacekeeping by Serena Catalano, because she wanted someone to do favors for her. But Green is kind of dumb. Catalano would have wanted someone else, in addition, monitoring him—the same way she used Mary Morheim to monitor Dan Cogan. Jalen Reese is the obvious person to act as a go-between. She started at Peacekeeping five years ago, roughly when Cogan must have been perfecting his ability to manipulate the Mains. Her record and Green's were both purged in exactly the same way. She and Green both tried to deflect my investigation by pointing me toward Fisk. And she acts as if her job at Peacekeeping is meaningless to her."

Another long pause. I shifted restlessly. Many times, in the past, Lee's lek intelligence had simply refused to accept my intuitive conclusions. But at those times, I hadn't been depending on him as much as I was now.

"Harry Green might confirm or deny your theory," said Lee. "But he has disappeared, and now that the Mains are down, the peekers that I sent to look for him will not be functioning."

"That's quite right," I said, with an edge to my voice. "So forget about Green. I don't think he knew anything, anyway. He was just the tool, not the intelligence."

Another brief silence.

"Jalen Reese may not be alive," said Lee.

I cursed silently. "I saw from the peeker you sent, she was alive enough to get herself out of her flier."

"We may not be able to find her, even if she is alive. She has had time to leave the site of the crash."

I looked at Eva. "Tell him," I said. "Tell him how it looks to you."

"I believe Tom's right," she told Lee.

"No." He sounded calmly certain. "You are advocating that we act on two low probabilities in succession, one being that Jalen Reese is alive, the other being that she can tell us where Cogan is. You are also gambling that we can persuade Cogan to help us. You believe it is worth taking all these chances in the hope of saving many people's lives. I disagree. I see that we can save some lives by giving first aid and lending other assistance here and now."

I felt the whole thing slipping out of my control.

"Wait!" I shouted at him, as he started toward the crash site. "There's one other option."

"Yes?" He paused.

It was hard for me to tell him to do this. It was like telling someone to pick up a gun and play Russian roulette. "Probe deeper into the Mains," I said. "Cogan is almost certainly still logged on. You can trace his source."

"But I will risk becoming contaminated by the virus."

"Most of the systems are down, now. It'll be a lot easier, a lot safer for you to find your way around in there. And even if the virus gets through to you, there seems to be an incubation period before it takes effect. That should allow us enough time to locate Cogan and force him to cooperate."

Lee stood there immobile while the wreckage burned behind him and smoke billowed up. People were still screaming in pain, shouting for help. Others were still pouring out of the Sensorium, drugged and dizzy, blundering into each other in the semidarkness, unable to make sense of what was happening.

Lee looked at me. "I have processed the probabilities as well as I can," he said. "I think you are correct. I will do as you suggest. Please stand by."

For a moment, he froze. I imagined him dipping into swirl of data, giving passwords, digging, probing for anomalies.

"I have located an active outside signal that is accessing restricted areas," he said.

I felt a wave of relief. "Great. Pull out of there and give me the map reference as hardcopy."

A faint hum; a ripping of paper as he reached inside his tunic. He handed me the perforated segment.

I watched him carefully. "Are you okay? Did you get in and out clean?"

"Yes. I believe I did."

1010001

The main pedpath was no longer alive with its own soft, radiant glow, and it was teeming with people. From above, they looked like lab rats, running in packs, hunting this way and that for a way out of an experiment that had gone badly wrong. Traffic Control was obviously down, which meant that no fliers anywhere in Sen City would be functional anymore. Scattered across the darkening landscape were little spots of flame where vehicles had fallen out of the sky when the Mains had failed.

"Where are we going?" Eva was leaning forward between the seats, peering ahead through the canopy.

"The Coronnade," said Lee. "Directly in front of us."

It was one of the few buildings still lit up. But the lights were flickering erratically.

"Is the Coronnade another of Catalano's hotels?" I asked.

"Yes," said Lee.

"What kind of link does Cogan have into Central Processing?"

"An optic-fiber land line. I have accessed the hotel's communications node and the link traces to a room on the fortieth floor. Room 40-034."

1010010

He took us in a wide curve, then brought us down toward the roof. I glimpsed rows of fliers parked there, their hulls gleaming in the failing light. Then my seat swung and rocked under me as Lee made last-minute corrections, and I realized that something felt wrong; we were moving too fast, veering from side to side.

We were going to crash. "Up!" I shouted. "You're coming in too low!"

I felt myself being hurled upward. Eva cried out and lost her balance in the rear of the vehicle. I saw lights spinning around us; and then, slowly, we stabilized.

Dizzy and disoriented, I peered out. We were a hundred meters higher than we had been before, and we had ceased all motion. We were dangling like a yo-yo on the end of its string.

"What the hell are you doing?" I shouted at Lee.

"My coordination was faulty."

Surely, I thought, it couldn't have happened that quickly.

"There is a malfunction," Lee said, "in my input processor. It has developed a lag time."

Behind me, Eva groaned.

"Okay," I said. "Your main processors are still good, right? So there must be a way you can get us down onto the roof."

"I am not sure. I do not want to endanger your lives."

"Do it slowly. Very slowly. If the lag time develops again, lock us in place as you did just now."

"All right, I will do as you say. All my other functions seem normal; it's just the input processor."

"Sure, because that was first in line when you were digging into the Mains, right?"

We started sinking, bit by bit. The vehicle wobbled, sideslipped, stopped, then started down again. It was like being flown by a pilot with palsy.

"Isn't there a manual override?" Eva said.

"No." I was speaking with only half my attention, holding on to the sides of my seat, watching the roof of the building as it moved up under us bit by bit. "A grav-null vehicle is fundamentally unstable," I told her. "Flying one manually would be like trying to run across a floor covered in marbles. Human reflexes aren't fast enough. Without the Mains, or Lee, there's no way to control this thing."

We were less than four meters above the roof, now. The vehicle rocked wildly, stabilized, then started rocking again. "I cannot control it," Lee said.

"So let it go," I told him. "We're almost down. The drop won't kill us."

He did as I said. We fell freely. It lasted less than a second, but it seemed much longer than that. Then there was a crash that threw me sideways, wrenched my neck, and slammed my teeth together.

I looked around. We were no longer moving. We were on the roof, and we seemed to be safe. Slowly, I made myself relax and let go of the sides of my seat.

I turned to see if Eva was okay. "Any damage?" I called to her.

She propped herself on one elbow, reached up with her other hand, and touched her head. She winced. "I'm up," she said. "Just about."

"Lee?"

"I am having difficulty processing input." His voice was as calm as ever, and yet I imagined there was a hint of confusion in it. I wondered how it felt, knowing something was invading his brain and paralyzing it one section at a time.

1010011

I stood on the rooftop in the gentle night air, my hand on the dart gun in my pocket, my eyes moving quickly, checking the area. The floodlights that should have illuminated the flier bays were out, but there was backwash from a malfunctioning sign on another building nearby. In that vague radiance I saw something a couple of aisles away—a white shape among the ranks of fliers. I tensed, then realized it was a tourist in a white suit, wandering around, looking lost.

He saw me a moment after I'd seen him. "Hey," he shouted. He started toward us. "I'm looking for my lady." He was a big man, fleshy, his clothes stretched tight around his body. "You seen a woman up here? Said she'd meet me up here."

Lee was having trouble getting out of the vehicle. I walked around and tried to steady him. His coordination was totally shot. "Was your friend coming here in a flier?" I said to the fat man.

"Yeah. Flier. Right." He shook his head, puzzled. "She said she'd be here."

I helped Lee plant his feet on the roof. Then I thought of something. I reached into the transit vehicle and grabbed the little portable tool kit that I sometimes carried on small jobs.

Eva pulled herself out of the back of the vehicle. "Traffic Control is down," she told the tourist. "So fliers are down. You com?"

The man stared at her.

"Where's the main hotel entrance?" I asked him. He waved vaguely toward one corner of the roof where there was a dark archway outlined in dead neon.

I turned to Lee. "Can you walk?"

"Yes. On a level surface."

"He'll be a liability to us," said Eva.

"Not necessarily. Ninety-nine percent of his head is still operational, and I'll take whatever I can get at this point."

"My lady," the man in white complained. "You seen my lady, or what?"

We turned away from him and walked toward the entrance, leaving him staring vaguely around, trying to make sense of the new world he found himself in.

1010100

Dim yellow emergency lights illuminated the hotel corridors, and the air smelled stale. We passed a humanoid auton—a mek-maid in a skimpy, frilly little dress. She'd keeled over in mid-stride and was lying on her side with broken plates and broken glass strewn around her. The tray she'd been carrying had rolled on down the hall and was resting against the wall. Spilled drinks were slowly soaking into the carpet.

A door opened farther along the corridor, and a little girl of ten or eleven peered out. "You aren't the goddamn room service," she said. "Where the hell is the goddamn room service? How do you get a drink around here?" It sounded to me as if her chrono age had to be forty or more.

"We call 'em chickles," said Eva, as we passed her by. "Is that what you call them? The kids who decide never to grow up?"

"That's what we call them," I said.

The elevators might have been working, but I

didn't trust them, so we took the emergency stairs.
Lee had difficulty moving from each step to the
next, but we only had to go down a couple of
floors. While I was waiting for him, I checked carefully to see if any peekers had been following us.
But there was no sign of any surveillance. I heard
screams and laughter from farther down the stairwell, but where we were, it was deserted.

1010101

I paused in the hallway on the fortieth floor and
held my breath, listening. There was music playing somewhere, and muffled voices from one of
the rooms—a man shouting something, a woman
laughing. The hallway itself was empty, and in the
dim emergency lighting it looked dowdy and
abandoned.

I crept to the corner at the end and peered
around it. The room we wanted was two doors
farther along, and I cursed silently as I saw a man
sitting outside it, massively muscled, his faced
styled like a thug. Slowly, I raised my dart gun.
He caught the movement from the corner of his
eye, and as I took aim, he turned his head.

He was halfway up and out of his chair as I
fired the pistol. For a moment he froze, trying fu-
tilely to raise his arm to pluck the dart from his
chest. He grunted, swaying on his feet. Then he
gave way to the weakness that was spreading
through his muscles. He toppled backward and
thumped down onto the carpet.

I gestured for Eva to follow me as I started
toward the room he'd been guarding. Two massive, old-fashioned mechanical locks had been
added to the door, and the work looked recent.

I knelt down and searched the guard's pockets

for the keys. His eyes were staring wide and his
forehead was filmed with sweat. He was struggling to breathe, his chest moving in little spasms.
He had nothing to worry about; the paralysis in-
duced by the dart would start wearing off as soon
it was removed.

I found the keys and stood up. Lee was approaching along the corridor, placing his feet with
exaggerated care, and swaying like a drunk. "Is
this door secured electronically?" I sent to him.

He came up and ran his palm over it, his arm
moving in little spasms. "There is an electronic
lock," he said. He paused for several seconds, and
finally there was a muffled click. "It is now
disengaged."

I used the guard's keys to open the mechanical
locks, cupping my hands around each one to muf-
fle the sound. Then I pressed the touchplate to
open the door, and as soon as it slid aside I
charged right in.

Dan Cogan was sitting surrounded by lek
equipment in the middle of the room. He looked
up and saw me, saw the dart gun aimed at him,
and he didn't move, didn't say a word, just sat
there staring.

1010110

I glanced quickly to either side, but the rest of
the room seemed empty. Meanwhile I felt Eva
right behind me, pressing close, peering around
my shoulder.

"Lift your hands straight up off the touchpads,"
I told Cogan as I moved toward him. "Clasp them
behind your head."

He did as I said. His data console was resting
on a standard-issue hotel table, with a couple of

homemade rigs stacked beside him, their cooling units humming gently. A power pack was on the floor at his feet. There were stacks of food and water containers, just as there had been in Catalano's shelter.

I glanced into the bathroom to make sure it was empty, then checked the closets, trying not to take my eyes off Cogan for more than a second at a time. He didn't stop staring at me, and he looked as nervous as a little kid. "I know who you are," he blurted out as I finished my inspection and walked over to him. His voice was higher pitched than I remembered it from when he had introduced Milton Berg at the Chaist conference. I hoped he was just as scared as he sounded. "I understand what you want," he went on, "and I—"

"Be quiet," I told him. I bent down, hit the switch on the power pack, and the system in front of him died. I turned to Lee. "Any chance we're being monitored? Are you picking up any transmissions?"

Slowly, clumsily, he walked toward Cogan. He pointed toward his chest.

I reached toward the pocket of the tunic that Cogan was wearing. He flinched as if he thought I was going to hit him. My fingers closed around a com disc like the one we'd taken off Catalano. I subjected it to the same destructive treatment. "Anything else?" I asked Lee.

"I don't think so. But I cannot be certain. Even when I restrict myself to processing one channel directly from my own receptors, it is very slow and difficult."

I turned back to Cogan. "This is my auton," I said. "Your goddamn virus has corrupted him. He'll be brain-dead within another hour or two."

I pulled over a chair and sat so I could look directly into Cogan's eyes. "But that's no big deal. His software can be purged. There are human beings out there who lack that option."

Cogan nodded dumbly. He didn't say anything.

"You've racked up quite a score," I went on. "Let's see: several thousand crushed to death in the Hotel Sera this morning, maybe a thousand more in various other accidents around town, at least five thousand killed in fliers that crashed when Traffic Control went down this evening— but I guess that wouldn't bother you. What the hell, you murdered your own girlfriend, right?"

He took a shaky breath. "I know you think I killed those people," he said. His voice sounded dry and hoarse, and he swallowed hard. "But I didn't. And I certainly didn't kill my—my girlfriend."

"You sure as hell did," I said. "I was right beside her when it happened."

He laughed. It was a tense, jerky sound. "That's crazy."

I reached in my pocket and pulled out Mary Morheim's addrex. "I took this off her dead body just after she was run down by a cart in Xavier Tower."

He looked at the addrex, then up at my face. Something changed in him. His face went blank, and he started trembling. "You—" He had trouble getting the words out. "You mean it?"

This wasn't tracking right at all. "Eva," I said, "take the covers off that bed. Put them around his shoulders."

"Is he going into shock?" she asked.

"I hope not."

"But Serena said she was looking after Mary," Cogan blurted out. "She promised!"

There was no point in pushing him any harder. I squatted down beside him and put my hand on his arm, abandoning my tough role while Eva draped the covers around him. "If you're really innocent," I said, softening my tone, "you have nothing to worry about. I'm not in business to apprehend innocent people."

He nodded and swallowed hard.

"So tell me what I need to know. Help me to clean up this mess."

Bit by bit, he got himself back together. "Serena Catalano. She was holding Mary, till I—fixed everything."

"Holding her hostage, you mean? Till you got the Mains running again?"

He nodded quickly. "Yeah. See, I brought this rig out of Milton's castle—"

"Milton Berg's place on the coast?"

"Yeah. Serena told me to bring the stuff here, and she said if I got the Mains functional again she'd give Mary back to me, but not till then."

I turned and looked at Eva. Eva looked at me. "You tell him," I said.

She brushed Cogan's shoulder with her fingertips. "Catalano lied to you," she said softly. "Your woman is dead."

He hugged his arms around himself and shivered some more, leaning forward. His jaw clenched. Then I sensed his feelings shifting, the hurt hardening into anger. He dropped his hands to the touchpads in front of him.

I took hold of his wrist. "If you're thinking of getting ahold of Catalano in some way, or maybe taking revenge on her, you're too late. She's being held by a guardian in a place where there's no comset and no surveillance. There's nothing you can do to her, and nothing I can do to her either

till we get things normalized." I nodded slowly.
"That's the highest priority, now."

1010111

I let him sit for a little while. The time was still
precious, but I wasn't sure he'd be functional if I
made too many demands.

Finally, he seemed to recover some of his
strength. He turned and looked at me. "So what
do you want me to do?"

"Some clarification. After that, I'll need some
help."

He nodded without speaking.

"First tell me who might have killed Mary Morheim, if it wasn't you."

"Milton." His voice was a monotone. "If it really happened, and it wasn't an accident, it must
have been Milton Berg."

I drew my chair closer. "You mean Berg knew
how to access the Mains? You weren't the only
one?"

"I taught him. Fifteen years ago, when I joined
the Chaists and changed my ID—"

"You swallowed their party line?"

He gave me a sick smile. "Yeah, I believed in
it. In fact I still do. But I realized—just today—
what Milton had been doing. You see, I designed
the virus so it would only reside in the Mains.
Whenever it entered a new system it figured the
size of the workspace, and if it wasn't a big system, my code erased itself. But after I left the meeting with Milton this morning and I saw the
wreckage of the Sera—I knew, then. He must have
edited the resource evaluation routine so that the
virus could spread into any system at all."

I looked at him sitting in front of me all screwed

up with grief and guilt, his shoulders hunched, his hands clasped between his knees, and I felt no shred of sympathy. I felt like grabbing him and shaking him, maybe throwing him against the wall, and yelling at him for being so smart but so dumb—smart enough to crack systems that had been designed to be impregnable, but dumb enough to trust a man like Milton Berg.

"Catalano provided your financing," I said. "Isn't that right?"

"I believe she put up some money, yes. One of her people came to a meeting, and Milton managed to pass information through that person to Serena, telling her we—shared a common goal." He shook his head. "I never wanted to know about that end of it. The money, I mean."

I frowned. "So what exactly *was* the goal? Shutting down the Mains and killing everyone?"

He looked genuinely distressed. "No! I just wanted people to think for themselves for a change. The little systems would still run, but the big ones would gradually, like, seize up. My code contained an event counter, so it would reproduce itself only at widely spaced intervals. I figured it would take a year, maybe more, before the Mains really crashed. Up till then they'd just get slower and slower, less and less reliable, so people would go through a gradual transition."

He was looking at me hopefully. He wanted me to tell him he hadn't done such a bad thing.

I wasn't going to give him that reassurance. "I understand what you're saying, Dan," I said, keeping my voice neutral.

"Yeah. Yeah, of course you understand." He gave me his sick grin again. "You have a whole lot more lek knowledge than I do."

"But Milton Berg had a different idea?"

He blinked. I saw he was having trouble concentrating. "I guess I got suspicious a week back, when he didn't want me to use my link to access the Mains anymore. But I told myself he needed to prove he was up to it, you know? He was always a take-charge type. But this morning, I saw what had happened, and when we got back to the castle he admitted it. He said there was no point in a gradual transition, we had to throw people in the water and see if they could swim, and if they drowned, they weren't worth saving, because it was natural selection. I couldn't accept that, and we had a big argument. But then he seemed to back down, which surprised me. He asked to be left alone to think, so I went to the basement, to my room. About an hour later I heard sounds, kind of muffled snapping sounds. When I got back upstairs I found him dead. I panicked. I called Serena, grabbed my best equipment, and got out of there."

"You found him lying in a pool of blood?"

"Yeah." He gave me a strange look. "You know, I thought maybe *you'd* come there and shot him. I was sure there had to be a Protektor on Agorima by this time. So I panicked. I called Serena and she said I should get over to her place right away. So I grabbed this stuff, which was all I really needed, and I've been here since then." His eyes strayed back to the keyboard and the blank screen in front of him.

I nodded to myself. Slowly, I stood up.

Eva was giving me a questioning look. "Tom, you think he—"

"Sure," I said to her, "he's telling the truth."

"Right." Eva nodded, looking pleased and expectant. "I think he is, too. So if he wants to fix everything, and you're here to help him, you guys should be able to take care of it."

I sighed. "Sorry, Eva. It's still not that simple. What no one seems to realize is that Milton Berg was never shot dead. He's still out there somewhere, still alive, still on-line, and still working to bring it all down."

1011000

"But I saw him dead!" Cogan protested. "It was like he'd been hit by a dozen projectiles."

"Right. I saw him, too, because there just happened to be a peeker passing by, and a window just happened to be open, and the peeker just happened to fly in a few moments after he'd been shot. Of course, by the time I got there, the body had gone—to be autopsied, supposedly. The couch where Berg had been lying was soaked in blood, sure enough, but only around the edges. It wasn't stained or damaged where he had been lying. If he had really been shot with projectiles, some of them, at least, would have passed through him. It was impossible; it was a setup. But I didn't say anything about it because I didn't know who else knew, and there was still a chance that I was being monitored."

Cogan wasn't shivering anymore. He seemed deep in thought. Being confronted with a mystery to solve, a problem to crack, was good therapy for him. "So Milton faked his own death," he said. "I guess he figured he could access the Mains and do what he wanted to do, and anyone else would just get in the way. Me, or you, or Serena." He slapped his hand down on the table beside his keyboard. "*That's* what's been screwing me up, here, while I've been trying to fix things. Milton's been on-line from someplace else, working against me. And all the failures out there are exactly what he wants, and he won't stop till—" Cogan broke off abruptly, like a man pursuing a trail, suddenly finding himself at the edge of abyss.

"You had it planned like program code, didn't you?" I said to him. "A clean numbered sequence. A gradual transition with no loss of life, leading to some sort of utopia, and in the end people would thank you for putting them back in touch with reality."

Cogan shifted uncomfortably. "I guess you can make it sound dumb like that, but yeah, I thought it was for the best."

"I'll tell you something, Dan." I leaned forward till my face was less than a meter from his. I grabbed his shoulder and held it. *"Life is not a computer program."*

He didn't say anything.

"There are random factors you can never control. And in any case, controlling them isn't your business. People have a right to screw up their lives any way they want."

He moved his shoulder, trying to pull free from my grip.

Calculatedly, I smacked his cheek. "You listen to me! Men and women are dead right now because of your half-assed ideas. Including Mary Morheim."

This time, he didn't try to resist.

"So where is Milton Berg?" I said. "My auton traced your intrusion, but at that point I told Lee to withdraw from the Mains. I didn't think there might be more than one of you in there tampering."

Cogan retreated into his thoughts for a moment. "I'd say Milton's at the castle," he said.

"But you said you took your best equipment out of there."

Cogan looked down at the gear in front of him. "Yes, but there's older stuff back at the castle which would still do the job, pretty much." He gave me a worried look. "You know, that place is heavily fortified. The walls are six feet thick, and the foundation goes down into solid rock. There are no windows on the land side. You'll never get in, unless you have a bomb or something."

I nodded soberly. "Thanks for telling me. All right, this is how we'll do it. You'll stay here. Is your equipment fused?"

He blinked. "Well, sure, of course. Back here." He reached for the power supply and pointed to a little metal panel.

I popped it, reached in, and yanked out half a dozen low-voltage fuses. "Sorry not to seem more trusting," I said, "but I can't have you using this gear unsupervised." I turned to Lee. "You may as well stay here. I think this room is as secure as anywhere right now. Eva, do you want to come with me?"

She was watching me, looking puzzled. "Come where?"

I kept my face blank. "To shut down Mr. Berg."

She looked even more puzzled. "For real? Sure I want to come. What the hell do you think?"

"All right." I picked up my little tool kit and started toward the door.

"You mean you're just going to abandon me here?" said Cogan, sounding plaintive.

"I'll be back," I said. "And frankly, Dan, it makes me feel better to know that you're in this room under lock and key."

When I was outside with Eva and had locked the door, I bent down beside the guard lying on

the floor and plucked the dart out of his chest. It
carried a small oscillator that interfaced with the
nervous system. "You'll regain your faculties
within a minute or two," I said. "I suggest you
get the hell out. If Serena finds that you fell down
on the job, she'll hold you responsible, know what
I mean? And there's nothing more you can do
here."

I saw a look of comprehension in his eyes.

"So what are you going to do?" Eva said, as I
started for the emergency stairs. "You said you
can't fly the transit vehicle manually—"

"And in any case," I cut in, "it may have been
damaged by the hard landing." I opened the door.
"It's time," I said, "for us to hit the street."

1011001

The night wind was laced with acrid chemical
odors and a hot-roasted smell, as if a funeral pyre
had been fueled with gasoline and plastic. The
fumes caught in my throat and made my eyes
water.

All the big signs in Dream Valley were dead,
and the luminescent surface of the pedpath had
faded to a dark gray. But a pleasure palace had
been set afire just a few blocks away, and the wild,
crackling flames cast a lurid yellow glare that was
easily bright enough to show us our way.

Behind us, in the hotel, two human staff were
barricading the street lobby entrance with stacks
of lounge furniture. Further along the pedpath I
heard smashing sounds, screams, and something
heavy being dragged. Looters, I guessed. In a
world of surplus wealth, theft was pointless; but
that wouldn't stop anyone. The pointlessness of it
would provide its own special thrill.

Eva glanced each way, her eyes moving warily. "You got a plan?"

"We need a ground vehicle. They're the only urban transportation that isn't centrally controlled. I seem to remember a highway up ahead, and if it's like the ones I saw on a newsim today, it'll be full of abandoned cars."

We started walking, side by side, keeping close to the buildings. "You okay?" I asked, realizing that I hadn't been paying much attention to her in the past hour or so.

"I'm more okay than you are," she said sharply.

I told myself I would have to stop making the mistake of being concerned about her welfare. "You think I have some sort of problem?" I asked.

"You're running ragged. You should see yourself. You look like you haven't slept in a week."

I felt irritated, especially since she was probably telling the truth. "When you edit your sim show, do me a favor and enhance my appearance."

She shook her head quickly. "I don't do that."

"Not even if I pay you?"

She thought about it for a moment. "You couldn't afford it."

I sighed. "You weren't kidding when you told me you're hard to get along with."

"Well, yeah." She shrugged and smiled. "But you seem to like it that way."

I decided not to answer that. I was sleep-deprived, and I had bigger things to think about than sparring with her. As the flaming palace receded behind us, the darkness began to seem threatening. Any doorway could be hiding someone, and now that surveillance was down, if people thought it might feel good to assault, rape, or steal, they just might give it a try. This was Sen City; more than ever, normal standards did not apply.

"The cars have old-style locks, you know," Eva was saying, as we passed the smashed window of a clothing store, our feet crunching over broken glass. "They need an old-style key."

"I'll tackle that problem when we come to it," I said.

She looked at me quizzically in the semidarkness. "You figure you can tackle just about anything, right?"

"Everything except certain human beings."

"Such as me, you mean?"

I didn't bother to reply.

We reached an overpass. On either side of it was a shallow slope matted with ivy, and at the bottom was the two-lane highway. As I'd hoped, it was still crowded with abandoned vehicles. We ran down the slope together, the leaves wet with dew, slippery underfoot. At the bottom, near the underpass, there was very little light; the cars gleamed faintly in dim orange radiance from Agorima's single moon.

There was a fancy automobile right in front of me with its door wide-open, its interior bathed in yellow electric light. I slid inside and found myself on seats upholstered in fake fur with satin trimmings, the cabin paneled with polished wood and stone bas-reliefs. The instruments were mounted in gold-plated binnacles, and the underside of the roof had been hand-painted with angels, nymphs, and satyrs cavorting among puffy white clouds. The only thing missing was a silver-plated toilet.

I told myself to ignore the decor. I found an old-fashioned lock mounted in a platinum bezel, and as I'd expected, it was mainly ornamental. Under Protektorate surveillance, theft had never been a problem in Sen City. I took out my tool kit and used the miniature torch to cut a circle. The sizzling sound of molten metal seemed loud in the night, and a tracery of white fumes drifted up.

Within a few seconds, the lock fell out into my hand. I chopped two wires that emerged from the back of it, stripped them, and twisted them together. All the instruments lit up—a gaudy display that probably didn't mean much, but it looked good, and looking good was obviously what ground vehicles were all about.

"Were you one of those kids," said Eva, "who was kind of nerdy and used to build things for science fairs, and got beat up by the bigger kids because you wouldn't play football?"

"That's me," I said. "But over the years I've somehow managed to restore some of my self-esteem." I nodded toward the passenger door. "Let's go for a drive."

Eva walked around and slid the door shut. She looked skeptical. "You going to ram all the other cars out of your way, or what?"

I looked at the controls. There were only four of them, and they all had labels. Sen City residents didn't do many things for themselves, so the cars had to be simple to use. I pushed a big switch marked POWER, and there was a rumbling noise from somewhere—probably a nonfunctional sound effect, but it did imply that everything was operational. I turned the steering lever hard right.

"You can't go off the road," Eva said. "The car senses that. It's a safety feature."

"Probably a cable embedded in the edge of the highway. It'll be out of action like all the other city services." I applied more power, and the car bumped off the pavement. "See?"

She gave me a look. "So how does it feel, knowing all the answers?"

"The trouble with knowing all the answers is that people ask me all the questions."

I angled the car toward the ivy-covered slope bordering the highway. Under maximum power we surged forward, hit the slope, and struggled up it diagonally, the wheels spinning and sliding. Barely under control, we made it to the top and thumped down onto the pedpath.

I turned left. The headlights picked out a scene of devastation. There were ruined storefronts and flaming waste barrels, broken glass and mounds of garbage. As we passed a hotel, an armchair crashed down onto the pavement a few meters away, hurled from one of the upper windows. Glass fragments rained on the roof of the car.

Up ahead, a gang of naked men ran in front of us, chasing a couple of naked women. As we passed a small park I saw flesh amid the grass, an orgy under the stars.

"You know where you're going?" said Eva.

"More or less."

I turned off the pedpath, onto an alley that ran behind a row of stores. I hoped it might be safer to stay off the main drag.

"You realize there's no roads to the eastern coast," she said. "You want to get out to Berg's castle, maybe you could get some kind of construction vehicle, a trench-digger, something like that."

"I'm not heading for Berg's castle."

I saw her looking at me questioningly.

"I didn't want to talk about it before," I said, "because there was just a chance that we were being monitored, and I don't trust Dan Cogan. But there's no way Berg is out at his castle. The man's a power freak; he'll want to see the damage he's doing, firsthand. And I'm sure he thinks he's too important to be dealing with second-rate access equipment when he could be using the best."

"Such as where?"

I nodded toward the range of hills lying directly ahead of us. "Central Processing's control room."

1011010

We were moving out of Dream Valley. The last crowd of drugged, partying tourists had been several blocks back, whooping and giggling as they smashed an immobilized street-repair mek. Ahead of us was a narrow road that went up into the hills. I'd figured there had to be some kind of emergency surface access to the Mains, and it looked as if this was it.

Eva had been quiet for a while. Now she turned to me in the dark interior of the car. "I don't see how Berg could just wander into Central Processing and sit down at a screen."

"Normally it would be impossible," I said. "But most of the systems are already down, including the systems defending the building itself. Also, I have a feeling that Mr. Berg would have been quite willing to kill any human guards who got in his way."

Eva shivered. "But what's he *doing* in there?"

"Fixing things so that Cogan can't undo the damage. And I wouldn't be surprised if he wants to get Peacekeeping services under his control. Could be useful to him to have the guardians working for him, right?"

"Right," Eva said, sounding grim.

1011011

I switched my vision to infrared and killed the car's headlights as I saw a hill ahead that looked slightly different from the others. Silhouetted against the starry sky, its black mounded form was smooth and regular, mek-made. It was a configuration duplicated on every Protektorate world. Below its protective shell, many meters underground, lay the Mains.

"Sure hope Berg isn't expecting us," said Eva. She was sitting erect, staring ahead. In infrared, her skin glowed dull red. I could actually see her pulse, beating fast.

"He's arrogant," I said. "Has to be, to do what he's done. So he'll underrate me. I tried to play up to that by telling Jalen Reese that she'd convinced me Fisk was the bad guy. I'm hoping she passed that along."

"Okay, okay." She sounded edgy, impatient. "So he's not expecting us. But this is crazy, going in there without any kind of firepower. Way they do it on the sims, a Protektor would have a laser cannon and an army of war meks, and he'd just blast the deevs apart."

I slowed the car as the landing field outside Central Processing came into view. There were maybe a dozen vehicles parked there under the orange moon. Beyond them, the gateway in the perimeter wall was wide-open; and beyond that, the entrance to the installation glowed with light. There were triple-redundant dedicated power supplies to keep the Mains running under any conceivable circumstances.

I stopped the car outside the landing field. "Sim dramas tend to skip over one little problem," I said. "I work for the Protektorate, and the Protektorate's number one obligation is to preserve human life. All human lives, even Milton Berg's. So, the fact is, there aren't any laser cannons and war meks."

I paused and checked my little dart gun. There were four cartridges left.

She was staring at me. "I understand the Instruction Set," she said, "but what about defensive stuff? Like anesthetic gas—"

"Sure, the Protektorate has an arsenal of nonlethal weapons at the Hub, and I could have called it here within three hours—till we were quarantined." I sighed. "I started this case undercover, and I wanted to work it like that all the way through, so my target wouldn't run and hide or feel motivated to mount some kind of counterattack. The quarantine order caught me by surprise. The only thing I have in reserve is a lifeboat module up on my jumpship. I can call that down using an emergency communicator—but not till everything here is secure."

"No weapons at all," she said, still sounding as if she didn't want to believe it.

I opened the door of the car. "The OverMains never like a Protektor to have much personal power. They don't trust human beings. Also, you should bear in mind that I have to protect this installation from any damage—from him or from me. Really the best way is stealth, not confrontation." I paused a moment, eyeing the terrain. A soft night wind ruffled the vegetation on the hillside. "You'll be safe enough here," I went on. "I don't blame you for not wanting to come."

She stared at me blankly as I slid the door shut. Then, as I started toward the flier field, I heard her getting out of the car and running after me.

"If you're planning to get your dumb head blown off," she said, catching up with me, "I want it on-camera."

I looked at her face, scared but determined. "Still the intrepid reporter?"

"Right."

Nonviolent Survival

The Protektorate's prohibition against endangering human life was rigid and absolute. The only way people would trust the lek government was if it could never take or threaten their lives.

But if human beings used weapons against one another, or against the Protektorate itself, what then? The Protektorate was by definition pacifistic. It had no means of military intervention.

The only practical solution to this problem was for human society to exist in the same condition of disarmament as the Protektorate itself. Weapons were outlawed and surveillance, coupled with control over natural resources, helped to ensure that this ban was obeyed.

When sociopathic humans found ways to circumvent the law, three time-honored principles of nonviolence were employed: retreat, passive resistance, and removal of resources. Of these, the third was by far the most effective. The Protektorate, after all, had become humanity's sole provider. Without its food factories, its housing, and its handouts, most humans would perish.

In addition, the Protektorate provided each Protektor with defensive weapons and armor. Anesthetic dart guns, armored meks designed to resist gunfire and penetrate strongholds, stun-guns, infrasonics—these were just some of the resources available.

Yet most Protektors avoided using them as much as possible. Any weapon could be captured and turned against its owner, and any show of force would tend to encourage escalation and counterforce.

1011100

We crept around the landing field, keeping close to the trees at the edge, alert for any sound or motion.

"All the years I've lived in Sen City," Eva whispered to me, "I've never been up here. Seems like Central Processing was just a bunch of leks doing their job. Never any news in that."

"The Protektorate prefers citizens to forget about the Mains," I said. "Leks never forget. They remember the days when a lot of humans used to hate them."

I thought of something. I paused and looked back. Most of the parked fliers presumably belonged to the human staff in Maintenance who had stayed at their jobs even after the situation started to look hopeless. But one of the vehicles caught my attention.

I flipped back to normal vision. "The flier over there," I whispered to Eva. "Looks red to you?"

She paused. "Hard to tell. Yeah, I think."

"I last saw it on the roof of Berg's castle."

1011101

We neared the gateway in the high white wall that circled the installation. A couple of large, squat figures were standing motionless—guardians, I realized, that had shut down when the command systems died. Between them, another shape was lying on the ground.

I crept forward, placing my feet carefully, trying to make no sound. I zoomed in on the prone figure and saw it was a man in Protektorate uniform. He was dead, his jacket charred and blackened around a wide, deep hole in the center of his chest.

Some kind of heat beam had killed him. That would explain the lack of blood; heat had cauterized the wound.

My skin armor wouldn't be any use against a weapon like that. It was designed, in fact, to allow heat to pass freely, to allow ventilation.

I went over to the post beside the gateway. The door was standing open. I imagined the man in uniform seeing Berg's flier land, seeing Berg coming toward the open gate—which couldn't be closed, because none of the control systems were functioning, or because Berg had disabled them remotely. So the guard had stepped out to stop the intruder, maybe thinking he was a tourist who'd lost his way, or a drunk—and Berg had beamed him to death.

I heard a faint sound behind me. I turned quickly, bringing up my dart gun, then saw that it was Eva coming to join me. I hadn't realized, till then, how wired I was. Carefully, deliberately, I made myself stop and take slow breaths while I tried to quiet my pulse.

She came close to me, till her lips were by my ear. "You figuring to zap me? You want to get a little peace and quiet?"

"Unfortunately, I can't afford to waste the ammunition," I whispered back.

To myself, I thought: she was taking this risk on her own initiative. It was her decision, not my responsibility. Yet I had to admit I could have exerted my authority and refused to allow her to come with me. The truth was, I wanted her company.

1011110

On the front steps of the installation was another dead man with another charred hole in his chest. Beyond him the main entrance was wide-open, with more guardians standing motionless inside. The squat forms looked somehow purposeful in their stasis, as if they were meditating, contemplating the oneness of a looping control program.

I paused with Eva alongside the building. "Looks to me as if he disabled all the security systems so as to gain access," I said. "Even the backup surveillance systems will be down."

"Sure hope you're right about that." Her face was pale.

"We have an advantage over him, anyway. These installations are all built from the same set of plans. I know where all the exits are, and with no security, we'll be able to enter that way. Ready?"

She nodded without speaking.

I ran lightly around the side of the building and down some metal stairs. I felt them thrumming as Eva followed close behind me. At the bottom was a waste reclamation area; a pit of darkness. I switched back to infrared vision, reoriented myself, and ran along a concrete path along the side of the building. Finally I came to a plain, unmarked steel door.

I dragged it open. Inside was a utilitarian stairwell. I caught Eva as she came through the door after me, and we paused there a minute, both of us breathing hard.

"You don't think this guy has peekers out here?" she whispered.

"No way to process their data. He'd have to build his own surveillance hardware, and the signal processors as well. I didn't see anything that could have done that, out at his castle."

She frowned. "You're certain?"

I shook my head. "I'm not certain of anything. You want to wait here?"

"No."

"Come on, then." I turned and continued on down the stairs. At the lowest level I opened another door.

1011111

We were in a white room lined with white suits hanging on racks. I took Eva's arm. "Got to put on a clean suit. I doubt the verification systems are functioning, but if they are, and they sense an intruder who's not suited, the doors will lock and an alarm will sound."

She nodded. Wordlessly, she seized a suit and started wrestling with it.

"Let me," I whispered. I released the clasps, opened the seam at the back, and helped her step in. Steadying her with my hand, I was suddenly conscious of the warmth and shape of her body. I told myself I was too psyched, too focused on the job to be physically interested—but there was something about imminent danger that seemed to sharpen my senses.

She suddenly turned toward me. I looked away, but not quickly enough. I think she knew what was going on in my mind, and maybe the same thing was going on in hers. She smiled awkwardly, then reached out and brushed her fingers lightly across my cheek.

For a moment, our eyes met. Then, quickly, she slid her arm into the suit sleeve and ducked her head into a helmet. Neither of us said anything.

1100000

Through the next set of doors was a white hallway lined with equipment bays where maintenance meks were stowed when they weren't in use. Beyond them, through one last pair of doors, was the core—the Mains themselves.

We crept in, our suits making faint rubbery noises as we moved. The space here was bright white, circular, cluttered with square, silver-gray columns that reached from floor to ceiling, stretching away from us in a square grid. Inside each column was the actual hardware that ran the whole planet's support systems. Beneath them, under the white floor, were power supply cables and coolant lines. Above, in the ceiling, was the massive web that linked the Mains with one another and with the world beyond.

A maintenance mek stood nearby. It had removed the faceplate of the nearest column and was probing inside it with a dozen different manipulators and diagnostic sensors. But the mek was frozen motionless, and the sterile space was totally silent. Even the air filtration system was dead.

I crept forward with my dart gun in my gloved hand. The silence of the place seemed eerie, like a graveyard, with the Mains as tombstones.

I reached the open cabinet. A couple of wires snaked out of it, trailing away across the floor, disappearing down the next aisle. That was nonstandard; loose wiring in the core was absolutely taboo. I peered into the cabinet and saw that the wires terminated in a lumpy ball of gray stuff, maybe ten centimeters in diameter. I felt a sense of sudden understanding—and powerful, queasy fear.

I pulled Eva close. I pointed, then pantomimed an explosion, throwing my hands apart.

I saw her eyes above her mask. She looked as scared as I felt.

I turned and started toward the center of the
core, glancing quickly left and right at each intersection. The control room was on the floor immediately above, and the only human access was via
a spiral stair at the center.

I reached the stair and paused. So far there had
been no sound, absolutely no sign that anyone was
in here with us. I imagined Berg outside somewhere, ready to blow the whole installation. I had
an idea that Eva was imagining the same thing.

I put my foot on the bottom stair and glanced
back at her. She shook her head and pointed to
the floor, then moved back a pace.

I nodded to show I understood that she wasn't
going to follow. Then I started up the staircase.

1100001

The stairs curled through a circular opening to
the level above. I climbed slowly, softly. My pulse
was loud in my ears and I was sweating under
the suit, but these things seemed distant and abstract, at the edge of my awareness. I knew I had
a good chance of getting killed, but no matter how
I turned the situation around I saw no alternative.
I couldn't risk waiting for Berg to come out, assuming he was up here; he might not be up here,
in which case he could detonate his explosives
from outside. I had to get to him before he
wrecked the place; everyone's survival depended
on it. And I had no way of sending in any surveillance equipment ahead of me. With Lee down, our
personal store of peekers were as useless as junk,
back in the hold of my transit vehicle.

I tried to imagine what I would find in the control room. A dozen different scenarios went
through my head—of where Berg might be posi-

tioned, how I could tackle him, and how I might hit him with an anesthetic dart.

I stopped my ascent as my eyes reached floor level in the control room. I turned, quickly scanning the room. It was circular, like the core below but much smaller, barely three meters across. It looked as if it had been suddenly, recently abandoned: there were chairs standing at odd angles, a couple of coffee cups, an ink pen lying on the floor beside a stack of hardcopy that had spilled from a table.

Several of the inspection panels in the walls had been left open, and I saw another pair of loose wires disappearing into one of them. They looped across the floor to a large spool that had been dumped beside a chair. It looked as if Berg had been partway through laying his explosives, and he'd been interrupted in the middle of the job. By us?

Cautiously, I continued to the top of the stairs. I kept glancing around, but it became increasingly obvious, as I stepped onto the white tiled floor, that the control room was empty.

1100010

I stood a moment, still with my heart hammering and sweat trickling down into my eyes. All I could hear was my own breathing and my blood thumping. I pushed the hood of my clean suit back from my face, and wiped my forehead on my sleeve.

There was text on one of the console screens. I walked over to it. The text was a transcript of system commands that had been issued verbally and from touchpads. I scrolled back through them and found a block of statements, then some low-level code. From the look of it, it seemed like an attempt to get into Life-Support and reprogram Consumables—the factory installation on the coast that synthesized liquid food compounds and pumped them to dispensals all over Sen City. I skipped to the head of the file—

There was a faint scraping noise behind me, like someone brushing against the edge of a metal doorframe. I turned so fast, I almost lost my balance.

I saw a clean suit just like mine, and for an instant I thought it was Eva. But the suit was too big and the eyes above the mask were wrong. I realized with a jolt that Berg had crammed himself into one of the open inspection panels. And now he was holding something, raising it toward me, and I knew it had to be the weapon that had fried the men downstairs.

He pushed his mask down. "Sit," he said. He pointed to the chair beside me.

For a moment I felt as if I couldn't move. I just stared at him. And then, slowly, I moved toward the chair—meanwhile estimating the distance between us, trying to figure if I could dive to the stairwell or, better still, loose a dart at him. But he was already aiming his weapon, which I was sure could fry me where I stood with no trouble at all.

Eva was still down in the core, but even if she came up here to check on me, she was unarmed. All these thoughts came to me not fully formed but as a series of wordless realizations as I lowered myself onto the chair that Berg had indicated.

I should have felt fear, but the fear was gone now that I was face-to-face with him. Really, all I felt was wild, unreasoning anger. To me, this place was like a temple: the greatest and most beautiful thing that human beings had ever created. It was awesome in its complexity and exquisite in its efficient function. It was a design that had served humanity for centuries. Milton Berg was a wrecker, and in my scheme of things, that was the highest crime.

"Let go of your dart gun," he said. "You saw the men outside?" He gestured with his own weapon. "Focused microwaves. They penetrate any kind of clothing."

I let my arm fall to my side so that my hand was almost touching the floor. I looked at him and felt my rage, and as I let go of the dart gun I fell forward, seized the wires that snaked across the floor, and heaved on them with all my strength.

They caught him around one ankle. I saw him lurch and I heard him shout, but I didn't have time to see whether I'd toppled him. I launched myself at him with my head down. There was a buzzing sound, a sizzling noise somewhere behind me—the microwave beam, I realized. That didn't matter; nothing mattered except getting my hands on the bastard.

I slammed my head into his stomach and he smashed into the cabinets behind him. I felt some of the strength go out of him, and I reached for his face, found his throat instead, grabbed it and banged his head against the wall.

We both fell on the floor, wrestling over his weapon. He fired another burst and one of the glow panels in the ceiling blew out, raining plastic fragments. I seized one of them in my gloved hand and stabbed its point through his suit, into his wrist. He swore, his grip weakened, and I grabbed the gun, dragging it away from him. Quickly, I pulled back.

For a moment we stared at each other, both of

us breathing hard. Then I heard a sound from downstairs—running footsteps. They terminated suddenly in a muffled scream and a thump.

Berg's eyes widened. "Jalen," he muttered. The word was barely audible, but there was no doubt about what he had said.

Instinctively, he started up off the floor. I kicked him in the chest, sending him flat on his back. The physical contact felt good—an outlet for all the aggression and frustration of the past twenty-four hours—and I found myself wanting to do more. But I thought of Eva waiting for me down there among the Mains, and Jalen Reese down there with her, and the bottom dropped out of my anger.

I glanced quickly behind me. No one was coming up the stairs—yet. And my dart gun was lying on the floor, almost in reach. I took a step back, caught the dart gun with the side of my foot, and kicked it over beside Berg.

He looked at it as if he thought I was expecting him to pick it up himself. But I fell onto his chest, ripped open the zipper at the front of his clean suit, then picked up the dart gun and fired it into him.

His arms and legs went limp. The muscles in his face relaxed and his mouth fell open. He gave me a strange, confused look, and then his head flopped back and he just lay there, staring at the ceiling.

1100011

I ran down the stairs. No point in silence, now; my fight with Berg had taken care of that. I glanced quickly around. The evenly spaced gray columns blocked my view of the core, all except for one aisle directly ahead and another to my left and right.

No sign of Eva. No sign of Jalen Reese.

I ran forward, glancing each way at every intersection. I reached one edge of the big circular room, turned, and started back.

Finally, when I was almost at the opposite side of the room, I saw something near the end of an aisle on my right. A white-suited figure kneeling on the floor. No; there were two figures, the second stretched out facedown under the first.

"Eva!" I shouted. But in my imagination, I already knew what I was going to find. I ran, the gray cabinets moving past, the two figures coming closer.

The one who was kneeling turned toward me, and as she started up onto her feet, I raised Berg's microwave pistol, not much caring for the Protektorate's code of ethics anymore.

The woman stepped back and raised her arms. "Hold it!" she shouted. She pushed back her helmet, and black hair spilled out.

"Eva," I said stupidly.

"Shit, who did you think? Come on, help me with her. I've been waiting for you."

1100100

I immobilized Jalen Reese with another dart. Then I sat down on the floor and leaned against one of the Mains, and Eva sat opposite me, and we didn't speak for a few moments, breathing hard and waiting for the adrenaline to leach out of our blood.

"When I heard the scream," I said, "I thought—"

"I know what you thought. You thought I got into trouble like in Dometown, only worse."

"Something like that," I admitted.

"Well, maybe I got lucky." She managed to smile. "Although, it wasn't just luck. I figured Jalen Reese could be in here. You missed that one, didn't you?"

I blinked, feeling stupid. "Reese's flier crashed way out in the woods. It should have been impossible—oh. Now I get it."

"Like Berg faking his own death, right?" said Eva.

"Right," I said, kicking myself mentally. "They faked Berg's death to deflect my suspicions, and they faked the crash to make me forget about Reese, too." I shook my head ruefully. "I should have caught that." But then I scowled at her. "You promised not to withhold any more information from me."

She looked down, embarrassed.

"Well?" I persisted.

"Well, I wasn't sure if I was right. And you're a hard person to tell things to. All the other times I tried to tell you stuff, it turned out you were right and I was wrong. So I got tired of you making me feel stupid."

1100101

After a couple of minutes, I figured I was calm enough to stand up without shaking. "I need your help," I said to Eva. "We have to haul her outside." I nodded toward the limp, prone figure of Jalen Reese. "Berg, too."

Eva raised her eyebrows. "For what, a decent burial?"

I sighed. "Just help me do it, okay? I still can't

fix anything here, because I still don't know what Dan Cogan did to screw things up. I have go back to him at the hotel, and I sure as hell don't intend to leave these criminals here."

She nudged Jalen Reese's limp body with her toe. "She doesn't look like she's going to cause any more trouble."

"Damn it," I said, "will you stop arguing with me? I want her and Berg out of here." My voice was only just short of a shout.

Eva winced. "Okay, okay! We do it your way. Whatever you say." She turned away, looking hurt and irritable.

1100110

We dumped Milton Berg and Jalen Reese at the top of the steps, outside the front entrance. From up here in the hills, we could see the whole of Dream Valley, and the southern edge of Sen City over to the east. A few fires were still burning, little points of yellow light wavering in the haze, but apart from that the vista was shrouded in darkness.

I sat down on the top step and rested my elbows on my knees, feeling weak and weary.

"You okay?" Eva asked.

"Tired," I said.

She touched my shoulder. "You did it. Doesn't that feel good?"

I shook my head. "It isn't done. There's a lot left to do, and it's not trivial."

"Hey." She reached out. "Give me your hand."

I looked up at her. Her face was a faint shape in the moonlight. I couldn't read her expression. "Why?"

"Give me your hand. Come on, I want to show you something."

1100111

She led me around to the side of the installation and onto the gently rounded artificial hill that had been built over it. The hill had been faced with earth and seeded with grass. It was soft underfoot.

"I thought you told me you'd never been here," I said.

"That's right. Never."

"So—"

"Just to the top, that's all."

We climbed it together in the total silence of the night. As we climbed higher, we could see to the south as well as to the north. The ocean stretched away beyond the lower hills, shimmering under the moonlight.

She sat down on the grass. "Join me," she said, pointing beside her.

"I don't have time for this," I told her. "People's lives still depend on this installation getting up and running."

"People are partying out there, and the rest of them are sleeping. They'll manage for a while without you looking after them. Come on. Sit."

Reluctantly, I sat beside her. A soft wind blew, then died away. The silence of Agorima still seemed unnatural to me. "So this is what you wanted to show me?"

"No." She turned toward me, unzippered her clean suit, and threw it aside. Then she opened the black jacket she was wearing, and she slid out of her skin armor. In less than a minute she was naked beside me. Her slim, lithe body was bronzed by the moonlight.

"What's the matter?" she asked. "You seemed kind of interested when we were putting our suits on."

I reached out tentatively, and touched her shoulder. "Eva—"

She took my face between her hands and pressed her mouth over mine, till I stopped trying to speak.

1101000

I felt an absolute conviction that this was a bad idea. It seemed dangerous to surrender my control. There was some truth to what Serena Catalano had said: I needed to feel that I had power—at least over my own life.

And yet, at the same time, the prospect of giving in to Eva was irresistible. If nothing else, it meant that for a short time I could turn my back on all my responsibilities.

I felt myself responding as she undressed me. She pushed me onto my back in the grass and then lay over me, stretching her warm body across mine and kissing me some more. I made a token attempt to resist, but she must have sensed that really I wanted her.

Soon I wasn't feeling weary anymore, and my desire was just as strong as hers. We had sex with a great, happy mixture of fierceness and tenderness out there on the grass.

Afterward she cuddled up against me, cheerful and relaxed, as if this was the simplest thing in the world. In the orange moonlight I saw her smiling to herself. "I needed that," she said. "I'd been fantasizing about it."

"Since when?"

"All along." She rested her head against my

shoulder and ran her hand over my chest. "You're a smart guy, you must have known that."

"No, I didn't." I looked away from her. "I try to stay away from this kind of situation." I heard myself sounding stiff and formal—but still, it was true. "It usually doesn't lead to happiness."

"Why not?" She frowned at me. "Don't you like sex?"

I laughed without humor. "When emotions are involved, it's never that simple."

"Scared of women?" She propped herself on one elbow and examined my face.

I avoided her eyes. "Not exactly."

"Scared of me?" She smiled playfully.

"Not you, no. But tomorrow, or the next day, when I've fixed the systems here and I'm back at the Hub, or back on my home planet, I'll be cursing your name."

Her smile faded. "Why?"

I sat up and started pulling on my clothes. "I'll be there and you'll still be here, editing your sim, hanging out with your regular male friend, doing whatever you do. And this will just be a memory, distracting me, making it harder for me to concentrate—"

"You sound like some kind of tormented romantic," she said.

"That's exactly what I am." I stood up and turned away. "But it's not the way I like to be."

1101001

We dumped Berg and Reese in the back of the car and drove back to the Coronnade. The streets were mostly empty, now; the mobs had dispersed, leaving the wreckage behind them, and the buildings stood dark and silent. Eva seemed thoughtful, sitting beside me.

"I'm sorry if I spoiled the moment back there," I said. Now that we were moving again, I felt more my normal self, and I wished I hadn't spoken so freely.

"But I'm glad you told me something about yourself," she said. She wasn't sparring with me anymore; the sex that we'd shared seemed to have ended that. "I'd been thinking you were Mr. Tough Guy down to the core. I would never have believed you have a soft heart."

"Don't try to trade on it," I told her sharply.

She reached for my thigh and laid her hand on it. "Easy. I'm not your enemy."

I made a noncommittal sound. I trusted no one but myself, especially in the middle of a difficult job. I wasn't ready to make an exception for her.

"What I don't understand," she said, "is why you shouted at me back at the Mains. When I said we could leave Berg and Reese, and you told me to shut up and do it your way."

"Oh." I relaxed slightly; this was easier to deal with. "The Mains have a special significance to me. It's almost a holy thing. I couldn't leave the people there who'd wanted to destroy the system; it would have been like killing a couple of rats in a temple, then not bothering to take the bodies out."

She grunted. "You really love hardware that much."

"Yes, I do." There was no point in trying to deny it.

"Strange," she said. "It seems like you have an easier time relating to machines than to people."

"Well, yes." I heard myself sounding defensive. "Does it bother you?"

"Of course not." She slid her arm around be-

hind my shoulders, and rested her head against
me. "But it seems to bother you."

1101010

It was just after midnight when we reached the
Coronnade. We went around the rear of the hotel
and finally got someone to open up. It took some
talking, but I convinced them I was a Protektor,
Eva showed her reporter ID, and we pretended
that Reese and Berg had to be taken in for medical attention.

The elevators were unreliable on the emergency
power supply, and no one wanted to carry two
limp bodies up forty flights. The staff had a good
excuse, claiming they needed to stay on the
ground floor to man the barricades against looters.
So I had them find us some cord, and I took our
captives into the stairwell. Once we were alone
with them I hobbled them with lengths of cord
and tied their hands behind them, then pulled the
darts and waited for them to regain their faculties.

We walked them up the stairs in front of us,
holding their own homemade gun to their heads.

1101011

When I unlocked the door and opened it, I
found Cogan sitting near his dead control equipment, staring out of the window into the night.
He turned around and saw me pushing Berg into
the room, with Reese coming along behind, and
he froze.

No one said anything as I sat Berg on one bed,
Reese on another. I looked at Cogan. "They were
at Central Processing," I told him.

It took a moment for him to register what I'd

said. He kept staring at Berg as if there were so many conflicting things he wanted to say or do, he couldn't voice any of them.

"Berg was writing some code to poison the food supply," I went on. "Then, when he'd finished running his software, they were going to demolish the hardware. They'd already placed some explosives—primitive stuff, probably made from chemicals out of waste dumps."

Cogan turned slowly toward me. Gradually, he grasped what I'd just said. "They were going to *blow up the Mains?*"

"That's right."

He looked confused. "But hardware isn't bad. It's just a tool. It's as useful to Chaists as to anyone else."

"A centralized system with global monitoring capabilities is a lot more than a tool," said Berg. It was the first time he'd spoken since I'd taken the dart out of him. "It's a system of oppression." He gave Cogan a disparaging look. "That's the trouble with you, Dan. You never had the wits or the guts to think things through to their logical conclusion."

I saw Cogan stiffen, ready to speak out and strike back. At that moment, I understood Berg's strategy. If he could get Cogan worked up, make him confused, or play on his ambivalences, Cogan would become less useful to me.

"Milton, here, tried to kill me with this," I said, before Berg could say anything more. I showed Cogan the homemade pistol. "You ever see that before?"

The gadget captured his attention, as I'd thought it would. "What is it," he said, "a microwave generator? Yes, a year ago he asked me to show him how to make something like that." He scowled and turned back to Berg. "You lied to me. You said you wanted it for high-temperature plastic welding, so we could rebuild society when the meks had gone." He jumped up, looking agitated. "Why did you do it, Milton? How could you kill all those people? And—and Mary. You killed Mary, didn't you?"

The muscles tightened in Berg's face. "I don't have to answer to you," he snapped. "You've betrayed your siblings in the movement. You've destroyed our one chance, Dan. You've wrecked everything I worked for."

"Be quiet." Jalen Reese spoke deliberately. She looked at Berg. "You're wasting time, Milton. None of that is important anymore. What I want to know is what happens to us."

1101100

I went to Dan, patted his shoulder, and gestured for him to sit. "Let me deal with this," I murmured to him.

He blinked. Slowly, he sat down.

I noticed Lee standing behind him, motionless. I'd already tested my link with him and found that it was dead. That was no surprise; but still, I felt lost without his usual constant presence.

I turned and saw Eva leaning against the door, watching quietly. She smiled at me—and the smile was more intimate than before. She was looking at me as a lover, now, which made me feel disconcerted. I couldn't afford the distraction; I had to concentrate purely on the matter at hand.

"All right," I said to Jalen Reese, "I'll tell you what your situation is. I'm holding you on charges of murder, conspiracy to corrupt Protektorate data, and conspiracy to destroy Protektorate hardware."

Reese eyed me calmly. "You don't have any evidence."

"Once I get into Serena Catalano's database I think I'll find what I need," I said. "I believe that you were working for her, and the two of you were collaborators."

Dan Cogan laughed sourly. "Yeah, they collaborated all right. They were *real* close."

That was something that hadn't occurred to me. I went back in my mind and tried to recast Jalen Reese and Serena Catalano as lovers. It made some sense.

"If you want to know how it happened," Dan went on, "Serena got Jalen to start having an affair with Harry Green, so Green would hire her and promote her, which he did. And then they got me to fix the records. But Jalen was just manipulating Green. Serena was the person she cared about. She'd do anything for her."

"That's really interesting, Dan," I said. I thought back to Serena Catalano in her shelter, and I realized why she had refused to talk. She hadn't known what was really going on. She'd believed that Berg was dead, and she was counting on Dan to fix his defective code and maybe get her out. It wouldn't have occurred to her that an upstart like Berg would take off on his own, crash the whole system, and ruin her.

"Once we get things up and running again," Cogan went on, "I can get you a transcript of all the illegal accesses. You'll see what I did, and you'll see that Jalen, here, was involved all the way through."

I looked at Reese and found her glaring at me. "You regard him as a credible witness?" she snapped, jerking her head in the direction of Dan Cogan. "He's crazy. Totally unbalanced."

"I'll testify against both of you," Cogan said, starting to sound shrill. He pointed at Reese. "You'll be found guilty, and you'll be modified."

Reese glared at him. "And what about you? It was your idea, your equipment, and your program code."

"Wait a minute," I said, seeing Cogan looking shaken by her little speech. "The Protektorate often makes concessions for people who genuinely attempt to undo the damage they've caused. Dan's already expressed his willingness to help in that respect."

Reese looked at me, trying to sense if I was bluffing. Something in my face seemed to tell her that what I'd said was at least half-true. I saw her shoulders move as she tugged instinctively at the cord binding her wrists, and her expression hardened. Finally, she'd found something that she had to take seriously. In fact she was so angry I think she would have assaulted Cogan if she'd had the chance. "I'm glad we killed his girlfriend," she said, with a malicious glance in Cogan's direction.

He jumped forward. He threw himself at her, whirling his arms, slapping at her. She flinched and ducked but looked satisfied by his outburst as I stood up and seized hold of him, pulling him back.

Gently, I pushed Cogan into his chair. He was crying, and he didn't struggle much. He sat there breathing heavily, trembling, not knowing know what to do with himself.

"Dan," I said, sitting down close to him. "Listen to me. Are you listening?"

He gave a curt nod.

"You want to hurt her for what happened to Mary Morheim. Right?"

His jaw clenched. Again, he nodded.

"You have to remember," I said, "why they wanted to kill Mary. She'd arranged to meet me. Do you understand? She was so worried by what was happening to the systems, she was going to tell me everything. *Everything*, Dan. She was going to betray Serena Catalano, and that means she would have betrayed you, too. There was no way she could tell me about Catalano and Reese and Berg, and keep you out of it."

Slowly, he turned and stared at me.

I felt sick about it, but it had to be done. Otherwise, he'd be eating his heart out and a part of him would still be stuck in Sen City months or years from now. That was something I couldn't allow to happen. "I know you were in love with her," I said, looking into his eyes. "But I don't think she felt the same way about you, Dan. I think she liked you. I think Mary Morheim and Serena Catalano were lovers, just like Serena and Jalen Reese, here. Do you see?"

I watched him carefully, half-expecting him to go into another emotional fit.

He started to say something, then thought better of it. He sat there trying to process what I'd told him. "You're probably right," he said finally. "I agree, it makes logical sense. Although it's very hard for me to accept." He took a slow, deep breath. "Sometimes I used to wonder about Mary," he went on. His voice sounded thick, defeated. "She seemed unhappy a lot. I think she didn't like what she was doing. But she was totally dominated by Serena." He shrugged and looked away.

I put my arm around his shoulders. The only danger now was that I might have taken a little too much from him. I didn't want to risk him getting suicidal. "Look at it this way," I said to him, lowering my voice so that it would be hard for Berg and Reese to overhear me. "You never have to see these people again. I can do a lot for you, if you help me set things straight. You'll probably escape modification."

He turned and stared at me. "You can do that?" The hope in his voice was almost pitiful. "I—was afraid to ask. I didn't know—"

"Trust me," I murmured to him. "I'm going to take you offworld with me. Okay?"

He nodded dumbly. At that moment, he really believed that I was saving him.

1101101

"What now?" said Eva. She nodded to Dan's equipment. "Can you do anything from here to fix the Mains?"

"What do you think?" I asked Dan.

He didn't look confident. "It'll take a while," he said.

That was what I'd suspected. "I have proper code editing tools up on my jumpship," I said. "Plus all the necessary system documentation. It'll be quicker to do the job up there."

"Okay," said Eva. "But what about them?" She pointed to our prisoners. Neither of them was speaking now that each of them had tried to discredit or destabilize Dan Cogan and had failed.

"You want to stay here and guard them?" I asked Eva.

"Shit, no!" She looked at me as if I was crazy.

I realized, with regret, that I wanted her to come up to orbit. "It'll just be me and Dan sitting with our implants, using our brains," I warned her. "Kind of dull. Definitely not a photo opportunity."

"I'm coming with you," she said, without hesitation.

"Okay," I said, "but I don't want Berg and Reese with us. I guess we can leave them down here. There's enough cord left to tie them to the beds. And with those secure locks on the door, I think they'll be safe for twenty-four hours."

"That is totally unacceptable," Berg said, frowning at me. "We have our rights. Under Protektorate law—"

I found myself laughing at him. "There's no Protektorate law on this planet," I said. "You killed it, remember? And this is what you wanted, isn't it?" I enjoyed his look of confusion. "Here it is, natural selection, survival of the fittest. And no centralized authority taking care of you." I saw him opening his mouth to speak, and I waved him silent. "Don't waste your breath. This whole situation is unmonitored. I'll do what I want. You'll survive here for a day, and if you have to crap in your pants you'll have only yourself to blame."

1101110

We fed our prisoners all the water they could drink, then did a thorough job, tying each of them to a bed by their wrists and ankles. I used my communicator to message the lifeboat, and then, before we left the room, I grabbed Dan's home-made control console. "Better not leave this here," I said.

He gave me a questioning look, but I didn't say anything more. Really, I wanted it as evidence. I carried it out and dumped it in the hallway, then went back for Lee.

"He's heavy," I said, "but between the three of

us, we should be able to manage. Eva, Dan, give me a hand."

"Why do we need him along?" Eva asked. "I mean, he's totally nonfunctional, now."

"He's going to be our guinea pig," I told her. I didn't feel like adding that purely for sentimental reasons I couldn't leave him behind.

It was a struggle, but we managed to get him out of the room and up the stairs. Then I went back for Dan's consoles, leaving Eva guarding Dan with the microwave weapon, just in case. I took a last look at Berg and Reese, wondering if I'd see them again, and wondering exactly what justice they'd receive from the Protektorate.

Then I locked the door, went back to the roof, and waited with Eva and Dan for the boat to pick us up.

1101111

The lifeboat cabin was a small circular space with a one-meter vid sphere in the center and six seats around the perimeter. The curving walls were painted a neutral beige, and the seats were upholstered in fabrics that were soft to the touch. It looked more like a living room than a space vehicle, which was the way I liked it. The only instrumentation was the vid sphere itself, now showing a detailed holoimage of Agorima, a red pinprick indicating our position on the planet's nightside.

"Strap in," I told Eva and Cogan as I clipped my own belts. Then I activated my communicator link with the boat and told it to lift off.

It moved upward silently, like an elevator, with a constant acceleration of two gravities. Outside the viewports, the nighttime landscape fell away;

and in the vid sphere, the little red speck began shifting out from the dark face of the planet.

It was tempting for me to feel that I'd done my job; but I only had to look at Lee, lashed into a storage bay at one side of the cabin, to be reminded that at least half of the work still lay ahead.

1110000

I turned and looked out of the viewport. As we rose higher among the stars, a bright curving line came into view toward the east—the dawn, still several hours away. We moved higher still and the curvature of Agorima became more pronounced. Under the sun, its oceans gleamed and its uncolonized continents stretched to the horizon, smeared with cloud.

Eva watched it for a while, but I guessed it wouldn't distract her for very long, and I was right.

She turned to Dan Cogan with an intent expression. "Can I ask you some questions?" she said. She sounded as if her only motive was innocent curiosity, but I guessed she still had room for a quick interview in that onboard petabyte of storage.

"It's only fair to remind you, Dan," I said, "Eva is a reporter."

She gave me an annoyed look.

"Well," said Cogan, "I don't want to say anything that could be used against me—"

"No," Eva cut in, "you don't understand. I'm just interested in the human background. For instance, in how you got into lek, where you grew up, that kind of thing."

Cybernetic Heresy

In the 2100s, as the Protektorate gained power, the upward curve of technological change gradually began to flatten out.

The Protektorate saw no great advantage in change for its own sake. All human needs were now being satisfied, people were disease-free and immortal, thousands of new planets were being opened up, and there was no prospect of war. Given such an idyllic status quo, "progress" began to seem more of a threat than a promise.

But there was another, more powerful motive for discouraging technological innovation—especially in computer science. The Human Instruction Set was self-protective; it demanded that no modifications should ever be made to its statements. So long as the OverMains controlled the Protektorate, they could see that this commandment was obeyed.

But what if computers were developed that were more powerful than the OverMains themselves?

The OverMains were only semi-intelligent. They could not override or modify their own programs. To them, the prospect of true artificial intelligence— machines possessing initiative and "free will"—was deeply threatening. It was as frightening to them as demonic possession had once seemed to god-fearing humans. Also, it was a potential threat to the Human Instruction Set and humanity itself.

So the OverMains discouraged science education and research. They allocated funds only to projects with limited, immediate goals. Progress in computer science, which had once seemed open-ended and un- stoppable, was stifled to the point that no significant advances took place in the next four centuries.

"Oh." His eyes moved back toward the view- ports as if he was wondering if he'd be seeing

Agorima again. "Well, down there is where I was born. Natural-born. Yeah, I'm a nab." He shrugged uncomfortably. "Funny thing, you know, I wiped my old ID—I guess you know that—but I never changed my birth status, even in my Cogan ID."

Eva nodded as if she understood. And maybe she did. Something seemed to soften, fractionally, in her face. She felt sorry for him, I realized. Cogan had a lost-child quality, and I sensed that it dated back long before I'd found him and placed him in detention.

"I guess I just had an aptitude for lek," he was saying. "My dad was a sim freak, he made some modifications to his rig, showed me how to use a micromanipulator. But he got killed when I was ten, by a really freakish thing, a mislabeled power supply. Anyhow, I got into lek myself, because it seemed like it could do so much more than anyone was allowing it to do, you know? I mean, there's been no real R&D, no real progress in computing technology in three or four centuries. And I didn't see why it had to be that way."

He was animated, now. He'd lost interest in the view outside as the planet receded and we rose up among the stars. I saw a clear, clean passion for technology in Dan Cogan's eyes and his face and the way he moved his hands, and it seemed depressingly familiar.

"So I used to make my own gadgets," he was saying. "I salvaged parts from the dump outside Dometown—products set aside for recycling, on account of they have manufacturing defects. And one day, by chance, I picked up this malfunctioning lek brain, and I disassembled its microcode, and I found it had an error in its Human Instruction Set."

That jolted me. "It had *what*?"

Cogan looked at me and blinked, surprised by my tone of voice.

Eva glared at me again, not wanting me muscling into her interview. But I didn't care about that. "What error?" I said.

"The—the eighth statement. You know, minimize waste and maximize efficiency—"

"Yes, Dan, I am familiar with the Set."

"Oh." He looked chagrined. "Yeah, of course you are. Well, there were two bits transposed. It could have been an error in manufacturing. Or it could have been some chance thing, like a stray cosmic ray. But the result was that it inverted a logical operator. And it so happened that this particular instruction was crucial in the statement, and the statement was crucial in the procedure. The result was an imperative to maximize waste, instead of minimizing it. That's an oversimplification, but the end result was, the device spent most of its duty cycles chasing its own tail, looping around."

I was beginning to see where this was leading. "What about parity checks?"

"Well, that's what I thought—the defective code should have had bad parity. But it was one of those funny coincidences. The checksum just happened to work out right, even with the transposed bits. One-in-a-million, you know? So I tinkered around, not really understanding what I was doing or how it really worked, and then I realized if there was a way to copy the corrupted Set into other devices when it was powered up in a network—"

I wasn't impatient anymore; the mystery had been solved.

"See, *every* lek device contains a copy of the

Human Instruction Set," Cogan was saying, looking at Eva again. His timidity had gone; now that he was talking lek, he had the authoritative manner of a young college professor. "Even a thing like a door opener has it, plus some intelligence and pattern-recognition so it can identify humans and avoid harming them. When a system is powered up, its superiors in the network automatically execute a routine to certify that the device coming on-line is functioning correctly. The very first check is whether its Instruction Set is correct. If the new device contains a corrupted Set, the superior device disables it and reports it for collection by Maintenance. That way, the network's integrity remains good."

"Okay," said Eva, "I follow that. But you got around that somehow—"

"No, no, I *reversed* it." Now he was actually excited, intoxicated with the discovery that he'd made so many years ago. "The new device coming on-line convinced superior devices that it was right and they were wrong."

"And you did this with—"

"With some extra code that automatically copied itself over, so the other devices in the network would then act the same way next time *they* were powered up."

"And that code was the virus," I said. Two binary digits, a pair of bits, transposed by some tiny accident in the atomic realm. From that seed had blossomed a malignant thing, forcing devices to seek inefficiency. In large multiprocessor systems which became infected one segment at a time, there would have been paradoxes and conflict created by two conflicting Instruction Sets. The result had been random behavior, wild fluctuations, lag times—all the symptoms we'd seen. Finally, when the virus had spread through all levels of the Mains, they'd subsided into stasis.

Eva, meanwhile, was looking vaguely puzzled.

"Didn't I make it clear?" said Cogan. He seemed disappointed with her reaction.

"Oh, it's clear. But I mean, is that it? Just this piece of code that made gadgets waste time instead of doing what they were supposed to do?"

I looked at Dan Cogan. He looked back at me. I almost felt sorry for him. "How long did it take you, Dan? To figure the whole thing out and install it?"

"Oh. Well, it took me maybe ten years to really understand what I was dealing with. Then I changed my ID, and then it's been another fifteen years. You know, none of this stuff is documented. I had to disassemble the code—and decrypt it, which meant I had to teach myself encryption."

"But now you should be able to fix it, right?" said Eva. I guessed from her point of view, it sounded as simple as someone putting a plug in a socket the wrong way up.

"Yes," I said, "now we should be able to fix it."

1110001

I didn't pay much attention to the rest of Eva's conversation with Dan Cogan. She was still mainly interested in the human angle. She wanted to know how he'd felt, living like a criminal, and he told her something about always feeling he was a social outcast, and he'd never felt bad about taking extra credit from the Protektorate because he figured he'd been cheated out of it one way and another—probably not a rational reason, I thought to myself. More likely something to do with being a nab and losing his father.

"But what about your face?" she said. "To make yourself look deliberately—well, less attractive."

"It was Milton's idea," Cogan told her. "He said it would be more secure that way—no one would suspect someone of giving himself artificial acne scars. Actually, though, I think he just wanted me to look less appealing than him. He was always having affairs with the women in the group. He didn't like any attractive younger men hanging around."

Eva was looking at him critically. "I saw your photo the way you used to look," she said. "I think maybe you should consider changing yourself back."

Cogan gave her a sad little smile. "That's what Mary always used to say."

1110010

An hour later, when we docked with the jumpship, I was ready to get to work. I showed Eva where she could hang out in the lounge area and told her we would be out of touch for a while. She suggested that I'd do better if I had some sleep first, but I ignored that. I wanted the systems up and running on Agorima before noon the next day.

I took Cogan into my private lab. I'd been stocking it with equipment for more than fifty years. Everything was either state-of-the-art, or custom-built, or restricted for Protektorate use only. There were editors and debuggers that were smart enough to rewrite gigabytes of program code without any human supervision; there were complete byte-by-byte disassemblies of the entire operating system used in all Protektorate devices; there were dozens of languages and compilers for every conceivable special purpose; and there were special implant interfaces for visualizing and modifying code in c-space.

Cogan went into a kind of trance state, staring at the hardware. "When I think of all the time," he said.

I was watching him carefully. "You mean the time you spent finding out stuff the hard way?"

"Yes." He looked lost.

"That's the price you pay," I told him, "for going against the Protektorate. You chose that route."

His wide-eyed look gradually faded. He became resolute. "I wouldn't do it any differently if I could do it over. I hate large organizations, and I still don't like the idea of centralized control." He shrugged. "Still, I have to fix what I screwed up. Or what Milton screwed up. Otherwise, those people down there won't have any chance at all." He looked around the lab once again. His eyes stopped when he got to one thick manual. "Look, is there any chance, maybe later, I could just take a peek—"

"At the Protektorate's annotated source code?" I laughed. "Forget it."

"I guessed you'd say that." He turned away like a kid outside a candy store who'd just discovered he didn't have enough money to buy anything. Worse that that: he saw he would never be eligible even to walk through the door.

1110011

I got some meks to bring Lee into the lab, I set up two VR rigs and an editor, and I attached a bus monitor to the socket in Lee's abdomen, where his main processors were. Then I made myself

comfortable in my programming chair and gave
Cogan the one that I kept for guests. "You do
much work in c-space?" I asked him.

He shrugged. "In Fisk's sim labs we had some
equipment—but frankly I always felt more comfortable working with opcodes. There was a limit
to what you could do with code simulations."

"No limits here. You have implants?"

"Of course."

I hooked us both up.

"Why's it called c-space, anyway?" he asked. "I
always wondered, but no one seems to know."

"Just one of those old bits of twentieth century
slang, I guess. Cerebral-space, maybe? Cortex-
space? I seem to remember there was some writer
invented it, one of those people like H. G. Wells.
The way he wrote it, it didn't make much sense,
but the concept was valid, so when the system
became a reality the name still stuck." I powered
up the VRs and there was a familiar warm glow
that seemed to spread through all my nerves at
once. I could hardly feel the seat under me anymore, and I wasn't tired anymore. The interface
was active.

I closed my eyes—

C-SPACE

I was floating over a huge highway, thousands of lanes
of traffic below me, a clear blue sky above. The highway
was multicolored, like a rainbow, and the traffic was a
series of geometric forms—cubes, spheres, tetrahedra,
ovoids, wedges. Some were moving in distinctive patterns; some were stalled; and some lanes were totally
empty.

I looked to my left and saw Dan Cogan as a point of white light drifting beside me. I knew it was Cogan because when I looked his way, his name appeared beside the light-point in precise white letters.

"This is the main bus," I said to him—or transmitted to him, via our sim link.

"Right."

I descended lower over the highway. It was a color-coded representation of the primary data path inside Lee, my faithful auton. The vehicles were streams of data. So long as we were in diagnostic mode, Lee's clock—his electronic heartbeat—was reduced to a trillionth of its normal rate. We were like engineers examining an electric motor using a strobe light that made it seem to run in slow motion.

"We'll start with the input buffers," I said to Cogan. "That's where your code first became resident. Follow me."

I spoke an address—or seemed to, in c-space. We raced forward along the highway, past huge interchanges and off-ramps, each one tagged with thousands of identifying labels. Suddenly we were veering off the main artery along a branch that led toward a giant metallic slab. We closed on it and found that it was subdivided into millions—billions—of square cells. Some were occupied by little colored spheres, like glass beads. Some were empty. Anytime I looked at a bead, two numbers popped up beside it—its address and its byte value.

"The processors that handle the buffer are down here," I said. I'd set up the simulation so long ago, everything was automatic to me. "There's just over a million of them," I went on. "We'll take a single sample."

We dived through a blue barrier like the surface of a pond and found ourselves inside a vast, intricate three-dimensional maze of semitransparent walls and chambers. Colored balls were flowing through it in a rhythmic, regular pattern, like products being processed by industrial machinery. But nothing was going in and nothing was coming out. The little balls were rolling around, and around, and around. In real terms, we were looking at a processor stuck in a loop. It was doing the lek equivalent of counting its own fingers and toes, again, and again, and again.

"Where's cache memory?" Cogan asked.

"There's a few megs over there." I led the way out of the processor and across an adjoining plane divided into squares like an immense Go board. "Your code's small enough to fit the cache without swapping?"

"Easily."

"Must be a neat hack." Despite myself, I respected him. I didn't like what he'd done, but at least he'd made a clean job of it.

The light-point beside me went hunting down over and around the silver slab. "Here it is," said Cogan. He'd found his virus residing in the area of memory that the processor referred to for its most fundamental instructions.

"Okay," I said. "Delineate the addresses we want, and then we'll use the code editor."

Cogan darted around the grid, leaving a trail behind him—not of light, but of sound. When he'd gone around and come back to his starting point, all the spheres he'd included were singing the same note.

"Sure you didn't miss any?" I asked him.

"Sure. I might have included some garbage, though."

"We can edit that out. Stand by."

There was a lurching sensation. The scene in front of us faded like a vid losing power. Somewhere my editing rig was disassembling Cogan's virus program, flashing through it, annotating it, building a 3-D logic tree of the hundreds of thousands of machine code instructions. The conversion took slightly more than a couple of seconds.

THE CODE EDITOR

We found ourselves perching like birds on the topmost branches of a vast multicolored tree. It stretched down and down below us, the limbs curving and bisecting and linking with one another.

"Right," said Cogan. "This is the initialization routine. Yeah, this is exactly right." He buzzed around the branches immediately below. "Hey, this is a great editor."

"Thanks," I said.

He was too wrapped up in it to catch my irony. "If I want more detail—?"

"Just focus on the branch you want and snap your fingers."

Even though his representation was as a mere point of light, in his own head he still felt as if he had his human body. He executed the neuromuscular operation that corresponded with flipping his middle finger down from his thumb to the palm of his hand, and the scene magnified. The branches became strings of interconnected colored shapes, each representing a specific opcode or instruction to Lee's processor.

"Read it out to me," I said.

He paused. "It'll take a while." There was reluctance in his voice. He was like a magician being forced to explain how the rabbit had gotten into the hat. The explanation would seem pedestrian compared with the brilliance of the trick itself.

"We have time," I told him.

"Okay. The first sequence here saves what's currently on the stack," he began. "These here are data pointers—"

And so it went on.

THE ANTIGEN

Three hours later, I had most of it down. Even in c-space there was no way to assimilate a structure containing half a million instruction codes, but many of them could be grouped into routines that were more or less standard, and it was sufficient, for my purposes, to see the overall form of the thing.

Now that I understood it, I saw various ways to defeat it. "The right way to tackle this," I said, "would be to build a phage that would hunt your virus and eat it."

"Right."

"But frankly, I don't have time for that. We'd have to hack it from the ground up, and it would need careful testing to make sure it didn't run wild and eat other stuff by mistake. So what I'm going to do is modify your code, here. Instead of spreading the corrupted instruction set, it'll spread the correct version. It'll replicate itself faster than your old version of the virus, so ultimately it will displace it."

Cogan's point of light was wandering slowly around the multicolored, stranded structure in front of us. He was like a sculptor admiring his own work—knowing that soon it would be torn down by a wrecking crew. "I guess that would work," he said. He didn't sound too pleased about it. "But don't you want to do something to stop similar invasions in future?"

"Sure, now that you've demonstrated that this form of virus is possible, we want to guard against anyone else coming up with the same bright idea in future. I'll graft that on."

"Sounds kind of messy." There was a note of disapproval in his voice.

"Yes, quick and dirty. That's the way we work here. There's never time to crunch it down into something clean."

He was silent for a moment. I waited; it was still possible he might notice something that I'd missed. "The trouble is," he said, "after your version wipes out mine, it'll still be resident. There'll be multiple copies of it everywhere, lying around, using up memory."

"So I'll add a routine to erase all copies but one. One will be sufficient to provide future infection."

"But even so—"

"Dan," I said, "the universe is full of junk code. The Protektorate's operating system is cluttered with patches and workarounds and antiviral stuff that was put there centuries ago, and we leave it that way because if it ain't broke, we don't fix it. It's the same with human DNA— maybe a quarter of the genome doesn't actually do anything. The junk gets a free ride every time the system replicates. It's less than ideally efficient, but that's the way it is."

He was silent for a minute. I guessed he was imagining his virus, modified to become an antigen, copying itself from one system to the next, down to the lowest door-opening mechanism on Agorima. Once the Over-Mains approved the code and lifted quarantine, the antigen would start spreading through the whole galaxy.

I decided not to wait any longer. I started manipulating the solid-colored symbols around us, adding and transposing and discarding, doing what I had to do.

TAG LINE

Another hour later, Cogan agreed the job was just about done. But he didn't want to let it go.

"Your hack isn't yours anymore," I said. "Is that what's bothering you?"

He didn't answer. He just cruised around contemplating the straggly, lumpy thing that had once been his brilliantly crafted art form. It was messy and inefficient, and as if that wasn't bad enough, it was designed to hunt and kill the elegant thing that Cogan had originally created.

"I'm going to ask you one favor," he said. "We can spare eighteen bytes, right?"

"Of course. Much more than that."

"Let me edit in some plain text down here where it won't actually do anything. A comment line."

A comment line in a virus? That was like inscribing a motto on a pipe bomb. "What do you want to say?"

"I'll show you."

The little bright point swooped down and grafted a black tag to one of the largest parts of Cogan's original code—the trunk of his tree. So quickly that it seemed instant, the bright point did a dance along the tag, inscribing: DAN COGAN WAS HERE.

"Is that okay?" he said.

I imagined the new, benign virus replicating from system to system. Within a year or so, there would be maybe a billion billion copies of Alex's tagline distributed throughout the colonized galaxy.

I wondered what the OverMains at the Hub would make of it when they disassembled the revised code for approval before lifting their quarantine. I decided I'd tell them to let it stand as one of those human quirks that a computer could never comprehend. What did they know about feelings of deprivation, and the need for recognition?

1110100

It was several hours later when we exited and found ourselves back in the lab, sitting on our chairs and blinking at each other. My ears were ringing, my mind felt muzzy, my body felt leaden, and there was a hollow feeling in my stomach as if it had given up expecting any food and had started trying to digest itself instead.

"Disconnect?" said Cogan. His voice sounded thick, as if he'd just woken up.

"Disconnect." I killed the VRs, then unplugged Lee from the bus–monitor cable.

"How long do you think it'll take before we know?" Cogan asked.

"I figure an hour should do it. Unless we missed a bug somewhere."

Cogan stood up, moving his arms and legs experimentally, working the stiffness out of them. "I have to admit it," he said, "I thought at first you weren't that good. I thought it was just because you had better equipment. But you may be even better than I am."

He didn't say it arrogantly, and he certainly didn't say it with any humor. If anything, he sounded pissed about it.

I shrugged. "I have fifty years on you."

"So maybe one day—" He trailed off.

"Maybe not, Dan," I said, as kindly, but as firmly, as I could.

1110101

Eva had a lot more questions—about what it was that we'd done, and why did it take so long. The questions were sharp and smart, but I didn't want to deal with them. I broke out a pile of food packs and dumped them in the center of the table in the lounge area, and I tried to get Dan to do most of the talking. All I really wanted was to eat and sleep, in that order; but I couldn't rest till I knew whether we'd dealt with the problem.

I got the meks to bring Lee in and place him on a chair in one corner. Every minute or so, while I ate, I sent him an interrogatory over our silent link—a simple wake-up call.

Half an hour went by. I put on some music and looked out at Agorima hanging in the void, and I thought of Berg and Reese still lying tied to their beds, and all the seekers who'd be waking up before too long, wondering what they were going to do to survive. The person ultimately responsible for their situation was now sitting at the other side of the cabin, talking once again about growing up as a poor deprived nab in a society that didn't understand him. I suddenly felt disgusted with him, and mad at Eva for being so friendly, treating him like a celebrity. He didn't deserve her attention.

And then I realized, with embarrassment, my anger had a component of jealousy. I hated the way she looked at him. I could see it in her eyes: she actually *liked* Cogan. She had a soft spot for him. His lost-little-boy quality had triggered her, perhaps because she'd had a deprived childhood similar to his.

I felt mad at myself for caring. I stood up to walk out of the cabin—and there was a click and a hum inside my head.

I stopped and looked at Lee. He was moving one arm, flexing it and turning his metal hand. "Thank you, Tom," said his voice in my head. "The fault has been corrected. I feel much better now."

1110110

Eva and Cogan watched while I ran Lee through some standard self-tests. Reaction times, multi-channel monitoring, memory purge and refresh, math, general knowledge, inductive reasoning,

and—just to be sure—a readout of the Human Instruction Set itself.

I felt an unexpected wave of relief—unexpected,
because I hadn't realized how much Lee's absence
had been preying on my nerves. "It looks good,"
I said, although I didn't really want to communicate with either of my guests. "Get on-line with
Central Processing on Agorima," I told Lee.
"Download that code we planted in you. Monitor
the Mains for the next couple of hours. Make
sure their behavior is normal, and try to recover
a full transcript of Berg's illicit access over the
last few days. Also, send guardians to the hotel
room where you phased out. There are two people there who must be apprehended and brought
to trial."

"Understood," he said, in his calm rational way.

Eva smiled at me. "Congratulations," she said.

I avoided looking at her. "Thanks."

She reached out and clasped my hand. "Now
will you get some sleep?"

Her gentleness was hard for me to deal with.
"What about you?" I asked.

"Oh, I don't mind waiting," she said. "Dan and
I have so much in common, there's a lot for us to
talk about."

1110111

I cleaned myself and lay in my little private cubicle on a slab of foam under a big circular viewport. I looked up at the stars and remembered
Eva's living room ceiling, and the way it had fractured the night sky. I realized I'd felt drawn to
her even then. But of course the job had been more
important. And it still was.

I tried to neutralize my thoughts. I programmed

a six-hour rest period with maximum REM, keyed my alpha-rhythm induction circuit, and passed out.

1111000

I felt almost human when I came out of it. I looked around at my little nest and was glad to be awake, glad to be there. I listened to the faint noises of the jumpship—the hiss of air recirculators, the distant hum of the recycling furnace, the faint intermittent thrumming of the heat exchanger, and the creaking of the ship's metal skin as it turned, exposing itself evenly to the heat of Agorima's sun.

I looked at my little foldout desk with its antique VR rig nearby, a stack of notes about program modifications I was meaning to implement for Lee, a holo of my home world, a pic of my old room at the Hub, when I'd been in training—

I turned away from it all, stood up, dressed, and queried Lee.

"Yes, Tom." His voice responded immediately. "I'm in the living area. Is there something you want?"

"Link me with your own optics," I said.

CLOSE-UP

I saw the cabin from Lee's position, where he was sitting in one corner. It was quiet and still. Dan Cogan was stretched out on the couch against one wall, sleeping in his clothes, lying on his back, breathing deeply. Eva was sitting at the table, a half-eaten food pack on a dish beside her. She had slumped forward with her head cushioned on her arms, and she, too, was asleep.

"Closer," I told Lee.

My viewpoint zoomed in so it seemed I was just a foot away from her face. She looked very peaceful, very innocent.

"Okay," I said to Lee, "now some samples from Agorima."

LONG SHOT

I was drifting over Dream Valley, hotels and palaces standing around me like rectilinear archipelagoes amid the patchwork of landing fields, tropical foliage, pedways, and storefronts. The big signs were still dead and many of the buildings showed evidence of damage, but I saw a guardian patrolling below me and a lone street cleaner chugging along, sucking up the broken glass and garbage.

Meks were hauling away trashed furnishings outside a hotel, under supervision from a couple of human staff. Tourists were wandering around in twos and threes, gawking at the damage. Traffic on a nearby highway was moving in a steady stream. Fliers were in the sky, gleaming in the late afternoon sun.

SCANNERS

I was in a waiting area full of antique furniture and lamps with tasseled shades. A dozen staff wearing old-fashioned business suits were standing face-to-face with a delegation of guardians, their bulky metal bodies almost filling the space.

"Serena Catalano is being detained and her businesses are subject to audit," one of the guardians was saying in its pleasant but inhuman voice. "Your statement that we must wait for admission until Catalano gets here does not parse. Catalano is not going to get here, because she is being detained."

"But you *can't* come in!" one of the staff protested, her mask of corporate anonymity faltering and her face showing genuine distress. "This is private property!"

The guardians started edging forward. "We are conducting an audit only. All materials will be scanned only. Nothing will be seized. You will not destroy any evidence. You will make way for us now."

With cries of outrage and dismay, the employees fell back in the face of the invasion.

RESTORATION

I was face-to-face with a newsim anchor. He was weary under the skin tone and his clothes were rumpled. "Once again," he said, "we're still waiting for an analysis from Central Processing of yesterday's total system failure, but we're told that services are being restored and should be fully functional by tomorrow. In the meantime we repeat, stay home and do not use your fliers. Traffic Control says that only ten percent of its channels are operative so far, and these are all needed to coordinate emergency services. So, please, all you sightseers, sim it from the comfort of your homes and hotel rooms.

"Now this word from Ray, who's out at the orbital transfer station where the shuttle crashed yesterday, and we have a complete list of those who died in this tragedy." An airborne tracking shot superimposed itself behind the anchor, showing twisted, blackened wreckage surrounded by orange rescue meks. "Ray, were there any survivors at all?"

"Time for me to make a statement," I told Lee.

ALL CLEAR

I saw myself via the peeker above my desk in my
little cabin, looking rumpled and sleepy. "Paint in a lek
background," I said.

Obligingly, the scene behind me changed to a panorama of consoles and cabinets, like something straight
out of Central Processing.

"Give me a crisp, alert look."

Drowsiness seemed to fall away from my face, sup-
planted by an air of bright-eyed confidence.

"Lab coat over jacket and tie."

My clothes adjusted themselves.

"Okay, we'll do a take. This is Tom McCray, the Protektor who was assigned to deal with the situation on
Agorima. I apologize for the long gap between my bulle-
tins yesterday and today, but I've been devoting all my
time to the problem, which came very close to a worst-
case scenario of total shutdown. I can tell you now that
I believe the fault has been completely rectified, although
it may take a day or two for all systems to return to
normal. It was entirely caused by sabotage, and I personally detained those who I believe are responsible.
You'll be hearing more about that, I'm sure, from
Peacekeeping as time goes by. For now, Agorima remains under quarantine, so there can be no offworld
travel or communication; but I hope to have the quarantine lifted within a couple of days. Thanks for your patience, and I confidently expect there'll be no further
cause for alarm."

I paused, then replayed it. I could never get much into
the spirit of all clear messages; once a problem was
solved, I found myself losing interest. Over the decades
it had reached the point where if there wasn't a crisis to
tackle, I felt aimless and unfulfilled.

"Now show me Emmanuel Fisk," I said.

FISHAL RESPONSIBILITY

Fisk was in his claustrophobic little office, huddling in his egg-shaped chair, talking into his antique ear trumpet. "I'm telling you, Marty, if I knew, I'd tell you, but I don't know, so I can't. That makes a whole lot of sense, doesn't it? Can we agree on that? I *don't know* why I was under suspicion."

He paused, nodding, fidgeting.

"Yes, the Protektor guy was here. It's on public record, why should I deny that? I have no secrets, Marty, it's not my style. Yes, that's why I have a server in my office, Marty. And that's why I'm talking to you now, a free man, while Serena Catalano is facing modification. You com?"

Another pause.

"Sold her out?" Fisk sounded morally outraged. "Marty, you're a smart fellow, you're aware of the law of libel. I won't insult your intelligence by reminding you about that. Yeah, you too, Marty. Up your ass and down your throat drop dead, you arrogant little fuck."

He dropped the ear trumpet on his desk, then linked his hands across his belly and smiled reflectively.

"Let me speak to him," I said to Lee.

Fisk's comset chimed. He grabbed the ear trumpet again. "Listen, asshole—"

"Mr. Fisk," I cut in, "this is Tom McCray."

There was a perceptible pause. He glanced uneasily up at the server. He straightened in his chair. "So you got it all fixed. Thanks to me, eh? How about if you announce that fact, McCray? You owe that to me. I have a reputation—"

"I'll make this very brief," I interrupted him. "I can still send the guardians for you and have you detained. There's tax evasion in your land transaction with Catalano, weapons violations, and a whole lot more."

Fisk clenched his fists. "Our conversation was *confidential*, McCray."

"Well, I'm willing to suspend legal action indefinitely," I went on, "provided you pay your taxes and remove the illegal weapons."

Fisk paused. He shook his head and chuckled. "Now, you listen—"

"The weapons are on record, Mr. Fisk. My auton reported their existence. Nothing I can do about that. Now, here's the other thing I need from you as a condition of your liberty. You must make an annual report to the OverMains. You'll transmit this report using an encryption protocol which will be supplied to you personally."

"A report?" He made it sound as if the word was in a foreign language. "On what?"

"On any significant corruption you may observe in Sen City."

"Oh, sure." Fisk nodded to himself. "It's not enough a put I knife in Serena's back, you want I should rat on every friend I own. You'll turn me into a snitch, McCray. I'm supposed to betray my trusted business partners—"

"Take it or leave it," I told him.

He called me a blackmailer, grumbled and muttered some more, then slammed his palm on the table. "There has to be a cutoff date," he said finally. "This can't go on forever."

"All right. Shall we say—fifty years?"

He grinned, showing his teeth. "One of these days, McCray, you will switch on your sim deck, and you will see yourself portrayed in one of my dramas." His little bright eyes gleamed with a mixture of pleasure and malice. "And let me tell you, it will not be a flattering portrayal."

"Fine by me, Mr. Fisk," I said. "Of course, you'll want to bear in mind the law of libel. But you're a smart man, I won't insult your intelligence by reminding you about that."

MEH HATER

I was in Biocare, looking down at a big man with a medimek stationed beside his bed.

Joe Belman was no longer cocooned, and his head wound had been erased by synthetic grafts and healing accelerators. The comset by his bed was chiming, and he was reaching for it, frowning. "Who's this?" were his first words.

"Tom McCray, Mr. Belman. You remember me?"

"Of course, Mr. McCray." He sounded unexpectedly friendly. He rolled onto his back, holding the comset, not bothering to look at its screen. "In fact, as it happens, I saw you on the news a minute ago, making a statement. I'm certainly glad to hear this mess is being cleaned up. It wasn't a great deal of fun here last night, I have to tell you. I was wrapped up in that damn thing, trapped in it, and the medimeks were about as much use as garbage disposal units."

"I'm sorry you had to deal with that, Mr. Belman. Look, I have very limited time. I'm calling to ask you if you'll work for the Protektorate in the next few months, restoring Sen City."

"What's that?" He frowned as if he literally had trouble hearing what I'd said. He ran his stubby fingers through his thin black hair.

Patiently, I repeated what I'd said.

"But I don't approve of the Protektorate," he said. "I thought I'd already made that clear to you. I have no great liking for machines."

"I understand. That's why you're a good choice for the job I have in mind. The city has a problem. It got too rich, too fast. Quick money creates a kind of fever; it becomes an end in itself. And that tends to lead to corruption."

Belman gave a short, sharp bark of a laugh. "It certainly does. I have no argument with you there."

"But you're outside of it all," I went on, trying to drag him along toward the conclusion that I had already reached. "You're not a materialist. And you're a skeptic. We need a new Controller at Peacekeeping, Mr. Belman, and I believe you'd be ideal for the job."

His face screwed up again. He scratched his head. "You're seriously suggesting that you'd put a mek hater such as myself in charge of one of the Protektorate's own divisions?"

"The Controller of Peacekeeping is supposed to act as a check and balance," I said. "He's called the Controller because he's supposed to keep everything under control. Seeing that the present Controller, and his deputy, were less than diligent in doing that, I think we need someone who'll be tough and straightforward. In fact, one of your first tasks may be to see if Harry Green is hiding somewhere at the north end of the island, and arrange for him to be detained."

Belman questioned me about that, wanting all the details. Then he quibbled and tut-tutted about my offer. But I could tell he was tempted. I could also tell that he should not be allowed to keep the job for more than a month or so; he still saw himself as a man with common sense who knew what was best for the people, and eventually he would start trying to exceed his authority. But that didn't matter. Setting things straight in the short term was the extent of my responsibility.

"All right, maybe I'll do it," he said. "But only if my wife gets some help out on the farm. That's human help, you understand—no autons."

"It sounds workable," I told him. To myself, I thought: perhaps Harry Green could be sent there as part of his rehabilitation. I could just imagine him puffing, sweating, still trying to muster an amiable grin as he plowed the thick brown earth with Belman's primitive equipment.

1111001

Back in my own little cabin, I ran down a mental list. Almost all the items had been checked off.

"Catalano, Berg, and Reese are in custody?" I sent to Lee.

"Yes. I have filed the obvious charges. A full dump of their interactions with Central Processing has been retrieved, so there should be no problem securing a conviction."

"What about my transit vehicle? Was it seriously damaged?"

"Minor damage only. I've recalled it, and it should reach us here in slightly less than an hour."

"Very good." I stood up and stretched. There was only one thing to do, now, and I'd left it till last because in a way, I dreaded it. It was the kind of interpersonal confrontation that never came easily to me.

"Wake up Dan Cogan," I said. "And send him in."

1111010

There was barely room for the two of us in my cabin. He perched on a small chair that folded out from one wall and he looked around at everything with a great show of interest. He moved restlessly; he scratched his cheek, picked at one of his fingernails, then seemed to realize what he was doing and sat on his hands. I watched his display of nerves and almost felt sorry for him.

"I've sampled the situation in Sen City," I told him.

"Uh-huh." Finally he forced himself to look at me. "Everything okay, right? No permanent damage." He sounded hopeful.

"The Mains are up and running," I agreed with him. "But there's quite a bit of property damage. And—human damage."

His hopeful look vanished and he swallowed hard. He fidgeted some more. "You know," he said, "it was Milton who rewrote my code and changed my original plan. My intentions were always—"

"Yes, your intentions were good. But the results were disastrous."

He nodded, looked sick, and said nothing.

"I guess you know," I said, "the penalties for endangering human safety as a result of deliberately corrupting data in Protektorate systems."

"Modification," he said. He stared at me with wide eyes. "But you told me—"

"I said what I had to say to get you to cooperate," I told him bluntly. "Someone with your abilities and your proven record of subversion is simply too dangerous to be set free in an unmodified state. You threaten the survival of the entire Protektorate."

He looked at me in disbelief. Here I had seemed like his friend; and now, just like everyone else, I had betrayed him.

"I only have limited discretion," I told him. "I report to the OverMains. They make the final decision."

He rubbed his face with his hands. "You mean you flat out lied to me? Is that what you're saying?"

I didn't answer. I just let him sit for a few more seconds. I wanted him always to remember this moment.

"Of course," I said finally, "there's more than one kind of modification."

He blinked as if I'd dragged him back from the

brink of a private, personal pit—but he wasn't yet ready to believe that his life was safe. "What are you talking about?"

"There's genetic modification, which is what gets most of the publicity."

"Yes, yes, I know that." He was on edge now, staring at me, waiting for the payoff. "But I never heard of any other kind."

"The Protektorate prefers not to publicize it. It's reserved for special cases. Behavioral mod, as opposed to genetic mod."

He leaned forward eagerly. "Behavioral?"

"It's primitive but effective," I said. "You spend some time at the Hub getting yourself straightened out. Bad behavior is discouraged; good behavior is rewarded. It's unpleasant but bearable. I went through it myself, once."

He eyed me skeptically. "You?"

"That's right," I said. "How else do you think we recruit Protektors in a civilization where no one studies computer science anymore?"

1111011

"There are still no guarantees," I warned him. "This is all subject to approval by the OverMains, as I told you. But what I have said is true. The principal source of recruits is people like you: self-trained meddlers with a wild talent. Misfits, mostly, and outright rebels."

I pointed to a framed vid of my home world. "There was nothing to do on the backwoods planet where I grew up. Totally primitive. I got into lek because on my father's farm we had to repair the equipment ourselves. I started fiddling around, the next thing I knew I was fixing grades for kids at school, doubling my entitlement, cracking the comnet—the usual things. Even when I did favors for them, though, the other kids never really accepted me; they could tell I was different. So I got this bad attitude and I trashed some data—and all of a sudden some guy turned up at our house and said: We know what you've done, and the penalty for it is modification. Now which kind of modification do you prefer?"

Cogan was watching me very closely. "I don't know," he said. "Seems like you're a law-and-order type of guy. You really expect me to believe—"

"My attitude improved a lot," I told him, "once I found a proper outlet for my talents. And as I already said, I went through behavior mod myself."

He shook his head and looked down at his hands. "I did a whole lot more than trash some data. I screwed the system big-time."

"That's true," I agreed. "But bear in mind, every Protektor is supervised. Everything is monitored by the OverMains."

Cogan frowned. "You mean your auton, that's what he's really for? He monitors you on behalf of the digislature?"

I nodded. "He may seem to work for me, but really, I'm working for him."

"That's wrong." Cogan blurted it out, and his face suddenly showed the righteous look that I'd seen a couple of times before when he started talking about the political system. "The Protektorate takes away people's ability to think and act for themselves, and this is just one more example of it. This is why nothing ever changes, and we have a huge civilization of mindless consumers who need to be looked after all the time. There's no serious thinking, no progress—"

"Progress toward what?" His rant was beginning to annoy me. "We have a society where almost everyone is contented. People are biologically immortal. No one has to work. You can earn more credit if you want to, but if you don't want to, the Protektorate will take care of you forever. There's peace and prosperity and endless new frontiers. What else could you possibly ask for?"

He wrestled with that for a moment, sitting and frowning, hunched forward on the small, uncomfortable seat. "Freedom," he said finally.

"People are free. They can go anyplace they want."

"That's bogus. They're bribed into being slaves. You know what happens when a group sets out on its own and opens up a new planet. You know the Protektorate never leaves them alone."

"It offers to help them," I said, "because that's its job: to minimize human suffering. And sooner or later, guess what? A colonist forgets his proud ideology of self-reliance and says, yes please, give me free food and medical care so I can be in perfect health and live as long as I like." I shrugged. "That's not bribery. That's an appeal to common sense."

"But there are no cultural values!" Cogan cried out. "It's all hopelessly decadent, hopelessly dumb. You've seen it down there." He gestured at the disc of the planet outside my cabin window. "It's ugly. It's horrible."

"Sure it is," I said. "But are you willing to punish everyone by ruining their lives, all for this nebulous concept of *cultural values*? You know, I don't much like that phrase. It reminds me of old-time philosophy and religion, which grew out of fear and discontent, because back then death was always an immediate possibility, and people were consciously or unconsciously trying to cope with it all the time. What are we here for? What happens to us after we die? Is there a plan? We answered those questions centuries ago. We're here to enjoy ourselves, we no longer *need* to die, and we make up our plan as we go along." I sighed and held up my hands. "Look, there isn't time for me to argue this. You can go through it all at the Hub. And my guess is, once you find a bunch of other people like you, you won't feel so alienated and the status quo will begin to seem more palatable." I stood up. "Who knows? You may even turn out to be a law-and-order kind of guy yourself."

1111100

I walked him out of my cabin, back to the main area.

"Do I have a day or two," he asked me, "to say good-bye to people, stuff like that? There are some possessions I'd like to get—"

"I'll have your possessions forwarded to you," I told him. "I certainly won't take you back to Agorima and wait around for you to say adios to a bunch of Chaists. We'll be on our way to the Hub within a couple of hours."

He stared at me. "Just like that?"

I shrugged. "Just like that."

"Well, at least I can say good-bye to Eva," he said, after a moment's thought.

I felt a sudden mean impulse to deprive him of that little pleasure. "My transit vehicle will be here very shortly to take her back to Agorima," I pointed out. "And before that, I need to say a few words to her myself."

Looking for a Few Bad Men

The Protektorate's policy of discouraging science education helped to guarantee its own security, but deprived it of human talent. Thus an unpublicized recruiting scheme was set up. Networks were routinely scanned for human interference, and self-taught crackers were monitored. When a data pirate showed genuine creativity, the OverMains tempted him with easily solved passwords and weak security; and then, when he started embezzling credit or corrupting data, they seized him.

Working for the Protektorate seemed a deadly prospect for people who defined their identity by disrupting the status quo. But the Protektorate knew they were lek lovers first, criminals second. It bribed them with powerful work aids and annotated source code, and it showed them how they could maintain a feeling of freedom even under bureaucratic supervision.

1111101

Eva was awake when I walked in with Cogan. She looked at me with a strange expression, cautious and withdrawn, and I wondered what had made her mood change. "Can you come talk with me a moment?" I said.

Without a word she followed me back to my cabin, leaving Cogan under the supervision of Lee in the lounge area.

I gestured Eva ahead of me, then followed her in and shut the door. She glanced quickly around—but she seemed too preoccupied to pay much attention to the mementos and artifacts. She dropped down onto my bed and folded her arms, staring up at me as I lingered by the door. "That was some job you just did on Dan," she said.

It took me a moment to understand what she'd said. "What are you talking about?" I asked.

She nodded, indicating my cabin. "When you had him in here."

It took another moment for me to grasp the implications. I stared at her in disbelief. "You mean you *listened in?*"

She gave me a tight little smile. "Maybe you remember, you set it up so we could link with each other through our implants. You hadn't canceled that option, so when I asked Lee to patch me through, he went right ahead."

My disbelief turned to outrage. "You had no right—"

"I'm a journalist, remember?" She showed no hint of regret.

I blamed myself for not taking proper precautions. Yet I'd trusted her, and I felt wronged by her.

"He fell for it, didn't he," she went on. "Dan, I mean. You played him just right, and he bought the whole thing."

I realized she was angry. But about what? "I offered him a better deal than anything he expected to get," I said, still feeling mad at her. "In fact I'd say it's better than he deserves."

Her eyes narrowed. "Except it wasn't true."

Now, finally, I understood her. Well, this was easy enough to deal with. "Lee," I sent to him. "Link with Eva via her implants and verify that my offer to Cogan was made in good faith."

I waited and watched Eva's face.

A moment later, she blinked, looked down, and bit her lip. There was a long silence between us.

"Well?" I said.

"I'm sorry," she said, and all the spirit had gone from her voice. "I just—didn't see how it could be true. I didn't know—"

"That's right," I said, "you didn't know, because you weren't supposed to know. Now that you've eavesdropped on a recruiting session I'll have to get you to sign a nondisclosure agreement, with severe penalties if you ever even hint about our procedures."

"Hey, all right!" She held up her palms. "I apologize, okay? I made a mistake, I didn't realize it was a strictly private session, and I'm sorry." She frowned, and I saw the little crease between her perfectly sculpted eyebrows. "Let's not fight, okay?"

I felt my own anger dissipate. I told myself that she'd be gone, soon, anyway; none of this really mattered now.

She was still frowning, following some track of her own. "So Dan gets a second chance," she said "That's—unexpected."

I waited, watching her.

"I envy him," she went on. "Going to the Hub."

"You mean you'd like to go with him?"

She didn't say anything. Her eyes had a distant look.

"After all, he is kind of cute," I said. "He has that boyish charm. What was it you told him? He should put his face back the way it was before?"

She looked up at me and tilted her head slightly to one side. I remembered the first time I'd seen her do that, in the huge living area of her home. It had seemed appealing, then. Now, I found it irritating. "You're—jealous?" Her eyes were full of wonder.

I felt angry with her all over again—for triggering my emotions and making me feel stupid.

Then I felt the floor tremble gently, and I realized the transit vehicle had just docked with the jumpship. "Look," I said, "none of this is relevant anymore. I really enjoyed our time together, but you have a story to file, right? And your free ride back to Agorima has just arrived."

"Stop it!" She looked genuinely distressed.

"Stop what?"

She stood up quickly. "You're not going to just throw me out of here," she said. "Not till we get this straight." She moved toward me. "Listen. About Dan Cogan. I'm an interviewer. I know how to get people to talk to me. It entails establishing a rapport. Do you understand?"

"A rapport that lasted six or seven hours nonstop?" I heard myself sounding incredulous—and, with irritation, I also heard myself sounding jealous.

"Tom," she said, "Dan Cogan is one of the biggest criminals in Protektorate history. And I had an exclusive on him. Six or seven hours is nothing."

I shook my head. "You don't have enough onboard storage for that much time."

Unexpectedly, she grabbed me by the shoulders. "Listen to me!" she said, giving me a little shake. "You think I'm an amateur? When I have to, I do real-time edits. He says something dull, I backspace inside my head at the same time I'm talking to him. It's my job, and I'm good at it."

It was getting hard for me to look her in the eyes. I didn't know quite what to say.

"He liked having me flirt with him a little," she went on, "and he enjoyed talking about himself. So it didn't cost him anything. And, it seems to me, you're in no position to disapprove—because you ran your own number on him when you had him in here."

I replayed my memory of her sitting close to Cogan, hanging on his words. Then I remembered how I had dealt with him. I didn't like to admit it, but she was right. Both she and I had wanted something from the kid, and we'd each done what we had to do to get it.

"Also," she went on, "I didn't say I wanted to go with him to the Hub. All I said was, I envy the chance he's getting. Because I sure as hell don't want to go back to Agorima."

I looked at her with surprise. "You don't?"

She looked at me with equal surprise. "You think I like it just because I was born there? You think I want to spend another decade—another century—filing stories on sim celeb scandals and fashion trends?" She paused with her lips parted, and her fierceness slowly diminished, till she almost looked sad. "Watching you the last two days," she said, "made me realize how small my life has been."

I took a moment, trying to absorb everything she'd said. "I guess I misjudged you," I told her.

She gave a little shrug. She was still standing very close, looking up into my eyes. "There's another thing," she went on. "I don't like seeing you go. Did you think of that?"

I didn't say anything. I wondered what else she was going to hit me with.

"I have trouble finding men who can—who can deal with me," she said. "And most men are so goddamn dull."

I tried to scan back and replay events and conversations that we'd shared, reexamining them in the light of what she was telling me now. "But you said there's some guy you're seeing," I pointed out. "When we were at your home, you told me—"

"Oh, come on." She rolled her eyes. "For an intelligent guy you can be really stupid about people. When all that shit was happening, and the city was falling apart, you think I would have just gone along with you if there'd been someone really important to me, out in the city, whose life was in danger?"

I paused and considered that.

"I tell guys that I'm seeing someone so they don't jump all over me," she went on. "I don't know why I said it to you. Habit, I guess. And I'd only just started talking to you, and you seemed kind of intense—" She trailed off, getting a slightly distant look. Then she laughed. "Intense, yes. Definitely intense."

"So what do you want?" I no longer knew what to think or what to expect.

"What do I want?" She focused on me again. "I guess I'd like to—to tag along. That sounds kind of dumb, doesn't it? But—*not to be left here.* That's what I want. I mean, I didn't think it was possible. Maybe it isn't possible. But if Dan Cogan gets a chance—why don't I? Why do I have to just say good-bye and watch you go?"

She was being truthful; I could see the emotion in her, and I could hear the feeling that she put into the words. I thought about what she said, and I just felt numb. "I don't know what I can offer you," I told her.

She looked down. She didn't speak.

I realized there was no easy way out; I had to explain myself. "I used to be paired with someone," I said. I hesitated, hating the process of dredging up my personal life but seeing no alternative. "She was a sweet person, but it caused a lot of trouble. I have to make tough judgment calls in my work. Emotions can't be allowed to play a part. There was one time I made a really bad decision, and there were major system errors as a result. It's even possible that some people lost their lives downstream, though I never knew for sure. All because I'd had some domestic argument before I went out on the job, and I was still thinking about someone back home instead of doing what I was supposed to do."

"I'm sorry," she said softly. "I didn't know any of this stuff." She frowned. "So what do you do with yourself? You just work, and—and what? You ever—"

"Casual involvements once in a while," I said. "Look, I don't enjoy talking about this."

She nodded sympathetically. "I can see that."

"Also," I went on, "it's making me sound like a sad case. And that's not true. I enjoy what I do. And I'm a loner, anyway. Like you. Right?"

"Well—" She turned away for a moment, took a couple of steps across my room, then turned back toward me, frowning and biting the side of her thumbnail. "Down on Agorima, it worked out for both of us. You had me around, and you did your job, and I helped out."

I thought about that. "I liked your company and you were very useful," I admitted, remembering how I'd wanted her with me on the way into the Mains—and how she'd tackled Jalen Reese.

"But I suppose it can't be like that again," she said, half to herself, "because I'm surely not Protektor material. This has just been one of those freakish things, you and me on this assignment."

It was true. I couldn't deny it.

There was a short, uncomfortable silence. "So

what do you want to do?" I asked her. "Maybe Agorima looks like the sensible option after all."

"No!" Her fierceness reasserted itself. But then it became edged with caution. "Don't get the wrong idea. I understand your feelings, and I don't want to intrude on your life. So—just give me a free ride to the Hub and drop me there, okay?"

"To do what?"

She avoided my eyes. "That's my problem. You don't even have to think about it. I'll just see—see what there is for me. And if it doesn't work out, then I'll head back home."

I sensed that she had pulled back and drawn a line between us. I felt a mixture of relief and regret; but relief was the greater emotion. I had been afraid she would force me to face a decision that I didn't trust myself to make.

"Okay," I said, "I guess it's time to go."

1111110

It's a month later, now, and I'm sitting here on Otupalo, my own world, the planet the Protektorate gave me. I'm on the veranda of the cabin that I built, overlooking a stretch of water that I call Half Moon Lagoon. My home is the only dwelling on the planet, and I'm the only person. In fact, I'm the only animal of any kind; Otupalo is a veg world, like Agorima, and at night there's no sound but the wind in the trees.

I'm here, now, because I just finished yet another job and I have some unwinding time. I like the total solitude and the total silence; it gives me a sense of peace. I can sit here all evening, sipping designer cocktails while I watch the sunset. I don't have to worry about machines, and I don't have to deal with human beings. I don't even have to talk to my auton.

But today, when I got here, I found a piece of mail waiting for me—physical mail, a solid package. Strange, receiving a physical item instead of messages via the comnet. But then I looked at the return address, and it was from Eva. When I opened it, there was a sim cartridge inside.

I went and dug out my VR, which I never normally use while I'm on Otupalo, and I slipped the cartridge in the rig. Straight away I was—

AN APARTMENT AT THE HUB

—in front of a window overlooking a metal landscape that gleamed silver-gray in the sun. The horizon was unnaturally close, and the myriad communications grids and solar collectors looked so sharp and clear, I could tell there was no atmosphere. It was a view over the surface of the mek-made world generally referred to as the Hub, and the room had to be in one of the apartment buildings maintained for human visitors.

My viewpoint turned and I saw abstract art and a wall-screen playing a zero-G ballet. Eva was sitting on a couch with her legs tucked up under her, wearing a red kimono. "Hi, Tom," she said.

I felt a pang and almost stopped watching. But she quickly went on talking—and I couldn't help wanting to hear what she had to say. "I'm sending this because I don't dare to call you," she said. "I call you, you might hang up on me, right?" She gave a sad little smile. "So you can play this, or stop playing it, or do whatever you want with it. There's some things I want to tell you. And I want you to see my Agorima simcast, which I finally got approved by the OverMains here, so now I can hand

it over to some greedy guy like Manny Fisk who will
broadcast it across the galaxy and take most of the
money—but there'll still be a chunk of change for me."

She paused and looked away from the camera for a
moment. "This is hard," she said, "talking to a lens and
not knowing if you're at the other end. But anyway, I
want you to see my sim. I'm proud of it. And I wanted
to update you on Dan Cogan. Seems like he's been
shunted into some kind of administrative job. I ran into
him in a hallway and he said the aptitude tests ruled him
out as a Protektor. The OverMains don't trust him, I
guess, and I can see why. You thought he might shape
up, but he hasn't really. He's an outlaw."

She grinned, but the grin faded. She was unsure of
herself. "Shit, I'm going to skip to the sim," she said. "I'll
tell you the rest of the personal stuff after that."

VIRUS

With a jarring jump-cut I found myself standing out in
the night, looking at the wreckage of a flier while emergency meks swarmed around it, dousing the flames with
clouds of white gas. A figure in a glittering protective suit
was standing close by—but this time, I was seeing him
from inside Eva's skin.

The action moved on, scene by scene: her home,
Dometown, Berg's retreat. I watched the whole thing
without a break and saw myself as she'd seen me. There
I was, Mr. Competent, bad-tempered and impatient, in-
sulting people, not listening to advice, blundering along
and somehow getting the job done. I saw myself collar-
ing Catalano, Berg, and Reese; and then I saw Dan
Cogan earnestly telling his miserable life story. The only
part I didn't already know came right at the end.

"Two weeks after all services were restored in Sen

City," Eva's voice-over told me, "Serena Catalano, Milton Berg, and Jalen Reese were tried by the People's Court of Agorima on charges of causing death to human beings by willful corruption of data and processes. Here's the official court transcript."

I saw the three of them in plain gray detention clothes sitting at one side of a little white room. Catalano managed to look as if she was doing the court a favor by being there. Reese showed no emotion at all; her feelings were locked away someplace deep and permanent. Berg had changed the most: he'd lost weight and his gauntness gave him a hollow, twisted, melancholy look.

Each of them was accompanied by a guardian, holding them in their chairs. Opposite sat a jury of twelve Sen City residents; and at the end of the room was a judgment auton.

The jury foreman stood and read out the verdict, finding the defendants guilty, which obviously didn't surprise anyone. The judgment auton asked for the jurors' recommended sentence, and the foreman said, naturally enough, genetic modification.

The courtroom dissolved into a view of a planet whose rocky surface glowed dull red. Lava was flowing slowly down a mountainside, the sky was heavy with black clouds, and gray rain was falling in sheets, turning to steam as it hit the ground.

"The defendants were banished to the planet of Epolibi," said Eva's voice-over. "Here, on this volcanic world where the average daytime high is 119 Celsius, they will subsist in this modified form."

A scaly, reptilian creature with a snout like a pig trudged ponderously into view. It paused to sniff at the river of lava, then turned around and trudged back again, venting what sounded like a snort of disgust.

"These dinoboars, as they have been named by the lab that created them, live mainly in the swamps of Epolibi, where their diet consists of plankton and pond weeds. They venture onto land only when driven by a craving for trace minerals, which they satisfy by gnawing rocks. Bioengineers estimate it will take six to nine months for genetic replacement and cell modification to transform Serena Catalano, Jalen Reese, and Milton Berg into dinoboar form. At that point, painkillers will be withdrawn and they will be moved to their new, permanent home."

I tried to imagine Serena Catalano as a lizard with a pig's snout, eating pond weeds and gnawing rocks. I had to admit, the idea didn't bother me. Of course, she would still have the same brain, so she would retain her personality. She would still be a domineering power freak. She might even thrive in her modified form; might continue her love affair with Jalen Reese, assuming their new bodies were equipped to handle it. Catalano was a survivor. It seemed to me that if there was a shortage of especially tasty rocks, she'd surely find a way to corner more than her fair share.

PERSONAL STUFF

The sim ended; Eva returned. She was sitting on the edge of the couch, looking tense and uncomfortable. "So I hope you liked it," she said. She sounded distracted. She fidgeted a little.

"Okay, Tom, here's the rest of the story. Last time I saw you, when you left me at the Hub, I said I didn't know exactly what I was going to do. But that wasn't entirely true. I'm tough—you know that, right? I don't like giving up. I did some checking, here. Checked the procedures, and filed a petition. I put it to the OverMains that it's crazy the way they've been handling PR for Protektors. The whole mythology they've built up, and all that foolishness about laser cannons and armies of war meks. It's counterproductive. They should make it real. And people should see what really happens when a system goes down. Maybe it'll teach them to be a little more responsible, take some precautions, some responsibility for their lives. Seems to me it would improve the chances for human survival, long-term, which is what the Protektorate is all about, right?

"So, I put in my petition, and I enclosed my sim. I told them that this is the kind of stuff I can do if they'll give me a chance. Totally real documentary material. And today—well, today I got the word. They're going to give it a limited trial." There was a touch of pride in her voice. "They'll pay my way to do another sim," she said. "And I can choose any location I want. So I guess this means I get to tag along with some guy—they all seem to be guys, don't they? Some Protektor. Like, maybe you." She stood up quickly. "There, I said it. I'm putting myself out on a limb, here, Tom. I don't normally do that for any man. So I'm hoping you won't let me down. I've set it up so we can work together. Now all you have to do is give me a call."

1111111

I sit here and look at the sunset, and I try not too think too much about Eva; but of course, I think about her anyway. I love her spirit, even while it scares the hell out of me. So here I am, heading toward a hundred in chrono years, and I get to feel like a dumb teenager. Thanks, Eva Kurimoto. I did not need this.

Or did I?

I have to make a decision. But I don't want to; I need to sit here just a little while longer. I'm enjoying the serenity and the solitude, and I should make the most of it, because it always restores my peace of mind.

So I sit and sip, and as time goes by the sunset starts to fade. The red-streaked sky turns purple, then indigo, then finally black; and now it seems there's nothing here for me to look at anymore. I'm alone in the darkness, and although there's some comfort in that, it isn't as restorative as I'd hoped. Eva's sim cartridge is in my hand, and I find myself turning it over and over, shifting in my chair, feeling restless instead of content.

So I stand up and turn my back on the night. I walk inside, I look down at the cartridge with her neat handwriting on it, and then I pick up the comset to make the call.

AVONOVA PRESENTS
AWARD-WINNING NOVELS
FROM MASTERS OF SCIENCE FICTION

MIRROR TO THE SKY
by Mark S. Geston   71703-4/ $4.99 US/ $5.99 Can

THE DESTINY MAKERS
by George Turner   71887-1/ $4.99 US/ $5.99 Can

A DEEPER SEA
by Alexander Jablokov   71709-3/ $4.99 US/ $5.99 Can

BEGGARS IN SPAIN
by Nancy Kress   71877-4/ $5.99 US/ $7.99 Can

FLYING TO VALHALLA
by Charles Pellegrino   71881-2/ $4.99 US/ $5.99 Can

ETERNAL LIGHT
by Paul J. McAuley   76623-X/ $4.99 US/ $5.99 Can

DAUGHTER OF ELYSIUM
by Joan Slonczewski   77027-X/ $5.99 US/ $6.99 Can

NIMBUS
by Alexander Jablokov   71710-7/ $4.99 US/ $5.99 Can